CRIME

(AND LAGER)

(A European Voyage Cozy Mystery —Book Three)

BLAKE PIERCE

Blake Pierce

Blake Pierce is the USA Today bestselling author of the RILEY PAGE mystery series, which includes seventeen books. Blake Pierce is also the author of the MACKENZIE WHITE mystery series, comprising fourteen books; of the AVERY BLACK mystery series, comprising six books; of the KERI LOCKE mystery series, comprising five books; of the MAKING OF RILEY PAIGE mystery series, comprising six books; of the KATE WISE mystery series, comprising seven books; of the CHLOE FINE psychological suspense mystery, comprising six books; of the JESSE HUNT psychological suspense thriller series, comprising fifteen books (and counting); of the AU PAIR psychological suspense thriller series, comprising three books; of the ZOE PRIME mystery series, comprising six books; of the ADELE SHARP mystery series, comprising ten books (and counting); of the EUROPEAN VOYAGE cozy mystery series, comprising six books (and counting); of the new LAURA FROST FBI suspense thriller, comprising three books (and counting); of the new ELLA DARK FBI suspense thriller, comprising six books (and counting); of the new A YEAR IN EUROPE cozy mystery series, comprising three books (and counting); and of the new AVA GOLD mystery series, comprising three books (and counting).

An avid reader and lifelong fan of the mystery and thriller genres, Blake loves to hear from you, so please feel free to visit www.blakepierceauthor.com to learn more and stay in touch.

LEFT TO HIDE (Book #3)
LEFT TO KILL (Book #4)
LEFT TO MURDER (Book #5)
LEFT TO ENVY (Book #6)
LEFT TO LAPSE (Book #7)
LEFT TO VANISH (Book #8)
LEFT TO HUNT (Book #9)
LEFT TO FEAR (Book #10)

THE AU PAIR SERIES
ALMOST GONE (Book#1)
ALMOST LOST (Book #2)
ALMOST DEAD (Book #3)

ZOE PRIME MYSTERY SERIES
FACE OF DEATH (Book#1)
FACE OF MURDER (Book #2)
FACE OF FEAR (Book #3)
FACE OF MADNESS (Book #4)
FACE OF FURY (Book #5)
FACE OF DARKNESS (Book #6)

A JESSIE HUNT PSYCHOLOGICAL SUSPENSE SERIES
THE PERFECT WIFE (Book #1)
THE PERFECT BLOCK (Book #2)
THE PERFECT HOUSE (Book #3)
THE PERFECT SMILE (Book #4)
THE PERFECT LIE (Book #5)
THE PERFECT LOOK (Book #6)
THE PERFECT AFFAIR (Book #7)
THE PERFECT ALIBI (Book #8)
THE PERFECT NEIGHBOR (Book #9)
THE PERFECT DISGUISE (Book #10)
THE PERFECT SECRET (Book #11)
THE PERFECT FAÇADE (Book #12)
THE PERFECT IMPRESSION (Book #13)
THE PERFECT DECEIT (Book #14)
THE PERFECT MISTRESS (Book #15)

CHAPTER ONE

London Rose was startled when the floor lurched slightly beneath her feet and everything seemed to begin sliding sideways. The faces of several other people in the passageway registered alarm, and the little dog at her side let out an anxious yap.

What could be happening to the boat they were on? The *Nachtmusik* was always very steady, and its motion along these European rivers was seldom noticeable.

Then London realized where they must be right now.

Smiling at the passengers, she said, "Don't worry, everything's fine. Remember, the captain sent out a memo about this turn. Come up to the Rondo deck with me and I'll show you what's going on."

This should be a nice change of pace, she thought.

Her duties as Social Director had been particularly hectic today. Whenever they were in port, many of the one hundred passengers aboard either joined a planned tour or took off on their own adventures. When the *Nachtmusik* was traveling between ports, it was up to London to make sure they were entertained.

Actually her job was even more complex than it had been in past years, when she had worked on huge ocean tour boats, but she loved the variety of it. And she'd been delighted to discover that the position included a certain amount of status and some definite perks.

Now London picked up Sir Reggie, her Yorkshire Terrier, and led the small group to the elevators and spiral stairway that accessed all of the passenger levels. They walked up one flight to the open-air top deck.

Sure enough, an impressive sight awaited them. Their vessel was slowly revolving almost completely around. Though smaller than most riverboats, the yacht-like *Nachtmusik* was built in that long and low style and London knew that this was no small navigational feat. The pilot was definitely demonstrating the ship's state-of-the-art maneuverability along with his own skills.

The fresh breeze on the Rondo deck ruffled London's short auburn hair as she led her group over to the port railing. She and the passengers peered into the late afternoon sunlight as she put Sir Reggie down on the deck and began to explain what they were seeing.

"You're looking at the Old Town of the city Passau, Germany, extending out onto this small peninsula. Passau is known as the *Dreiflüssestadt*—the 'City of Three Rivers,' and you can easily see why. In fact, you've got a wonderful view from here."

London's voice was almost drowned out by the ship's machinery, which was working harder than usual. She spoke louder to be heard above the noise.

"We've just sailed out of the mouth of the Inn, the river to your left. Far over to your right you'll see the mouth of the tiny Ilz River. We are now where the Inn and Ilz join the Danube, the river between the other two. Once we get turned all the way around, we'll sail upstream along the Danube on our way to Regensburg, the next stop on our cruise."

The passengers murmured with admiration at the ship's unusual motion—the sharpest and fullest turn it had made since their initial departure from Budapest, Hungary, a few days ago. The boat seemed almost to be rotating on some invisible axis, like the needle of a gigantic compass.

But the sight of the ancient city of Passau itself was even more interesting than the navigational feat—and certainly more charming—with its stone buildings, red rooftops, and multiple spires. It occurred to London that those homes and other buildings along the shore had been casting their reflections on these rivers for hundreds of years. Long before that, tribal people and then Roman colonists had lived on this very waterfront.

She loved this aspect of her job—these expeditions into both the delightful present and the rich past of European civilization. So far on this trip, she had learned lots of remarkable facts and captivating legends. She had seen some beautiful things ...

And some ugly things, she reminded herself.

At two of their stops, people had died and London had found herself in trouble with the police. She shook off those memories and turned back to the passengers who were waiting to hear what she had to say.

London began to point out the buildings.

"Over there in Old Town you'll see St. Paul's, the oldest church in Passau. Nearer to us are two white spires of the Baroque St. Stephen's Cathedral, topped with copper onion-shaped domes. The cathedral

2

houses what is said to be the world's largest church organ. And over there you can see the fourteenth-century Gothic tower, the Old Town Hall. And on that hilltop overlooking the city from the other side of the Danube ..."

London interrupted herself as she noticed another group of passengers gathered nearer to the ship's bow. There she saw the ship's historian, Emil Waldmüller, giving a lecture of his own.

London smiled and said to her group, "Perhaps we should go hear what my colleague Herr Waldmüller has to say. He knows much more about all these things than I do."

As London's group gravitated toward Emil's circle, she heard a woman's voice speak sharply.

"Miss! Come here!"

Not sure who was being called so harshly, London turned and saw a woman reclining in a deck chair near the railing. She was middle-aged, tall, and long-limbed, with a shock of curly hair that seemed to be trying to leap off the sides of her head. She'd been reading a paperback book, apparently uninterested in the wonderful sights at hand.

London had learned the names of all the hundred passengers of the *Nachtmusik*, so she knew this was Audrey Bolton.

"Didn't you hear me?" Audrey complained, glaring at London. "Honestly, it's so hard to get the attention of anybody who works aboard this dreadful ship!"

London bristled internally at the remark. Although she hadn't really talked to Audrey Bolton since she'd first boarded the *Nachtmusik* back in Budapest, she'd heard from several members of the staff that she was difficult to get along with—and impossible to please.

London walked over to the reclining woman and asked pleasantly, "How may I help you?"

The woman peered disapprovingly at Sir Reggie over her sunglasses.

"To begin with, I don't like dogs," she said. "And I don't like sharing my expensive vacation with one."

London tried not to look as startled as she felt. Sir Reggie was practically a celebrity aboard the *Nachtmusik*. It was rare for a passenger to complain about him.

Fortunately, Sir Reggie seemed to detect the woman's disapproval. He let out a slight whine and crept away to join the group of people listening to the historian. Two of those passengers immediately leaned

3

down and welcomed the little dog with a pat.

"Humph." Audrey Bolton snorted at the sight. "That horrid little animal doesn't bite, I hope."

"No, he's perfectly friendly," London said.

"I'll take your word for it. Just keep him away from me."

"I'll do that," London said. "What else may I do for you?"

A frown fell over the woman's angular features as she pointed to a nearby magazine rack.

"If you don't mind very much, miss, I'd like you to fetch me a magazine."

The word "fetch" startled London a little, as if Audrey Bolton were addressing Sir Reggie instead of her. As wide-ranging as London's job had turned out to be, it had never included "fetching" things for passengers. She wasn't used to being called "miss" either. But she reminded herself of her professional motto.

The customer may not always be right, but the customer is always the customer.

London smiled her brightest smile.

"I'd be glad to," London said. "Which would you like?"

Audrey Bolton's eyes narrowed grimly over her tilted-down sunglasses.

"Why, *The New Yorker*, of course," she said, sounding as if London ought to have already known that.

"Right away," London said. She walked over to the rack and took out a copy of *The New Yorker*, then walked back and handed it to the woman.

Audrey scowled at the magazine and held it back out toward London.

"This issue is quite out of date," she said.

London looked at the date on the cover. This was obviously the most recent issue of the weekly magazine they would have on board. For a moment, she didn't know what to say.

Just take a deep breath, she told herself.

"I'm sorry to disappoint you," London said. "We'll pick up the latest issue at the very next opportunity."

At least I'm being truthful about it, she thought. She knew the staff would pick up publications and other paper mail when they were in port.

"Well, that won't do," Audrey growled. "That won't do at all."

Then the woman stared off into space as if deep in thought. London wondered whether she should just apologize again and try to excuse herself and leave.

Finally Audrey Bolton said, "Bring me the latest issue of *Cosmopolitan*."

Feeling a little worried now, London walked back over to the rack and took out the latest issue of the monthly magazine. She glanced at the cover and saw that this one was definitely not out of date.

She handed this magazine to Audrey, who frowned at the cover.

"These articles look boring," she said.

London had to swallow back a laugh. Was she really being held responsible for the editorial content of the magazines in the rack?

"I'm sorry," she said again, as seriously as she could manage. "Would you like me to look for something more ... to your liking?"

"No, you'd never get it right."

Glancing at her wristwatch, the crotchety woman added, "Anyway, I haven't got time for that sort of thing."

Haven't got time? London wondered.

She asked cautiously, "Do you have somewhere you need to be?"

Audrey smiled condescendingly.

"Regensburg would be nice, wouldn't it?" she said.

London squinted curiously.

"I'm not sure I understand," London said.

"Well, Regensburg is where we ought to be today, isn't it?" Audrey said. "If we weren't so desperately behind schedule, I mean. Instead, we're just now sailing past Passau, which we should have done yesterday."

London winced again. Hardly any passengers had complained outright about the recent delays in the boat's itinerary. Clearly, Audrey Bolton was going to be an exception.

London said, "Ms. Bolton, on behalf of the staff and crew of the *Nachtmusik*, and also on behalf of Epoch World Cruise Lines, I apologize for our delays. Due to circumstances beyond our control—"

"You mean people getting murdered left and right?" Audrey interrupted.

CHAPTER TWO

London breathed slowly, trying not to get agitated. This woman was definitely testing the limits of her professional poise.

The *Nachtmusik*'s passengers weren't getting murdered "left and right." One passenger, the elderly and ill Mrs. Klimowski, had been killed in a cathedral back in Gyor, Hungary. Her death had hardly been a case of cold-blooded murder, just an attempted robbery gone horribly wrong. Still, it had resulted in a full day's delay in Gyor until the killer had been apprehended, mostly through London's own investigative efforts.

Then of course there had been that incident in Salzburg, Austria, when the *Nachtmusik* had been delayed again over the suspicious death of a local tour guide. It was true that London had come all too close to getting killed herself while solving that mystery. But nobody aboard the *Nachtmusik* had been at fault.

London was sure that it would be useless trying to explain all that to Audrey Bolton.

"Our trip has been disrupted by a couple of unfortunate tragedies," London said.

"That's one way of putting it," Audrey replied.

"We've done what we can to make up for lost time," London continued. "For example, we spent only one day in Vienna—"

"A very poor decision," Audrey said, interrupting again. "Vienna has to be savored to be enjoyed. I for one felt terribly cheated. Surely there were—and are—better ways to make up lost time."

Like what? London almost blurted.

But she didn't dare ask the question. Besides, she knew that Audrey was going to answer it anyway.

Audrey steepled her fingers together and looked thoughtfully over the Danube.

"For example," she said, "why didn't we skip Salzburg altogether? We would have avoided getting mixed up in that horrible mess there."

Skip Salzburg? London thought with disbelief. *Mozart's hometown?*

It would have been unthinkable, of course. For most of the passengers, that visit had been richly rewarding. The delay had just presented them with more opportunities to enjoy everything—ranging from music and history to the wonderful foods of that city. And anyway, there had been no way to foresee the trouble they were going to run into there.

Still glaring up at London, Audrey shrugged.

"Well, it's not too late to try to get things back on track," she said. "Why don't we just do Regensburg as planned tomorrow and skip Bamberg the following day? It sounds to me like a perfectly boring place. That will save us another whole day. Then we can arrive in Amsterdam right on schedule."

Skip Bamberg? London thought.

Was it really feasible to pass by one of Germany's most beautiful towns, with a medieval center that was a UNESCO World Heritage Site?

Not that the choice was up to London, anyway. Bamberg had been scheduled by Epoch World Cruise Lines, and the necessary adjustments to the timing of their visit had already been made.

And that choice certainly wasn't up to this woman either.

But Audrey made an authoritative nod.

"Yes, we should skip Bamberg. We *must* skip Bamberg. I insist upon it. Be sure to tell the captain."

London's mind boggled at the thought of suggesting to the sturdy and good-hearted Captain Hays they had to cancel their stop in Bamberg, solely on the whim of a single grumpy passenger. He'd surely scoff at the very idea.

Right now, though, London found nothing amusing about it. She had to wonder what Audrey Bolton did in everyday life that gave her such an assumption of authority.

"You *will* tell the captain, won't you?" Audrey demanded.

London stammered, "I—I'll be sure to convey your opinion to him."

Audrey frowned again. Apparently she'd wanted London to make more of a commitment than that. Then she shrugged again and opened her magazine.

"That will be all," she said to London. "You may go."

As anxious as she was to get away from Audrey Bolton, London felt too nonplussed to even move for a moment or two.

She saw that her little group of passengers was still standing with the others who had gathered to hear Emil Waldmüller's lecture. Some of them had apparently picked up drinks from the little café near the pool on the ship's bow, and they all appeared cheerfully attentive. Even Sir Reggie was sitting there tilting his head as if fascinated by every word the man had to say.

London had always admired the tall, dark-haired ship's historian. He was a handsome man in a rather bookish style, and at the beginning of the tour she had found herself developing something of a crush on him. His intelligence and knowledge were impressive, and his sophisticated Old World manners could be charming, despite his tendency toward haughty aloofness.

Nevertheless, London had decided she should not get romantically involved with either the German historian or with the Australian chef, a man she found attractive in quite a different way. She was determined to stay focused on her job. If this very first Epoch World Cruise Lines riverboat tour wasn't successful, the company would probably fold and her own future prospects would become quite murky. She might even be faced with the prospect of returning to Connecticut and settling down like her sister had. London had chosen to embark on this new adventure, and she very much wanted it to continue.

She stepped closer to the group to hear what Emil was saying, but just as she got there, the listeners broke into a round of applause of appreciation, and Emil took a modest little bow. His lecture was obviously over, and his audience headed off in different directions.

"I'm sorry I missed what you had to say," London told him.

Emil looked at her with an even more distant and preoccupied expression than she'd seen on his scholarly features before.

"You did not miss very much," he replied rather formally. "I was just pointing out the Veste Oberhaus, the medieval fortress overlooking the city. I was also giving a short account of the city's history—its origins as a Celtic settlement, how it became a Roman colony, how it became a religious center for the Holy Roman Empire, its role in medieval trade and commerce, and ... well, et cetera, et cetera, and so on and so forth, and ..."

He added with a haughty smirk, "I believe the American expression is 'yada yada.' He stood there for a moment, as if unsure what to say next. Then he spoke curtly, "And now, if you will excuse me, I must get back to the library."

He fairly brushed London aside and headed toward the stairway.

As she turned and watched Emil march away, London wondered if she should hurry after him. She knew she had annoyed him with her theories about the tangled mysteries they had encountered. But he had actually helped her solve Mrs. Klimowski's murder by recognizing the true value of a stolen object, which no one else had thought important.

London looked down at Sir Reggie, who had come over to her side.

"Why do you suppose he's acting like that?" she asked the dog.

The furry little terrier let out a slight grumble, as if he was also baffled by Emil's behavior.

As the dog gazed up at her with big brown eyes, looking much more like a teddy bear than like a canine, London wondered how Audrey Bolton could possibly dislike him. And why had she thought that he might be vicious?

Of course, she reminded herself, it was true that Sir Reggie had taken a good nip at the pinkie finger of a man who had attacked her. And earlier on, he had tripped up a killer who was trying to escape. This dog might have started off life as Sir Reginald Taft, show dog and handbag pet, when he'd belonged to Mrs. Klimowski. But since he'd been with London, he'd turned into a lively and handy companion.

She bent down and petted Sir Reggie, thinking again about the historian's unexpected coolness.

I guess it doesn't help that I actually suspected Emil of murder, London reminded herself.

But she'd only suspected him slightly and briefly—and with justification. After all, she'd had to consider a lot of people and a lot of possibilities.

He's not the only person I was wrong about, London thought. *What's important is who I was right about.*

"Well, there's not much I can do about it right now, I guess," London told Sir Reggie.

She stood up and took out her cell phone to check for messages. Sure enough, she'd gotten three texts since the last time she'd checked.

The first one read: "Please find us a fourth right away."

A fourth what? she wondered.

Then she recognized the name of the sender as one of the ship's most enthusiastic card players. Two other names were listed at the end of the brief message, so they obviously needed a fourth player for a game of bridge. London ran several names through her mind and texted one of them to see if she was available.

The next text was from a couple who had decided they wanted to change the décor of their stateroom. Failing that, they wanted to move to another room. Well, all the staterooms were booked solid, but she'd go down and talk to the unhappy pair and see if housekeeping could accommodate some aspect of their desires.

Then there was the singer who wanted to perform in the boat's lounge and was looking for an accompanist. Seeing who that was from, London smiled. She'd be happy to help keep that particular singer occupied.

"Come on, Sir Reggie," London said to her dog as she headed toward the stairway. "We've got to arrange a little redecorating and also set up an accompanist for our friendly onboard kleptomaniac."

CHAPTER THREE

When London walked into the ship's Amadeus Lounge later that evening, she was hoping she had settled all of the issues for that day. The bridge game had worked out fine, and the would-be redecorators had settled for switching the artwork in their stateroom for a set of different pictures. But she was still uncertain about the event that was soon to take place. Although she had found the requested accompanist, she was uneasy about what kind of performance this particular singer might have in mind.

London hadn't had time for dinner, and she was hoping to settle in at the bar for nourishment and a chat with her bartender friend, Elsie Sloan. As she headed across the lounge, she noticed Amy Blassingame, the ship's concierge, at a table near a window. Although London waved, Amy quickly turned her head toward the window, as though she was only aware of the view. Since it was dark outside, London wondered just how interesting that view could be.

Maybe she didn't see me, London thought.

Of course it could be that Amy was miffed over something and just didn't want to see her.

London sighed. She was Amy's boss, but she always hoped to keep a friendly relationship between them. Unfortunately, she and Amy had been at odds during much of the voyage so far. She thought maybe she should go sit down with her and try to be friendly.

Or should I just get a sandwich first? And a drink?

Before she could make a decision, she heard tentative notes being played on a piano. She turned and saw Letitia Hartzer standing on a little stage on one side of the large open room. The accompanist London had arranged for her was already riffling a few notes on the keys.

Our resident kleptomaniac is about to sing, London thought with a smile.

London liked Letitia, despite her unfortunate character flaw. Thank goodness Letitia's thefts had been small and innocuous, and when she'd been caught she'd pledged never to take anything again. Now

11

Letitia wanted to do a cabaret act here in the lounge, and London had agreed to set that up for her.

"How is everybody this evening?" Letitia asked, smiling at the audience.

At least some people called out that they were fine. Others obviously weren't paying any attention, which of course wasn't at all unusual for a setting like this. London hoped Letitia understood that. The large Amadeus Lounge in the bow of the ship provided a variety of seating at tables of various sizes, clusters of chairs and little sofas, and barstools at the wide bar across the far end of the room. On the starboard side was a mini-casino. Between that and the bar was a piano and a raised platform for the occasional performance.

As she looked over the room, London realized that someone seated alone at a table definitely was watching Letitia closely, and probably not because of any anticipated musical skills. At least, London was pretty sure that the man was staring at the singer. It was always hard to tell exactly what Bob Turner, the ship's so-called security expert, was looking at. The man always wore those mirrored sunglasses, day and night, indoors and out.

Bob had been the first person aboard the *Nachtmusik* to discover Letitia's kleptomania. Now he sat staring at her with his arms crossed, as if he expected her to snatch up a saltshaker from one of the tables. After all, he'd caught her doing that very thing once before.

She looks nervous, London thought, hoping that Letitia hadn't noticed Bob's scrutiny.

London worried for a moment. The last time she had heard Letitia try to sing, the woman had humiliated herself by fumbling a Mozart aria.

Now as the pianist vamped an introduction, Letitia took a deep breath and seemed to gather up her courage. Then she burst into a wide, impish grin and launched into a rendition of Cole Porter's sprightly, slightly risqué classic, "Let's Do It, Let's Fall in Love."

London chuckled with surprise. Letitia was a tall, stout woman who usually wore the stern face of a dour society matron. She cut an incongruous figure in a long sequined gown, smiling and swaying to the jazzy tune. Letitia seemed to know it too, and she winked knowingly at the audience as she put a bawdy emphasis on each of Cole Porter's naughty double entendres.

The people near the little stage broke into smiles, and even some

12

customers who hadn't seemed interested in listening now began to pay attention.

Letitia's going to be a hit, London thought happily.

Deciding that food and drink would have to come before Amy, London made her way toward the bar. As she passed near Bob's table, he gestured to her, so she stopped and leaned over to hear him.

"Where's my partner in crime-fighting?" he asked.

London knew that he was referring to her dog. Bob had come to consider Sir Reggie an investigative colleague. But the little Yorkshire Terrier had stopped following London around a while ago, and she assumed he'd returned to her stateroom. His doggie door gave him the freedom to come and go as he pleased.

"I guess he decided to turn in early," London replied.

"Yeah, we private eyes need our rest," Bob said. "But I'm still on duty. Got to keep a sharp watch on our delinquent lady yonder."

London just nodded and continued on her way toward the bar. She was pleasantly surprised to see that Captain Hays himself was sitting on a barstool chatting with Elsie, the head bartender. It was unusual to see the portly, middle-aged Englishman away from his post on the bridge or some business meeting in his office. Now his walrus-style mustache wriggled cheerfully as he and London exchanged playful salutes when she sat down next to him

Elsie had obviously seen London coming. The two had been friends for many years, and they'd worked together on lots of cruise ships. As soon as London got there, Elsie set a cocktail glass with a reddish drink in front of her.

"Your Manhattan, just as you ordered it, ma'am," she joked.

London took a sip and savored its hearty rye flavor sweetened slightly with vermouth.

"Excellent as always," London said.

Then she turned back to the captain. "Are you actually taking a break?" she asked him.

"Of sorts, and only briefly," he said.

Raising his glass he added, "Sometimes I have to fortify myself with lime and tonic water. Don't tell anybody you caught me drinking on duty."

Elsie winked at London, put her hand beside her mouth, and silently mouthed the words, "Not a drop of alcohol."

London laughed.

13

"Your secret is safe with me, Captain Hays," London said.

"I'm sure I can trust your discretion," the captain said with a laugh.

Then London remembered the disagreeable episode that had taken place earlier today up on the Rondo deck.

"Oh, I'm glad I got a chance to talk to you, Captain," she said. "One of our passengers has a complaint that she asked me to bring directly to you."

"Indeed?" the captain asked, his bushy eyebrows rising with concern.

"Yes, her name is Audrey Bolton. She's very upset by the delays in our journey."

The captain let out a grunt of dismay.

"I can't say I blame her," he said. "I'm quite upset about it myself. I'm surprised more passengers aren't complaining. I only wish there was something I could do about it."

London shrugged slightly.

"Well, Ms. Bolton has a suggestion," she said.

"Really?" said the captain.

"Actually, it's more than a suggestion. It's more like a demand."

"I'm always keen on fulfilling passengers' demands. Tell me about it."

"She insists that we skip our stop in Bamberg. Her instructions are to sail straight on nonstop to Amsterdam."

Captain Hays drew himself up with surprise.

"What! Skip Bamberg?"

Then he added in a mock earnest tone, "A sweeping demand. And yet I suppose it *would* put us back on schedule. What is that motto of yours, London?"

"'The customer may not always be right, but the customer is always the customer.'"

"Words to live by. Well, I'll give new instructions to the pilot, then get right on the intercom and tell all the passengers and crew that we are following the explicit orders of … what was her name again?"

"Audrey Bolton."

"The orders of Ms. Audrey Bolton, and we're canceling our scheduled overnight stay in Bamberg. I'm sure no one will object. After all, orders are orders, and the orders of Ms. Audrey Bolton must be obeyed. In fact, we'll power up the engines and sail past Bamberg as fast as possible, at record-breaking speed."

The captain's straight-faced delivery didn't hide his mockery of the idea.

"Well, I promised her I'd tell you, and I did," London said.

"Well done, London Rose," he said, finally yielding up a chuckle.

"Seriously, Captain," London said. "I'm sure she's not going to drop this. What do you want me to tell her when she mentions it again?"

"Tell her to bring it to me personally," the captain said.

"I'll do that," London said.

"Jolly good!"

The captain finished his tonic water, then looked at his watch and got up from his barstool.

"Well, it's time for me to make my tipsy way back to the bridge," he said to London. "Enjoy your evening."

"I'll do that, sir," London replied.

The captain stopped for a moment to listen to Letitia, who had just begun a lovely and surprisingly sensual interpretation of Cole Porter's "I've Got You Under My Skin."

"Delightful singer," Captain Hays murmured with a smile. "Charming woman."

London smiled. She figured it was just as well that the captain didn't know about Letitia's penchant for minor theft. Then he made his way toward the exit, walking, of course, with a perfectly sober stride.

Looking over the room, London saw that even Bob Turner's lips were turned up in a smile. He was enjoying the performance in spite of himself.

Then she turned back to Elsie and said, "I'm starving."

"Would you like to order something from the restaurant?" Elsie asked. "I hear the head chef is not only a culinary genius but also a gorgeous hunk of an Australian."

London couldn't help blushing a little. Elsie had picked up on her attraction to the handsome Bryce Yeaton almost before she'd become aware of it herself.

"A sandwich would be nice. What do you recommend?"

"Since we're now in Germany, how about something of that nationality? A little while ago I had a delicious *Leberkässemmel.* I highly recommend it."

London laughed.

"I've got no idea what that is," she said.

15

"Trust me, you'll like it."

"All right, that's what I'll have," she told Elsie.

As Elsie texted the order down to the Habsburg Restaurant, London saw that Amy Blassingame was still sitting alone looking out that window. She was finishing what looked like a daiquiri.

"Have you talked to Amy tonight?" London asked Elsie.

"Do you mean our infamous river troll?" Elsie said.

London cringed a little.

"I wish you wouldn't call her that," she said.

"Sorry. She just rubs me the wrong way. And admit it—she rubs you the wrong way too."

London couldn't deny it, but she preferred not to say so.

Elsie continued, "And no, I haven't talked to her much. She just over came to the bar a few minutes ago and ordered her daiquiri and stalked away to her table. She was pretty much monosyllabic."

"She looks lonely," London said to Elsie.

"Well, she doesn't make it easy to be friends with her," Elsie said.

Maybe that's not entirely her fault, London thought. She knew that Amy was inclined to be abrasive, but perhaps that was because no one had put much effort into making friends with her.

"I think I'll go pay her a visit," she said.

"London, that's not going to end well," Elsie said.

"How do you know?"

"From experience. Don't you? She'll snap your head off for no reason."

London got up from her bar stool and picked up her drink. She felt that she should at least make a try at bridging the gap between them.

"I'll have my sandwich at Amy's table. Send it over with a nice cold German lager."

"OK. And good luck."

As London walked toward Amy's table, she felt sure that the concierge was definitely just pretending not to see her. And that didn't bode well.

Maybe Elsie was right, London thought.

Maybe this was a bad idea.

CHAPTER FOUR

When London stepped over to the small table where the concierge was sitting, Amy just kept staring out the window. The young woman's smooth helmet of short dark hair added to her severe, unwelcoming look, and London knew she wasn't the only staff member to have trouble getting along with her.

London stood there awkwardly for a moment, but Amy gave no sign of having noticed her.

"Hi, Amy," London finally said.

Amy looked around with a rather unconvincing expression of surprise.

"Oh, it's you," she said. "Hello, London."

Then Amy gazed back out the window again.

London stifled a sigh. Amy had resented London since before they'd even met, and not entirely without reason. Amy had been hoping to be hired as the ship's Social Director, and London had gotten the job instead. The daily pressures of working on a tour boat hadn't brought them closer together.

For that matter, neither had dealing with two murders.

It hasn't been an easy trip for anybody, London thought.

"May I sit down?" she asked.

At first Amy looked as though she might say no. But then she gestured noncommittally to the empty chair at her table.

"The chair's free," she replied.

Feeling more uneasy by the second, London sat down at the table. Amy took a sip of her daiquiri and kept looking out the window.

London could see that it actually was a beautiful view, with moonlight playing on a forested riverbank. Just coming into sight were the cheerful lights of a German town.

Less cheerful was Amy's expression when she turned to London and snapped, "I hope you're not here to tell me something else I've got to do today."

London was a little startled by the suggestion.

"Of course not," she said.

17

"Good. Because I'm off the clock."

Amy let out an exaggerated sigh of exhaustion. She turned slightly in her chair and kicked off her high-heeled shoes in a dramatic fashion.

"Honestly, London, you know how to work a woman half to death. I've been on my feet nonstop since this morning doing your bidding. I'm dead on my feet. I ache from head to toe."

London was a bit nonplussed. She didn't doubt that Amy had been working hard all day. So had London. But they'd had no one-on-one contact until now, and although London was technically Amy's boss, she hadn't given the concierge a single order today. They'd both been going about their separate tasks.

It's not like I've been cracking the whip, London thought.

"I just thought we could ... visit for a little while," London said.

"What about?"

London shrugged.

"I don't know," she said. "About ... things, I guess. Nothing in particular."

Amy shrugged and took another sip of her daiquiri and looked out the window again.

London wished she'd come prepared with a few items of meaningless small talk to break this hard, deep, cold layer of ice.

Meanwhile, Letitia had finished singing "I've Got You Under My Skin," and was making a segue into a swaying and finger-snapping rendition of Cole Porter's "It's De-Lovely."

London was relieved to have something to talk about.

"Sounds like Letitia's going to go through the whole Cole Porter song book," London said to Amy with a smile.

"Huh," Amy said. "I'd like to know whose idea it was for her to do this little act."

London's eyes widened.

Of course, it had been Letitia's own idea to do a cabaret act here in the Amadeus Lounge. But London herself had encouraged her and made all the necessary arrangements.

"You don't like the way she sings?" London asked.

"Oh, she sings just fine, I guess," Amy said. "But somebody should have warned the audience to hang onto their valuables."

She crossed her arms and added, "In fact, I don't know why you haven't put out some sort of APB so that everybody aboard knows they'd better watch out for her."

18

London was more than a little shocked by this remark. As far as she knew, Bob and Amy were the only other people aboard the *Nachtmusik* who knew about Letitia's kleptomania. They'd all agreed to keep quiet about it—or so London had thought. London hated the idea of exposing the repentant thief to the judgment of everybody around her.

"She says she's not going to steal anything else," London said.

"And you believe her?"

"I think she deserves a chance, anyway. Besides, she doesn't steal personal belongings."

"I know—just little items from restaurants and museums and such. As if that made everything hunky-dory."

London squinted with worry.

"Amy, you haven't told anybody about all that, have you?"

For the first time since London had joined her at her table, Amy grinned just a little.

"What if I have?" she asked.

"Please tell me you didn't."

Amy chuckled a little.

"Maybe I did, and maybe I didn't. You don't know, do you?"

Before London could say anything else, she saw Emil coming into the lounge from the ship's library. He walked with a spring in his step, so he looked more cheerful than he had when London had last seen him. He even smiled and waved slightly as he noticed that Amy was in the lounge, and Amy smiled and waved back at him.

Emil headed toward them, but suddenly he hesitated. Looking directly at London, he slowed his steps and frowned. Then he turned and walked back toward the library. Amy looked disappointed to see him go.

"What do you suppose is wrong with Emil?" London muttered.

"Why do you ask?" Amy said.

"He's been standoffish toward me since yesterday," London said.

"Maybe he doesn't like being accused of murder," Amy said.

London's mouth dropped open with shock and surprise.

"I never accused him of murder," she said.

"Odd. I seem to remember you saying something like that."

London's mind raced as she tried to understand what Amy meant. But then she remembered the scene right here in the lounge just a few days ago, when she'd been questioning a group of people to try to determine who had killed Mrs. Klimowski. Emil had been one of her

19

suspects—she couldn't help that—but then so had some of the ship's passengers. She hadn't accused anybody of anything, but she remembered how testy the historian had gotten toward her—even a bit sarcastic.

"I would be rather disappointed in your intellectual prowess if you did not include me among your roster of suspects."

Unfortunately, she'd had a sharper confrontation with him just yesterday over the murder of the tour guide in Salzburg. He hadn't reacted at all well to her admission that she suspected him.

"I think our little chat should end here," he'd told her. *"Kindly leave me alone."*

Of course, London and Emil had been alone in his library at the time, and Amy couldn't possibly know about Emil's frosty words toward her …

Or could she?

"Amy, what's going on?" London said.

"About what?"

"Well, *you* to start with. I know we haven't always seen eye to eye—"

"No, we really haven't."

"—but tonight you're being very odd. What do you know that I don't know?"

Amy laughed outright.

"You don't know, do you?" she said.

I wish she'd stop saying that! London thought.

Still laughing, Amy leaned across the table on her elbows.

"Honestly, London, there's *so* much going on around here that you don't know about. Don't you ever look right under your nose? Does somebody always have to tell you about everything that's happening? Can't you figure it out for yourself?"

"Can't I figure *what* out?" London asked. She could feel her frustration rising.

"There. That's just my point. You don't know, do you?"

Amy was smiling ear-to-ear, all happy and gloating. She pushed her empty glass aside and put her shoes back on and got up from her chair.

"Well, I'll just leave you to your unresolved curiosity. Goodnight, London."

Amy walked out of the lounge, leaving London alone at the table with what was left of her Manhattan. As she sat watching Amy exit, she heard a voice beside the table.

"Your *Leberkässemmel* and lager, *fräulein?*"

London turned and saw Elsie's smiling face. London's friend had arrived with a tray carrying her sandwich and a glass of beer.

"Thanks," London said. "Care to sit down for a moment? I seem to be alone all of a sudden."

"So I noticed," Elsie said, putting London's meal in front of her and then sitting down where Amy had been sitting. "Things didn't go well with the River Troll, I take it."

"Things went ... very oddly," London said. She took a sip of the delicious lager, then looked at Elsie intently.

"Elsie, do I strike you as ... well, hopelessly unobservant?"

Elsie laughed with surprise.

"Unobservant? Quite the opposite, I'd say. I doubt that you could have solved two murder cases if you'd been unobservant. Is that what Amy told you?"

"Amy didn't *tell* me much of anything."

London hesitated, then said, "Elsie, tell me the truth. Are there things going on aboard the *Nachtmusik* that everybody knows about except me?"

"I ... don't think so," Elsie said.

"You'd tell me about something like that, wouldn't you?"

"Of course I would," Elsie said. "Don't get paranoid on me, OK? And don't let whatever Amy said get to you. Enjoy your *Leberkässemmel*. I've got to get back to my customers."

Elsie got up and headed back to the bar.

London turned her attention to her meal—a simple sandwich served on a halved, hard wheat roll of *semmel*—"small bread."

She mentally teased out the meaning of the German word *Leberkäse* to be "liver cheese." London could see the thick slice between the buns looked something like ordinary meatloaf.

London took a bite. The meat was more finely ground than American-style meatloaf, but its crunchy brown crust around its edge was similar. London's happy taste buds didn't detect either liver or cheese, but she hardly missed them. Instead she relished a mixture of ground pork, bacon, and corned beef, all pleasantly flavored with coriander, marjoram, thyme, and other seasonings.

Real German comfort food, she thought.

And exactly what she needed after a long, hard day that hadn't ended especially well. She finished her sandwich except for a morsel of meat, which she wrapped in a napkin.

By then Letitia was wrapping up her performance with a delightful rendition of another Cole Porter tune, "You're the Top." London waved goodnight to Elsie, then left the lounge. Feeling a bit too tired for the stairs, London took the elevator down to the Allegro deck. When she opened the door to her stateroom and switched on the light, she was glad to see Sir Reggie lying fast asleep on the bed. If he'd been out at all tonight, he'd made use of his doggie door to return and make himself comfortable.

"Wake up, sleepyhead," she said, holding out the piece of *Leberkäse*. "I've got a treat for you."

Sir Reggie suddenly leapt to attention. London tossed a bit of the treat into the air, and Sir Reggie deftly caught it and ate it. London crouched down beside the dog and helped him to the rest of the treat.

"So how was your evening, buddy?" London asked.

Sir Reggie let out a yap that seemed to indicate he'd been having a good time. Of course London had no idea where he'd been or what he'd been up to.

Just something else I don't know, I guess, London thought.

London took a good hot shower and climbed into bed. As he always did, Reggie crawled under the covers and snuggled up beside her. London felt more and more relaxed as she lay there petting him. Still, she couldn't shake off a nagging annoyance at the way Amy had behaved tonight and that question she'd kept asking.

"You don't know, do you?"

Amy had seemed awfully gleeful about something she was keeping secret from London. Or was Amy keeping a secret at all? Had she just found a new way to push London's buttons?

Don't let it get to you, she told herself.

That's exactly what she wants.

Soon London heard the comforting rumble of Sir Reggie's soft snoring. And yet she still couldn't quite get to sleep. Finally, she realized what was on her mind.

Mom.

London's mother had left her father and sister and her back when she was fourteen. She'd said she was going on a trip to Europe, but she disappeared without a trace. Whatever had happened to Mom had been a family mystery for years. But the day before yesterday, back in

22

Salzburg, something had changed.

A woman named Selma had said she'd gotten to know Mom while she'd been living in Salzburg, working as a language tutor. According to Selma, when Mom left she'd said she was on her way to Germany. The woman hadn't heard from her since.

And now I'm in Germany, London realized.

Not that it really made any difference. London had no idea where in Germany Mom might be—or if she was still in Germany at all. She might be anywhere in the world as far as London knew.

She remembered what Selma had said when London asked if Mom had ever talked about her family.

"Whenever she tried to talk about you, she'd look like she was about to cry."

So why had Mom left in the first place—and why hadn't she come back, or at least told somebody where she'd gone and why?

It was late now, and London reminded herself that she needed her sleep. The *Nachtmusik* would arrive in Regensburg early tomorrow, and she and Emil would be leading a tour for the passengers.

She had to wonder, were she and the historian even still friends?

How would he behave when they were working together tomorrow?

CHAPTER FIVE

"It's been said that the devil himself has snatched certain souls from this very bridge," the ship's historian declared.

London joined in the general gasp of surprise. She and Emil were beginning their tour with twenty passengers from the *Nachtmusik*, and his words were quite startling on such a pleasant morning in this charming city. She looked over the faces in the group, some more familiar than others. Walter and Agnes Shick, a kindly elderly couple, were among them, as well as the less friendly Audrey Bolton. They were all about to step onto a wide stone structure built across the Danube River.

London herself didn't happen to know anything about the devil and this ancient bridge.

"And so, ladies and gentlemen," Emil continued, "you might want to exercise some caution before you walk across. Just a fair warning in case you would rather not take any chances. Would anybody like to go back to the ship?"

Of course, most of the passengers looked more amused than alarmed at the historian's announcement. They knew what London knew. With his characteristic dryness, Emil was teasing them with the promise of a good story, and nobody raised their hand wanting to go back.

"Ah, an intrepid group indeed," Emil said. "Well, let us plunge on into today's adventure, shall we?"

As they walked toward the picturesque buildings, towers, and spires of Regensburg on the other side of the river, London was pleased to see that Emil seemed to be in a good mood now. He hadn't joined her for breakfast in the Habsburg Restaurant as she'd hoped he would, and he'd barely said a word to her since they'd come ashore.

His silence worried her—not just because she didn't know why he was acting like this, but because it hampered their working relationship. She'd come along on the tour, as usual, to back him up and to help out with whatever the passengers might need. She had even left Sir Reggie back on the boat so she could concentrate on her job.

24

But she felt that the easy rapport she and Emil had developed while leading tours in other cities was missing. They both knew a lot about European locales and history, and usually they were able to slyly cue each other with a word or a nod or a smile as to which of them should do the talking at any moment.

Right now she sensed no such clues from Emil. Although he was walking right at her side, he was acting as if she wasn't there at all.

Even so, London thought it was probably time for her to chip in.

Smiling at the group, she said, "Well, I don't happen to know about any danger of having our souls snatched by the devil. I hope Emil will explain that before we get all the way across. But I *can* tell you that we are now walking across almost nine centuries of European history."

A murmur of interest passed among the tourists.

London pointed east where the morning sun glistened on the Danube.

"Before this bridge existed, the emperor Charlemagne himself built a wooden bridge over there, about three hundred feet downstream. That bridge didn't last, and this one was built between 1135 and 1146—a true masterpiece of medieval engineering that made Regensburg a cultural center that linked Venice with Northern Europe. Until about a hundred years ago, this was the only bridge across the Danube between Ulm and Vienna."

London pointed at a statue of a nearly naked young man mounted above the balustrade at the bridge's highest point. He was shielding his eyes with his hand and seemed to be looking toward a pair of spires in the Old Town.

"Perhaps Emil could tell us something about that interesting character," she said.

Emil nodded to her rather coolly, then broke into a smile again as he spoke to the group.

"He's called the *Brückenmännchen*, which means 'bridge mannequin,' and he's mounted on top of what appears to be a little toll booth. But don't worry, there's no charge for crossing the bridge, at least not now."

Walking closer to the statue, Emil explained, "The *Brückenmännchen* is thought to represent the young engineering prodigy who is said to have built the bridge in the first place. As you can see, he is looking over at the two spires of St. Peter's Cathedral. According to legend, he had good reason to keep his eye on those spires."

Emil leaned against the balustrade as the others in the group gathered around him to listen. London, too, was intrigued.

He continued, "Back in Regensburg's early days, a master builder and his young apprentice each took charge of two crucial construction projects. The master set to work building that cathedral over there, while his apprentice started building this bridge. The apprentice was rather—how do you say it in English?—'full of himself.' So he made a bet that he could finish building the bridge before the master could finish the cathedral."

Emil crossed his arms and chuckled.

"Ah, the arrogance of youth! Of course the young man soon fell behind schedule. Realizing that he was going to lose his bet, he summoned up the devil himself and made a deal with him. The devil said he would help him finish the bridge on time, but only if the apprentice promised he could take the first three souls to cross the bridge. The deal was signed—in blood, I suppose, as deals with the devil usually are. Naturally, the devil expected those souls to be very valuable indeed—presumably the mayor, the duke, and the bishop."

Emil smiled impishly at the group and said teasingly, "Oh, but I don't want to bore you with the rest of this silly story."

London laughed and said, "Don't you *dare* stop now!"

Emil looked over the group, apparently ignoring London's comment. But when several of the tourists eagerly agreed, he continued.

"Well, the devil sped the construction of the bridge along, and as completion neared, the young apprentice started feeling guilty about the deal he had made. He sought out a priest and confessed what he had done. Fortunately, the priest was a very smart fellow, and he noticed that the devil had unwittingly left a loophole in his contract."

Emil paused and smiled.

"Well, what was the loophole?" one of the tourists demanded.

"Yes, tell us!" another said.

"Unfortunately for the devil," Emil said, "he did not specify that the souls promised to him had to be *human* souls."

Emil then pointed to several peculiar statues that ranged along the bridge.

"You may have noticed the statues of certain creatures that have been fashioned here. Among them you'll see a donkey, a dog, and a goose. The apprentice made sure that they were the first three creatures to cross that bridge, and the devil wound up with their measly souls. He was furious, of course. And it is said that he still lurks beneath one of the bridge's arches sulking over how he was cheated, causing navigational problems with eddies and whirlpools like those you can see right below us."

London and the group lined up along the balustrade and looked down into the river. Sure enough, the water swirled menacingly around the pilings of each of the arches.

Emil finished his little lecture by saying, "Ever since then, the Danube has been hard to navigate along this stretch. Just ask our captain. He'll tell you it isn't easy sailing."

Indeed, London was aware that the *Nachtmusik* had had difficulties in docking. She thought that some of the passengers had probably also noticed the slight bumpiness of the ship's early morning maneuvers.

The group broke into delighted chatter about the legend they'd just heard.

London found herself impressed by Emil anew.

He's quite a storyteller, she thought.

She asked Emil jokingly, "Has the devil actually snatched any other souls off this bridge?"

"None that I know of," Emil said.

"Well, after almost nine hundred years, I imagine the coast is clear," London said to the group. "Come on, let's head on over into Old Town."

At the far end of the bridge, the group walked through an arch under a clock tower. As they continued along the street, several of the passengers came to a sudden halt.

"Oh, my!" one exclaimed. "What's that delicious smell?"

"The whole city smells like sausages!" another said.

London laughed. She knew that they were passing near one of the most historic restaurants in the world. But she considered it too soon after breakfast to stop there now—especially since beer was an outstanding part of the menu.

"It's a famous sausage kitchen," London told them. "We can come back later for lunch."

Several grumbling passengers broke away from the group and headed toward the restaurant anyway. And as London expected, a few of the others broke away from the tour to go exploring on their own. It made for a smaller and more manageable group for London and Emil to escort on into the city.

Their first destination was an ancient archway amid ruined walls and towers. The ruins of massive stone were eerily embedded in the walls of a building that must have been built there many hundreds of years later.

London explained, "This is the Porta Praetoria, the gate of the northern wall of an ancient Roman camp called the Castra Regina, which means 'fortress by the river Regen.'"

Emil added, "It was built in 179 A.D. by the Roman emperor Marcus Aurelius. It is one of only two surviving Roman gates north of the Alps."

Then they led their charges a short distance to St. Peter's Cathedral, with its Gothic spires and its tall facade adorned with statues.

Before they entered, London smiled as she told the others, "I'm afraid the legend he told about this cathedral and the bridge can't be entirely accurate. You see, construction on this church started in 1260—more than a hundred years after the completion of the Stone Bridge. So there couldn't very well have been a race to get them built."

"And probably no deal with the devil, I suppose," Emil added dryly. "A pity."

He turned abruptly and strode away.

London hurried after him. She had only intended to point out that the contradiction in dates that made the legend historically inaccurate—as many legends were. But she had managed to annoy the historian again.

Apparently not noticing the tension, the tourists laughed and followed London and Emil into the nave with its arched, vaulted ceiling, its beautiful stained glass windows, and its countless carved images of St. Peter. Before they left the cathedral, they stopped to look at one of its most famous features—a charming statue of a smiling angel gazing protectively down from high on one of the pillars.

Their walking tour continued west through Regensburg's narrow, weaving streets and frequent plazas to the Old Town Hall, a three-building complex of Baroque and Gothic architectural styles with a tall, ornate clock tower. Emil led the way into an enormous old meeting chamber with severe-looking wooden benches and a high timbered ceiling.

Emil explained, "Between 1663 until 1806, this was the meeting place for the Imperial Diet, a governing body of the Holy Roman Empire. Certain German phrases originated here. For example, *am grünen tisch sitzen*—'to sit at the green table'—means to take part in important decisions."

Putting his hand on the back of a bench, he added with a grin, "And on those extremely rare occasions when a German procrastinates, we say he's putting something on *die lange Bank*—'the long bench.'"

Emil and London then led the group down into the cellars below the Old Town Hall, where they stepped onto a gallery overlooking a torture chamber. A veritable factory of horrors, the room was cluttered with familiar grim devices like stocks and the rack, but also with stranger tools and machines too frightening even to think about how they must have been used.

Emil explained, "It was here that heretics were forced to confess before they were sentenced to death. I don't imagine many of them held out too long before confessing to whatever heresies they were supposedly guilty of."

It was a relief to climb out of the dank cellar and step into the cheerful, sunlit streets again. As the tour continued south, one of the tourists called out.

"Listen! Do you hear that?"

London stopped walking and listened. For a moment, she couldn't hear anything over the sound of traffic and chattering pedestrians.

But then she heard it too—the sound of music wafting through the air.

It certainly wasn't the kind of music she'd have expected to hear in a historical town like Regensburg.

For a moment, London wondered whether she might be dreaming.

What is that music, exactly? she wondered, as she hurried in that direction.

And why are we hearing it here?

CHAPTER SIX

The bright, cheerful, and rather rowdy music sounded oddly out of place here among the quaint, stately, antique buildings of Regensburg. London noticed that several in the group were looking around with confusion on their faces. A few broke into laughter, apparently enjoying the contrast. Others, including Audrey Bolton, seemed less happy with the sounds.

But then, London thought, *I've never seen Audrey look happy with anything.*

Emil seemed to be the only person in the group who wasn't at all startled.

"Ah, I think I know what we are hearing," Emil said with a smile. "Follow me."

He led the way along a short, narrow street into a bustling square called the *Neupfarrplatz.* A small ensemble performing there included trumpets, trombones, a sousaphone, a clarinet, a banjo, and even a washboard being used as a percussion instrument. Other people gathered in the square seemed to be thoroughly enjoying the sounds those musicians were making.

"I believe we are hearing an American form of jazz called 'Dixieland,'" Emil said, speaking above the boisterous music. "And the tune, if I am not mistaken, is 'That's a Plenty,' and it was composed by Lew Pollack in 1914. Just listen to that web of intertwined melody lines—counterpoint, it's called. It is as intricate in its way as the Baroque music of Bach, Handel, or Vivaldi."

After pausing to listen for a moment, he added, "This particular type of performance, if I'm not mistaken, is Dutch 'old-style jazz,' which evolved in the Low Countries about the same time that the earliest American jazz was taking shape. Such American jazz greats as Cab Calloway and Duke Ellington gave some of their finest concerts in the Netherlands."

Tilting his head judgmentally, Emil added, "Call me a snob if you like, but I prefer traditional New Orleans style to this European offshoot. Still, this is better than no jazz at all."

I shouldn't be surprised, London told herself. Although the ship's historian sometimes seemed a bit stuffy, he had already proven himself a man of wide and eclectic tastes. She felt her admiration for Emil building up again. She missed the friendship they had shared, and wondered why he was being so touchy lately.

When the tune came to an end, Emil continued his little lecture as the instrumentalists readied for their next number.

"Although Regensburg is a long way from the Low Countries—and even farther away from America—it is quite an important European jazz center. My guess is that this ensemble is in town preparing for the upcoming annual Bavarian Jazz Weekend, when about a hundred bands from all over the world will congregate here in Regensburg. I understand the city can get especially lively then."

Emil nodded with approval as the band launched into another sprightly tune.

"Ah, the celebrated 'Tiger Rag.' An excellent selection. Alas, we do not have time to stay and listen. As you know, our ship is scheduled to move on this afternoon. Our time in Regensburg is short, and right now we must make a rendezvous with history."

Two more of their group waved goodbye and stayed right there, listening to the music. But London felt a tingle of excitement about their next stop on the tour—a literal descent into Regensburg's past.

At the southern end of the square, she and Emil led the group down a staircase and into a concrete tunnel with bare light bulbs hanging overhead.

Taking her turn at lecturing, she told the group, "We are walking through an air raid bunker used by the Nazis during World War Two," she said. Pointing to a row of stenciled letters along the wall, she added, "The word you see repeated here is *Neupfarrplatzgruppe,* the name of a resistance group that fought against the Nazis. The name has been written over and over again in their honor."

For a few moments they walked in silence, then London resumed speaking as they emerged from the tunnel into a maze of stairs and suspended walkways that overlooked an array of excavated sites.

"This subterranean museum is called the Document Neupfarrplatz," London told them. "It's an archaeological site where excavation began in 1995." As they wended amid fascinating underground ruins, she pointed out some specific ones. "Here you see the foundation of a Gothic synagogue."

31

Emil now spoke up.

"According to tradition, the presence of Jewish people here in Regensburg dates back before Christ. Starting around the eleventh century, this area was Regensburg's Jewish quarter, making this the oldest Jewish settlement in Bavaria."

Emil looked around the ruins thoughtfully before he spoke again.

"For several centuries, Regensburg didn't wreak the same persecution and intolerance upon its Jewish population that was so horribly widespread elsewhere in Christian Europe. Jews were relegated to a lower social status, but by decree they were also protected and defended from harm."

Emil sighed bitterly.

"Alas, this tolerance came to an end in 1519, when Regensburg expelled its entire Jewish population. The citizens razed the beautiful synagogue that stood in this spot."

London let the silence that followed hang in the air for a few moments before she led the group under a stone arch and farther into the maze.

"Now we're stepping even further back into history," she told them, "to when this site was home to the Roman military camp Castra Regina. You saw that old gate when we came into the town. These ruins give you a different look at Roman legion life."

Pointing to some wall foundations and the remains of an ornate tile floor, she continued, "We are standing where a high-ranking Roman officer lived back in the second century."

The group murmured with interest.

Emil added, "Further excavations may delve yet deeper into Regensburg's past. Long before the Romans came, the Celts settled here and called this place Radasbona. And before even that ..."

Emil shrugged and smiled.

"Well, I'll leave it to your imaginations. Suffice it to say that this ground has been inhabited for many thousands of years, all the way back to Stone Age times."

When the group was ready to leave these remnants of ancient cultures, London and Emil led them back up onto the sunlit Neupfarrplatz square. The jazz ensemble was still playing—an even more startling contrast than before.

Emil smiled and nodded in time to the music.

"Excellent!" he said. "'Basin Street Blues,' immortalized by the great Louis Armstrong."

He chuckled and added, "If I'm not mistaken, it was composed quite a few years after medieval times and the ages of the Celts and Romans—and yet those early inhabitants surely sang and played music of their own, century after century, millennium after millennium. Imagine what kind of music they made!"

The passengers who had stayed to listen to the performance rejoined the group.

"Great music," one of them commented.

"When do we eat?" another asked.

It was about noon now. London certainly felt ready for lunch herself, and she knew exactly where she wanted to go for it. She told the group they were now free to explore on their own, and reminded them to get back to the ship in no more than three hours.

She added, "Those who'd like a hearty German lunch can follow us."

She and Emil led the group back toward the Stone Bridge. As they neared the river, a familiar rich aroma filled the air.

"There it is—that delicious smell again!" one tourist commented.

"I'm really hungry now," another said.

London laughed and said, "Don't worry, you won't be hungry for long."

They turned a corner near the end of the Stone Bridge and arrived at a charming little building. It was shaped oddly, like a trapezoid, and it had a red-tiled roof and a large outdoor area full of picnic tables and benches overlooking the river.

This was obviously the source of that sausage odor that had enticed a few of the group away this morning. Fortunately, the lunch rush wasn't yet underway, so it wasn't terribly crowded.

Before London or Emil could explain to the group where they were, a cheerful voice called out.

"Willkommen im Historische Wurstkutchl!"

A stout, smiling woman wearing a black dress, a white old-fashioned apron, and a white fluffy hat came toward them.

"You are the Americans, *ja*?" she said. "From the boat that arrived just this morning?"

Members of the group said yes.

The woman continued in English, "Excellent! I am Hilda, your hostess, and I am here to welcome you to the Historic Sausage Kitchen of Regensburg. We have been continuously open for longer than any other restaurant in the world, maybe. We opened almost nine hundred years ago, in the year 1146, soon after the old Stone Bridge was finished. As you can imagine, the construction workers had worked up quite an appetite by then. We have been doing a thriving business ever since."

With an impish chuckle, she added, "Or so I have been told. I have not been working here quite that whole time. I do not want you to think I am *that* old!"

The tourists were amused, and many of them laughed aloud.

Hilda continued, "And we use the same mustard recipe created by Frau Elsa Schricker when she owned the place in the eighteenth century. We still make our sausages from pure pork ham, and we cook them the same way we've done for two hundred years, over an open grill. And we serve them over a bed of sauerkraut fermented in our own cellar. Come, let us make you feel at home."

Hilda led them onto the patio, where a group of similarly aproned women bustled around among the tables helping the tourists find places to sit. Not surprisingly, many of them chose the picnic tables with the best view of the Danube.

Before London could decide where to sit herself, she noticed the tall, gangly Audrey Bolton standing alone, staring out at the water.

She didn't look happy—but then, that was nothing new.

Judging from their unpleasant encounter yesterday, London knew that it might be impossible to cheer up this prickly woman.

I've got to give it a try, she thought.

CHAPTER SEVEN

London saw that Audrey Bolton even had a disapproving expression on her face as she gazed out over the beautiful blue Danube.

I wonder if she's going to complain about the color, London thought. *Or the rate of flow, or ...*

She brushed aside her own thoughts and smiled her best professional smile.

"Are you enjoying Regensburg, Ms. Bolton?" London asked.

The tall woman's curly hair bounced as she wheeled around to reply.

"As well as our brief stop here will allow," she said in a haughty tone. "But I understand that we will be leaving quite soon for our next stop."

"That's true," London replied. "But we have plenty of time for a nice lunch here by the river."

Audrey glanced around at the other passengers seated at the tables. Then she glared back at London. "I've been informed that our itinerary hasn't changed."

Uh-oh, London realized. *Here it comes.*

"That's true," London replied again, realizing she was being repetitious.

"I assume you told the captain we must skip our visit to Bamberg."

"I did," London said.

"And what did he say?"

London swallowed hard.

Just be truthful, she told herself.

"He said you should talk to him about it," London said.

Audrey let out a grunt of dissatisfaction. This clearly wasn't the answer this woman wanted to hear.

"Wouldn't you like to sit down?" London suggested.

Audrey crossed her arms and frowned.

"Yes, I would *like* too. But all the seats with a view of the river have been snatched up. I'm afraid you've bungled things again. If only you'd let the group know in advance we'd be eating here today, I could

35

have called ahead and reserved a table for myself."

London felt stumped, much as she had yesterday. How could she have anticipated this problem? She herself hadn't known for absolute certain where the group would be having lunch today, or how many people there would be. And she was pretty sure the peasant-style restaurant with its outdoor grill was too informal to take reservations.

But before London could think of what to say or do, she heard a friendly woman's voice nearby.

"Why, there's plenty of room out *our* table."

London turned and saw a pair of familiar faces—Walter and Agnes Shick, the kindly elderly couple. They were the only people sitting at this particular table with a view of the river. They both scooted over on their benches to leave plenty of room.

Walter smiled and patted the bench he was sitting on.

"Come on, make yourself comfortable," he said.

Audrey's frown deepened, as if he had said something offensive.

"I couldn't possibly impose," she told him.

"Nonsense," Agnes said with a warm smile. "You wouldn't be imposing at all."

"We'd like some company," Walter added. "We came on this trip to meet people—and I don't think we've gotten to know you. I'm Walter Shick and this is my wife, Agnes."

When Audrey didn't reply, London volunteered, "Walter and Agnes, I'd like you to meet Audrey Bolton. And she'd really like a seat with a view of the river."

"Be our guest," Agnes said.

Audrey's eyes switched nervously.

London felt as though she was starting to understand what made the woman tick. Audrey simply liked to complain—and to complain for complaining's sake. Apparently she didn't quite know what to do when people kindly offered to resolve those complaints. At the moment she seemed thoroughly stymied. Nevertheless, Audrey sat down on the bench next to Agnes.

London stood and watched for a moment as the couple set right to work trying to draw Audrey out with conversation. The woman wore a perplexed, deer-in-the-headlights expression.

The Shicks are such nice people, she thought. *They certainly deserve a pleasant vacation.*

Several days ago, she'd found out something strange about the

36

couple. Walter Shick had slipped her a note telling her that he and Agnes had been in the witness protection program for thirty years. In his note, he had implored London not to tell another living soul. His note had concluded with the unsettling words ...

Our lives might still be in danger.

London still found it hard to believe that anyone could possibly mean any harm to such a sweet and amiable couple. But she would never think of asking either of them to tell her more about their past.

As London turned to look for a place for herself to sit, she noticed that Emil was sitting at a table alone reading a book.

London felt a spasm of indecision.

Should I sit at the table with him? she wondered.

Given how distantly he'd been behaving lately, she wasn't at all sure she'd be welcome.

She walked over to his table and asked cautiously, "May I join you?"

Emil looked up from his book as if surprised to be spoken to.

"Of course," he said with a slight smile, then went right back to his reading.

He looked and sounded almost as if London were a stranger and he was only trying to be polite. She wondered whether it might be best to look for someplace else to sit, but she figured that just walking away would make things even more awkward than they already were.

As London slipped into a chair on the other side of the table, she saw that Emil was reading a collection of poems by Rainer Maria Rilke. She happened to like the early twentieth-century Bohemian-Austrian poet, although she'd only read his work in translation. She was tempted to break the ice by asking Emil to read her a poem aloud in the German original.

But Emil seemed to be taking no notice of her presence.

Instead, London picked up the menu and started to look it over.

She was relieved when a waitress dressed like their hostess in a black dress, white old-fashioned apron, and white fluffy hat came over and took their orders. Then the two of them fell silent again.

London was feeling more awkward by the moment.

"Emil, is there something wrong?" she asked carefully.

Emil lowered the book and squinted at her curiously over his reading glasses.

"How do you mean?" he asked.

Yes, that's what I'd like to know, London wanted to say.

Instead she said, "Well, things seem to be … a little off between us."

Emil tilted his head and knitted his brow.

"Off?" he said. "How so?"

London stammered, "I—I'm not sure, exactly. But you've been very quiet. Toward me, I mean."

Emil leaned back as if in surprise.

"Really? I was not aware of that."

He sat looking at her as if he expected her to explain herself further. For a moment, London didn't know how to put the matter into words. Then she remembered something Amy had said to her yesterday.

"Maybe he doesn't like being accused of murder."

Of course, as she'd told Amy at the time, London hadn't *accused* Emil of anything.

But even so …

She took a deep breath and said, "Emil, I'm sorry I ever imagined …"

"Imagined what?"

"Well, that you might have been guilty of … you know."

Emil's lips formed into a flicker of a smile.

"Oh, there is no need to apologize. You simply had to follow clues wherever they happened to lead you. And as it happened, they temporarily led you toward me. It could hardly be helped. It is—what is the English phrase?—'water under the dam,' as far as I am concerned."

Of course, London knew he really meant to say "water under the bridge." Sometimes she'd gently correct him over little mistakes like that. But that didn't seem like a good idea right now.

He shrugged slightly and added, "As for my being quiet … well, it is just my personality, I suppose. I can get quite introverted at times. Please do not let it bother you."

Then he lifted his reading glasses and went right back to reading his book.

Does that explain it? London wondered.

She'd only known Emil for a few days, which was hardly long enough to get a sense of his moods. And he certainly wasn't being deliberately unpleasant toward her, at least not at the moment. In fact, he seemed to be quite sincere.

I guess I'd better get used to his moods, she thought. She didn't plan to get involved with him, or anybody else right now. But she did hope to regain their good working relationship.

She gazed around at the rest of the people she'd brought on this tour. They were chattering and smiling and seemed to be having a good time—which meant that, between the two of them, she and Emil had been doing a good job. Even Audrey Bolton seemed to be carrying on a conversation with her lunch companions.

It was a lovely setting here on the bank of the beautiful Danube. Those spectral eddies swirling around the pilings of the ancient bridge made it almost easy to believe the fanciful story Emil had told about how it had gotten built. And the aroma of sausages on the grill promised that a satisfying meal was well on the way.

In fact, the waitress soon returned and placed their orders on the table. As London looked down into a dish of sauerkraut topped off with a generous row of grilled sausages, she wondered briefly whether she could eat the entire meal.

Well, I am pretty hungry, she realized.

Then she took a bite of the bratwurst. The taste of garlic was rich without being overwhelming, and the meat was smoky from being prepared on an open grill. Her taste buds detected just the right flavorings of pimentos, cloves, and marjoram. Elsa Schricker's legendary mustard was pleasantly flavored with honey and horseradish, and the bed of yeasty sauerkraut was also delicious.

She sipped the clear, foamy lager, which was cold and refreshing after the morning's activities. Everything seemed to be just right.

Yes, she decided, *I can eat it all.*

By the time London finished her lunch, Emil had gone back to reading his Rilke poems, and neither of them seemed to have anything to say to each other. Seeing that others in the tour group were still enjoying their meals and multiple drinks, she got up to take a look around the little restaurant building.

Peeking inside, she saw that the cooks were working cheerfully over their fiery grill. The hostess and waitresses bustled back and forth, keeping their customers happy.

On the outside wall of the building was a large bulletin board covered with a collage of messages and advertisements, including a poster announcing the line-up for the upcoming Bavarian Jazz Weekend. Some of the smaller messages advertised boat rides and personal tour guides and classes of all kinds.

Just before she turned away, one thumbtacked message caught London's eye. Although it was mostly covered over by other notices, its opening words captured her attention.

Sprachleher zu mieten.

Translating aloud, London said, "Language tutor for hire."

For a moment, she wasn't sure why those words gave her a peculiar chill.

Then she remembered the woman she met back in Salzburg telling her that Mom had been working as an itinerant language tutor.

London gasped aloud.

Is it possible ... ? she wondered.

She pushed aside the tangle of messages to view the entire note.

Language tutor for hire.
I teach mostly English, but other languages as well, for students at all levels, children and adults.
Contact Fern Weh.

London's heart sank. That was not her mother's name.

But she asked herself—what did she expect?

To accidentally come across a personal ad left by Mom herself? That would have been too amazing to believe.

Fern Weh, she thought.

She wondered whether the name might be Asian.

She turned and saw that her tour group all seemed ready to leave.

Without quite knowing why, she tore off one of the little dangling tags with Fern Weh's phone number and put it in her pocket. Then she and Emil gathered the group together, and they all headed back to the *Nachtmusik.*

London was glad to see that the passengers all looked well-fed and satisfied.

The next leg of this trip should be smooth and easy, she thought. *At least as far as the passengers are concerned.*

She'd been warned that tomorrow's leg of the trip might be rougher going. But surely their brand-new high-tech riverboat would be up to any challenge.

CHAPTER EIGHT

The *Nachtmusik* was sinking.

London felt it again—that odd sensation of slowly dropping downward. And she knew it wasn't just her imagination.

It was very late at night, and she was standing at the rail on the open top deck of the ship. All she could see was a massive, blank concrete wall that was weirdly illuminated by massive industrial floodlights.

Sitting by her side, Sir Reggie let out an unsettled little whine.

"I know, Sir Reggie," she said. "I'm having trouble getting used to it too."

The *Nachtmusik* was slowly descending, foot-by-foot, down into a lock on the Main-Danube Canal.

This was the ninth lock the boat had passed through since navigating from the Danube into the canal earlier that day. London had never been on this canal before, but she knew its route. It stretched between the Danube to the south and the Main River to the north, making it possible to travel by water all the way from the Black Sea to the North Sea. The *Nachtmusik*'s remarkable itinerary, rare among river tour boats, would be impossible without it.

She was finding it a strange experience, especially in contrast with their trip until now. Completed in 1992, nothing about the canal felt "Old World." It felt very modern, very man-made, and very different from the river cruise so far.

The canal carved a narrow, monotonously direct route through the hills, forests, and cities of Bavaria. In fact, it sometimes seemed more like a modern highway than a river. In places, the canal rose above the level of the land surrounding it. The waterway even bridged some highways on its own overpasses. More than once, London had glanced down from a deck or a window to see cars driving below her.

And then there were the locks.

Boats eventually had to be raised to more than 3,000 feet above sea level to cross this countryside. So from time to time the *Nachtmusik* had to stop between massive gates where the water was adjusted to the

41

next level. At first the locks had lifted the *Nachtmusik* higher and higher. But now the ship was descending, and it would continue to descend until its arrival in Bamberg.

Tonight the strange sounds and motions had made it impossible for London to sleep, and Sir Reggie had been restless too. They had joined a handful of passengers up here on the Rondo deck, where they could at least see what was going on. Now the others had wandered away, to bed or perhaps to the bar.

London stood listening to the rumbling and churning of the water and massive machinery as the boat slipped lower and lower along the wall of the lock. Sir Reggie whined again and nudged her ankle, so she picked him up in her arms.

"It will be easier going after we get to Bamberg," she told him. "I promise."

In a way, this descent seemed an eerie contrast to the tour group's underground visit to the Document Neupfarrplatz. The descent into that archaeological site had taken the group deep into European history, while this descent seemed to lead …

Where?

Nowhere, I guess.

For the first time since she'd arrived in Europe, London felt like she was a long, long way from home.

But where *was* home, exactly?

She didn't ask herself the question very often. But whenever she did, she realized she simply didn't know the answer. She'd been traveling for years and didn't have a permanent home anywhere.

And now she felt a growing desire to reach out to someone familiar.

A couple of nights ago, while the *Nachtmusik* was sailing between Gyor and Vienna, she'd gotten a call from Dad, who still traveled the world as a flight attendant. He'd called her during a layover in Tokyo.

Should I give him a call? she asked herself.

But she didn't know where in the world he might be right now or what time of day or night it might be for him.

Then there was London's older sister, Tia.

London had been visiting Tia and her three kids in Connecticut when she'd gotten the call offering her the job of Social Director aboard the *Nachtmusik*. She glanced at her watch and calculated that it was late afternoon in Gaitling, Connecticut.

Sitting on a deck chair, she put Sir Reggie back down, then took out

42

her cell phone and dialed Tia's number.

The phone rang a couple of times, and she heard Tia say "hello." But before London could reply, she heard an alarming crash, followed by the sounds of explosions and gunfire.

"Tia!" London exclaimed.

After a lot of clattering noise, Tia spoke again.

"London. Is that you?"

The sound of gunfire and explosions continued.

"Tia, are you all right?" London asked.

"Sure. Bret just overturned the end table. But nobody got hurt."

Then she said to her son, "Bret, Mom's talking with Aunt London. Go play with your sisters, OK?"

London realized that the clamor sounded the same as when she'd been at her sister's house just before this trip began. Seven-year-old Bret was Tia's youngest child. And now London realized that the ongoing racket must be Tia's daughters, ten-year-old Stella and twelve-year-old Margie, playing a video war game. Tia somehow managed to maintain her calm, or her detachment, thorough it all.

She heard Bret complain, "I want to talk to Aunt London too."

Tia let out a sigh and said, "OK."

Then London heard Bret's little voice.

"Hi, Aunt London."

"Hi, Bret."

"Where are you?"

"I'm traveling in Germany, sweetie."

"Where's Germany?"

"It's in Europe."

"Oh. Europe is over across the ocean, isn't it?"

"That's right."

"That's a long way away."

"I suppose it is."

London felt uneasy about this innocent little interrogation. She wished Bret would hand the phone back to his mother.

Then Bret asked, "When are you coming home?"

London felt a jolt of emotional surprise.

Home? she thought.

Does he really think of their house as where I live?

London supposed it might make sense in the mind of a little boy. After all, whenever London wasn't voyaging around the world, she'd often stayed with her sister and her family.

London was relieved to hear Tia say again, "Go play with your sisters, Bret."

"OK," Bret said.

A second later Tia was back on the phone.

"Bret misses you," Tia said.

"I know," London said.

"So do the girls."

Actually, London doubted that. Unlike little Bret, the girls had never shown a lot of interest in her.

"Where are you right now?" Tia said.

"On our way to Bamberg," London said.

"Is that in Germany?"

"Yes."

"Have you been enjoying Europe?"

London was a bit surprised by the question. But then she realized—Tia surely had no idea that London had dealt with two murders since they'd set sail from Budapest, much less that her own life had been in danger. Enjoying Europe hadn't exactly been her first priority.

"It's been fine," London told her.

"I'm glad."

But Tia didn't sound so glad at all, and London now more than half regretted reaching out to her.

"How are you and Bernard?" London asked.

"Pretty much like always," Tia said.

"And the kids?" London asked, still hearing the sounds of combat in the background.

"The same," Tia said. Then she said again, "They miss you."

Then came an awkward pause. London knew what she was supposed to say—that she missed Tia and her husband and the kids too, and couldn't wait to get back to Connecticut. But the truth was, London had barely given them any thought since she'd left. And she certainly was in no hurry to get back to Connecticut.

Then Tia said, "It's not too late to change your mind, you know."

"About what?"

"About Ian, of course."

Oh, that, London realized.

The night before the phone call offering her the job aboard the *Nachtmusik*, her accountant boyfriend Ian Mitchell had asked her over

44

an elegant dinner to marry him. Actually, he'd made his proposal more in business terms—as a "merger" that would be advantageous to both of them.

"Um, Tia," she said, "I think that ship has sailed—so to speak."

"What do you mean?"

London stifled a sigh. She didn't want to tell Tia how Ian had reacted when she'd called him from the airport to turn down his "merger," explaining that she was on her way to Europe instead.

"The deal is off," he'd said. *"I'm afraid the matter is no longer up for negotiation."*

And that had been that.

"Never mind," Tia said with a groan of resignation. "You'll never settle down. You're determined to follow in Mom's footsteps."

London's mouth dropped open.

Is that what I'm doing?

Following in Mom's footsteps?

Tia continued, "Not that we have any idea where those footsteps finally took her, or where she might be now. And I guess that's fine with her, no matter how we felt about it. All we know is she ... well, she didn't care enough about us to hang around. You seem to take after her that way."

London felt a deep tingling all over.

She doesn't know what I found out.

London wondered for a moment—was it a good idea to tell Tia? But surely her sister had a right to know.

London spoke cautiously.

"Tia, I ... I've got some idea of what happened to Mom."

"What do you mean?"

London took a long, deep breath.

"During our stay in Salzburg, I met a woman—her name is Selma—and she said she knew Mom. She said Mom has been traveling around Europe working as a language tutor. Mom tutored Selma's daughter in Salzburg for a few months. When she left, she only told Selma that she was on her way to Germany."

"Hold on a minute," Tia gasped.

Then London heard her sister say, "Out of the kitchen. Now. Close the door."

When the noise diminished, Tia said to London, "And that's where you are now. In Germany."

Well, Germany is a big country, London almost said.

Also, Mom might very well be in a different country by now.

"London, don't even think about it," Tia said.

"Think about what?" London said.

"Looking for her."

Did I say I was looking for her? London wondered.

Am I looking for her?

Tia continued, "She never wanted to be found. And I for one don't want to find her. And you shouldn't either. I'm sure Dad feels the same way. Think about *his* feelings, London."

"Tia—" London began.

"I mean it, London. Mom is just being true to her nature. Remember what she told us about her name?"

"No," London replied.

"She told us Barbara comes from the Greek word *barbaros*, which means 'strange' or 'foreign'—the same word 'barbarian' comes from. 'That's what I am,' she used to tell us, 'just a wandering barbarian at heart.'"

Yes, I remember, London realized.

She had been very little when Mom had said that, and she'd forgotten it. But now, for the first time in years, those words were coming back to her.

Suddenly London heard a raucous metallic clatter.

"Stop that, Bret!" Tia shouted.

But the noise continued.

"I've got to go," Tia said. "Bret's pulling all the pans out of the cabinet. Call me again when you get a chance, OK?"

Tia ended the call before London could say another word.

Meanwhile, the boat's slow descent had come to a stop, and the enormous metal gate in front of the *Nachtmusik* was sliding upward with a thunderous roar of machinery.

Sir Reggie nudged London's ankle again, and she picked him back up.

"It's OK, boy," she said over the noise. "Everything's OK."

But she didn't feel like everything was OK. Her conversation with Tia had left her rattled for reasons she couldn't quite put her finger on. It had something to do with what Mom had said about her name meaning "strange" or "foreign."

And now she found herself thinking about that advertisement she'd found posted at the restaurant back in Regensburg: *"Sprachleher zu mieten"*—"Tutor for hire." She reached into her pocket and took out the little slip of paper with the phone number on it. For a couple of seconds she wondered ...

What was the name on that ad?

Oh, yes.

Fern Weh.

At the time she thought maybe the name was Asian.

Looking into Sir Reggie's eyes, she said it aloud.

"Fern Weh. Does that name mean anything to you, boy?"

Sir Reggie let out a grumbling sound, as if he wondered the same thing.

Then London said it again and realized something.

"Fern Weh. Fernweh! It's one word, Sir Reggie! One German word!"

Sir Reggie grumbled again, as if he wanted more of an explanation.

It took London a couple of seconds to remember what that word meant.

"Of course," she said aloud. "It means 'wanderlust.'"

And now she'd been reminded that Mom's name meant "stranger" or "foreigner."

Were the meanings of those two names just a coincidence?

Or was it possible that Mom had posted that advertisement after all?

London struggled to make sense of her own thoughts.

Why Fern Weh? she asked herself.

Then she remembered something Selma had said about Mom.

"She seemed ... well, a little mysterious somehow. As though she just didn't want to talk about herself in any detail."

Might Mom have started traveling under an assumed identity?

It seemed like a crazy idea. But then, Mom was hardly what anyone could call a normal person.

London looked carefully at the phone number, wondering if she should call it.

Tia's words echoed through her ear.

"London, don't even think of it."

Maybe that was good advice after all.

"She never wanted to be found," Tia had also said.

But London suddenly realized—she didn't care. Mom had left a family behind. As much as she might want to disappear without a trace,

47

it wasn't her decision to make—not when her disappearance affected the lives of people she loved.

London set Sir Reggie down. Her fingers shook as she read the number on the slip of paper and punched it into her cell phone. She heard a couple of rings, then an automated voice.

"Die von Ihnen erreichte Nummer ist nicht in Betrieb."

London sighed aloud as she translated the words in her head.

"The number you have reached is not in service ..."

And of course, the message continued to advise London to try again if she thought she'd called this number in error.

London did try again, and she got the same message.

Staring at the phone, she inhaled and exhaled slowly, not certain whether she felt disappointed or relieved.

The *Nachtmusik* was now sailing under the gate between two massive towers. Spread before her along the canal were the lights of Nuremberg—an industrial area, hardly anything scenic.

She got up from the chair and said to Sir Reggie, "Let's go back to the room and try to sleep again, OK?"

As if in agreement, Reggie jumped out of her arms and trotted in front of her toward the elevator.

As they rode down to the Allegro deck, London remembered how the message on the bulletin board had been mostly buried under other ads and messages, and also that it looked yellowed and old. It probably had been posted quite a long time ago.

Anyhow, the number was out of service now. And of course, she had no idea whether "Fern Weh" really was Mom. The whole thing was a dead end.

London admonished herself to forget the odd message and focus on her job. She had plenty of things to take care of right here on the *Nachtmusik*.

Tomorrow they would be in Bamberg. Surely that would give her a nice break from any personal concerns. She was looking forward to a quiet and peaceful visit to a lovely historical town.

CHAPTER NINE

Strange and unexpected sounds drew London toward the rail on the Rondo deck.

What on earth ...?

Was that music she heard, or something else entirely?

She had first noticed the noise from her stateroom when she was doing research and planning today's tour while having a light breakfast. Sir Reggie had kept right on sleeping soundly after spending a restless night passing through the locks, so she'd left him there and hurried up to the ship's top deck.

Several passengers were already gathered at the railing, staring out over Bamberg and chattering with each other. When London joined them, she saw that the *Nachtmusik*'s crew was finishing up their docking procedures, tying massive ropes around the shore bitts and preparing the gangway. With its steep red roofs and half-timber houses and church spires, the town of Bamberg looked like the fairy-tale setting she had expected.

It did seem odd that so many of the people she could see on the waterfront walkway and adjoining streets were dressed in colorful costumes. Most were wearing folk Bavarian clothes, women in puffy outfits called *dirndls* and men in short pants called *lederhosen.* Others were more weirdly decked out as mice, snakes, some kind of bugs that she thought resembled fleas, and still other whimsical characters.

But strangest of all was the noise, like a gigantic band tuning up or playing dozens of different melodies at the same time.

Before London could ask anybody if they knew what was going on, she heard Captain Hays's voice behind her.

"Ah, the revelry is well under way! Capital! I wish I could join the festivities myself. Maybe I'll be able to get away for a bit later on."

Grinning with delight behind his walrus-style mustache, the portly captain joined London to look out over the railing.

"Captain, what's going on out there?" London asked him.

"Oh, I thought you knew," the captain said with a wiggle of his bushy eyebrows. "Today is the beginning of *Hoffmann Fest* here in

49

Bamberg."

"I didn't know there was going to be a festival here."

"You didn't? Well, I suppose you might not have heard. If we'd followed our original schedule, we'd have missed it. But there's a silver lining to everything, I imagine, including setbacks and delays—although I suppose I must draw the line at murder. The festival should be great fun for all. Meanwhile, I must get back to the bridge. Ah, the endless and burdensome duties of command!"

The captain turned and headed off toward his glass-enclosed bridge.

Now London was starting to get the picture. The local police investigations of two murders had set their voyage a full day behind schedule. If the *Nachtmusik* had arrived here yesterday, they would have found a charming and rather quiet historic Bavarian town. Today it was bustling and noisy. The cacophonous music was surely coming from many smaller ensembles playing at different places in town.

London couldn't wrap her head about what this development would mean for today's schedule.

And now all she knew was that some major and unexpected event was unfolding here in Bamberg, the so-called Hoffmann Fest. She was going to have to rethink today's activities. The town they were visiting was certainly lovely and historic, but it seemed that their visit would be anything but quiet and peaceful.

London decided she needed a fresh cup of coffee—and besides, in the Habsburg Restaurant she might even find a moment to chat with ship's chef and sometimes medic, Bryce Yeaton.

Just a brief friendly visit, she told herself.

She took the stairs down to the Adagio deck, but when she entered the restaurant, she saw no sign of Bryce. To her surprise, the room was quite crowded, and the festival seemed to already be under way there inside the ship.

A middle-aged honeymooning couple, Gus and Honey Jarrett, were dancing a sort of ragged polka among the tables while other customers watched in amusement. The overweight Gus was wearing harness-style suede suspenders, a green felt Alpine hat stuffed with feathers, and leather *lederhosen* pants that exposed quite a lot of his broad, hairy legs.

His wife, Honey, was dressed in a *dirndl* with a white puffy blouse, a low-cut bodice that made the most of her considerable bosom, and a colorful dress and apron that were way too short to be considered

50

traditional. She was wearing a feather-laden headband over her heavily dyed red hair.

Gus and Honey stopped dancing as soon as they caught sight of London.

"Hey, London!" Gus exclaimed. "Why aren't you in costume?"

"I—I don't have one," London said. "Where did the two of you get yours?"

"We brought ours with us," Honey said with a snap of her chewing gum.

Gus added with a laugh, "After all, we knew we were going to be traveling in Bavaria. We figured sooner or later we'd want to blend in with the locals. We didn't realize we'd have a chance to take part in a festival like this one. What luck things worked out how they did, huh?"

London doubted very much that Gus and Honey would succeed in "blending in with the locals," especially since she was pretty sure neither one of them spoke any German.

The couple took up their polka again, whirling back toward their table where they sat down. London thought they looked a little winded, but she was sure they would soon revive and have a good time joining the party that was going on outside.

London noticed that Emil was sitting alone at a table off to one side, sipping a cup of coffee. As she headed in his direction to discuss revising their plans for the day, her attention was caught by a gleam of morning sunlight reflecting off a pair of mirror glasses. She saw that Bob Turner was sitting at a nearby table and that he had two unusual companions there with him.

One was Sir Reggie, sitting on a chair and listening intently to the ongoing conversation. She'd left the little Yorkshire Terrier sleeping when she'd left her room, but he'd obviously made use of his doggie door and come out looking for companionship.

And probably for treats, she thought.

The other chair was occupied by an elderly man with squinty eyes and a hawklike nose. It was Stanley Tedrow, an aspiring mystery writer who was so reclusive that he rarely came out of this stateroom.

"I'm glad to see you out and around," London said to Mr. Tedrow as she approached them. "But maybe I shouldn't be surprised, since you've finished writing your novel."

"Oh, that," Mr. Tedrow said with a dismissive wave. "I tossed it."

"You what?" London said in astonishment, remembering how

51

intently he'd been working on his book, which he'd been sure would be a bestseller.

"I trashed it. Threw it out. I realized I got the whole thing wrong."

London stared at him. When she'd seen Mr. Tedrow just the night before last, he'd been so excited about finishing his novel that he'd told her the entire plot, spoilers and all.

Pointing at Bob, Mr. Tedrow said to London, "Do you know this guy? He's Bob Turner, the ship's crack security expert. Did you know he solved a real-live murder mystery pretty much single-handedly when we were back in Salzburg?"

London couldn't help but smile.

"Yes, I heard something about that," she said.

She already knew that Bob had been taking full credit for solving the mystery of the tour guide's death. Now it appeared that he wasn't even mentioning her much more considerable role in discovering the killer. She reminded herself that Bob actually had rescued her when she'd almost gotten killed while confronting the man.

In his usual monotone, Bob said to London, "I'm giving him a few tips about the art and science of criminal investigation."

Nodding toward Sir Reggie, Bob added, "And my canine partner might learn a thing or two as well."

"This guy is telling me all kinds of stuff I didn't know," Tedrow said to London. "That's how I found out that my novel was junk. I need to start the whole thing over from scratch. I can't wait to get back to work."

London tried not to laugh. During the short time since she'd first met Bob, he hadn't struck her as much of a detective in spite of his earlier years spent in criminal investigations. But she figured no harm was going to come from this budding relationship.

It might even be a good thing, she thought.

At least it meant that the normally dour and solitary Mr. Tedrow was out of his room and enjoying himself. It also gave Bob something to occupy himself with other than prowling around and taking unnecessary notes and photographs of other people's business, which he tended to do otherwise.

And of course, Sir Reggie seemed to be fascinated by the conversation as he sat there between the two men. Since London didn't plan on taking him out on today's tour, it was good to know he had something to keep him entertained.

"Enjoy the day," she told them, then continued on her way toward Emil, who was staring moodily into his cup of coffee. She ordered coffee for herself from a passing waiter and then took the liberty of sitting down with the ship's historian.

"Did you have any idea all this was going on?" London asked Emil.

"I should have," Emil said with a growl of dismay. "I have heard about this festival. I just had not thought about the date. It was not on our schedule."

"You don't sound very happy about it," London said.

"Are you?" Emil asked.

London didn't know what to say. She hadn't had a chance to consider the ramifications of this new development.

"Tell me about the festival," London said. "The captain called it the Hoffmann Fest."

"Well, then what do *you* suppose it is about?" Emil said a bit impatiently, crossing his arms and looking at London in his most professorial manner. "Surely you can figure it out."

London thought for a moment, then quickly realized that Emil was right.

She said, "It must be a celebration of E.T.A. Hoffmann—the composer and writer."

"And don't forget painter," Emil said.

"Right. He lived part of his life here in Bamberg. We're planning on visiting the house where he lived on today's tour."

Emil scoffed. "We will see how that works out. Our well-made plans for today are rather at the mercy of anarchy and chaos, I fear."

"I don't understand," London said.

"Suffice it to say, Hoffmann Fest ought to be a celebration of literature, music, and painting. But from what I hear, another aspect of German culture takes precedence here today."

"What's that?" London asked.

"Beer," Emil said with a smirk. "Bamberg is home to nine breweries. That's a considerable number for a city with a population of about seventy thousand."

Sipping the last of his coffee, he got up from his chair.

"I will meet you in the reception area shortly," he said curtly.

Without another word, he left the restaurant.

He's not being much friendlier today than he was yesterday, London thought.

As she sat wondering what the day might have in store, the waiter brought London her coffee. She sipped at it but realized the rich dark brew wasn't helping to clear her head.

At that moment, Bryce appeared out of the kitchen with a tray in his hands. The chef was obviously helping out the waiters during this unusual breakfast rush. She felt a little thrill when he glanced her way and their eyes met. But with no more than a nod and a discreet wave, he turned away and vanished back into the kitchen again.

London sighed, remembering what Emil had said just now.

"Our well-made plans for today are rather at the mercy of anarchy and chaos."

Even her wish for a simple spontaneous encounter had lost out to the hullabaloo.

She figured she'd better be ready for anything today.

Abandoning the rest of her coffee, London left the restaurant and headed up the stairs to the Menuetto deck. She thought that her tour group would soon be gathering in the reception area, so she might as well get there and be ready for them. She wasn't expecting a large number of passengers for the tour this morning, but when she got to the reception area, she was amazed to see the room filled with excited people. They were jammed against the big glass doors that led out to the gangway.

"Somebody get these doors open," one man shouted. Others muttered in agreement.

London gasped. She knew that the stewards were fastening the gangway into place just outside. Those doors would be opened as soon as the crew had the gangway secured.

But chaos seemed to be already in effect, and London was beginning to feel a bit panicked. If all of these eager people were signed up for the morning tour, how would she ever deal with so many of them? Would they even be able to hear what she had to say?

CHAPTER TEN

As London tried to reimagine her plans for the day, the big double doors at the end of the reception area swung open. She watched in astonishment as the mass of people surged through the doors and clattered down the gangway.

So they hadn't been waiting for her tour after all.

But what could be happening? She almost wondered for a moment whether the *Nachtmusik* was being evacuated.

Then she saw that a much smaller group was still there in the reception area, looking somewhat bewildered. Among them were a few familiar passengers, including Letitia Hartzer and Audrey Bolton.

Amy was waving her notebook, checking off names, and Emil stood there with them, looking rather cross.

"A lot more people had signed up for the tour," he said crankily as London walked toward them. "But these seem to be the only ones actually going with us."

London felt a wave of relief. What had looked to her like too much of a crowd to handle had actually been tourists eager to get to the festival on their own. So the tour was still scheduled, but just with this handful of people. She thought that this should make the tour easier to handle, even though one of them was already complaining.

"I had thought this was going to be a more sophisticated adventure," Audrey Bolton said. "Do all those upscale passengers really want to go a German beer fest?"

"You bet they do," Letitia Hartzer answered her. "And I will too. I just want to see a bit of history first."

Amy shoved the list of names into London's hands and left the reception area. It was clear from the marked-up paper that a lot who had signed up had changed their minds. London had to admit, after coping with two murders during the last week, a beer festival was likely to be a healthy way to let off steam. In the long run, it would probably improve morale aboard the *Nachtmusik*. She half-wished she could skip the tour herself.

"Emil and I appreciate your interest," she said to the small group that remained. "But I'll understand if some of you would rather join the festivities."

A man shrugged and said, "Well, I don't want to miss the partying altogether."

A woman said, "After all, the festival is part of Bavarian culture, just like the sights we're headed out to see. It's the kind of thing we came on this trip to experience."

Emil grunted discontentedly. But London knew that the woman was right. It would be a shame for any of the tourists to miss the festival.

"Let's do it this way," London said. "We'll keep our formal touring to a minimum. We'll take a look at the unique Old Town Hall, but leave the cathedrals for you to visit on your own if you want to. Since this celebration is all about E.T.A. Hoffmann, we'll focus on things pertaining to him. We'll finish quickly, and everybody can head off on their own to do whatever they like. Just make sure you're back aboard tonight before we set sail for Amsterdam."

Almost everybody smiled and nodded and murmured words of approval.

Then London realized she was making some important decisions without consulting her partner.

She turned to Emil and asked, "Does this plan sound OK to you?"

Emil rolled his eyes and frowned.

"Who am I to say otherwise?" he said.

Hardly a ringing endorsement, London thought.

She wished she knew why he was being so aloof.

The exit and gangway were now clear of passengers. and the group made their way down to join the locals and tourists who swarmed the streets.

"What a mess today is going to be!" Audrey complained. "We should have skipped Bamberg, just like I told you. But does anybody ever listen to my advice? No! And now we're about to walk straight into pure bedlam!"

London stifled a sigh. She thought that the bedlam in view seemed quite cheerful. At the base of the gangway, a German band had gathered to welcome the American tourists. The musicians were all dressed in *lederhosen*, and their instruments included a trumpet, a trombone, a tuba, and a couple of less familiar-looking horns, along with an accordion.

The tuba kept jaunty time with a steady old-fashioned *oompah,*

oompah, oompah while men and women in Bavarian costumes danced nearby.

As the group stopped to listen, Emil nodded his head to the music and grumbled sarcastically.

"Oh, yes. A revered and venerated classic, 'Bayern des Samma Mir.' It sets the tone perfectly for a celebration of an icon of German creativity like E.T.A. Hoffman. I fear that no translation can hope to capture the exquisite poetry of the lyrics, but they go something like this ..."

Then he recited in a tone of mock grandeur and loftiness.

"Bavarians, that's what we are!
Oh, yeah!
Bavarians, that's what we are!
Oh, yeah!"

Emil continued, "The words go on to praise Bavarian beer—'our liquid bread'—and Bavarian beer purity laws. The song was recently performed—'covered,' I believe is how you put it in English—by the death-metal rock group Rammstein. I cannot say it was an improvement. But let us soldier on."

He led the way across the *Inselstadt,* the island between the two arms of the Regnitz River that formed the center of the city. As they wended their way along narrow streets among half-timber houses and buildings, they encountered plenty of revelers. Most of them were dressed in the usual *dirndls* and *lederhosen,* but some were in stranger gear.

Even Emil's frown disappeared at the sight of a man wearing a black half-mask and a tight-fitting outfit all covered with diamond-shaped patches, and carrying a long, flat stick.

In fact, the historian almost smiled.

"That is Harlequin," he told them, "a stock character from the traditional *Commedia Dell'Arte.* The stick he's carrying is a 'slapstick.' It is designed to make a loud slapping sound, so he doesn't have to hit other actors very hard in order to make a lot of noise."

"But what does he have to do with E.T.A. Hoffmann?" Letitia asked.

Emil said, "Hoffmann was a composer as well as a storyteller and painter, and he wrote a ballet about *Commedia* characters called

Harlequin."

Emil pointed to a group of brightly dressed people moving about in a strange mechanical manner, almost like wind-up toys. Their "leader" was dressed in a brightly colored Turkish costume.

Emil explained, "Those people are dressed as characters from Hoffmann's story *Automata*, which deals in part with remarkable machines that imitate the actions of people. An early example of science fiction, in its way."

Then Emil actually became animated when a woman dressed in rags approached. She wore a bushy gray wig and a long fake nose with a wart on it, and she carried a basket of apples.

"Would you like to buy an apple, young man?" she asked Emil in German.

Emil waved her away as he replied in German.

"Begone, old woman! Go turn into a beet!"

A beet? London was startled by his rudeness.

But the costumed woman let out a wild, gleeful cackle.

"Then away with you, child of Satan!" she laughed. "Run into the crystal which will soon be your downfall!"

Emil laughed as the woman hobbled away. He turned to the group and explained, "The lady and I just acted out a scene from Hoffmann's novella *The Golden Pot*—although if we'd done it accurately, I would have knocked her whole basket of apples to the ground. I was playing a young student named Anselmus, who winds up imprisoned in a crystal bottle—among many other strange adventures."

Emil pointed to a group of three young women doing a shimmying dance while dressed in full bodysuit leotards all covered with green sequins.

"For example," Emil continued, "those attractive young ladies are enchanted snakes, the daughters of an alchemist named Lindhorst, who is actually a magical salamander exiled from the lost continent of Atlantis. Once Anselmus is freed from his crystal bottle, he will marry Serpentina, the loveliest snake of the three. Oh—and the apple seller really will turn into a beet."

Proceeding on their way, the group passed an ensemble of men playing the most gigantic horns London had ever seen. Each of the instruments was about three yards long.

"Those are alphorns," Emil grumbled less cheerfully. "They were invented to send messages up in the mountains. Alas, they are also used as musical instruments of a sort."

When they arrived at the bank of the Regnitz River on the far side of the island, a quaint and peculiar sight awaited them—the *Alte Rathaus*, or the Old Town Hall.

"Why, the whole building looks as though it was dropped into the river!" Letitia cried.

"In a way, that's not far from the truth," Emil replied with a chuckle. "When Bamberg's original town hall burned to the ground, the Bishop of Bamberg refused to grant land to build a new one. So the builders literally put up a building on stilts in the middle of the river—a building that grew and developed over the centuries until it became its own artificial island."

The *Rathaus* was a startling mix of architectural styles, from ornate and stately looking to medieval half-timber. Emil led them across an old stone bridge that connected the riverbanks and literally cut through the building in the form of an arched passageway. The building's façade was completely covered by beautiful fresco mural paintings portraying heroic figures. Emil explained, "The original murals were painted by Johann Anwander in 1755, but they have been restored and repainted many times over."

"The figures look so lifelike," one man observed. "They appear completely three-dimensional, although I know they are actually flat."

Emil chuckled again.

"Interesting you should say that," he said. "Look here."

He pointed to a painting of a cherub.

As they all stared, Audrey commented, "That's not just an optical illusion."

One of the little angel's legs was sculpted from stone and stuck out from the wall. Audrey actually joined the others in their laughter.

London smiled. At last, Audrey seemed to have found something entertaining.

After they viewed the frescoes on the other side of the building, Emil led them back into a nearby street. He shuddered with disgust, but made no comment as they passed by another peculiar musical ensemble. Several women standing along a table were lifting up little bells and ringing them, managing to produce a semblance of the old Dixieland tune "When the Saints Go Marching In."

They soon approached a narrow little house squeezed between two other residences.

"This is where E.T.A. Hoffmann himself lived with his wife between 1809 and 1813," Emil explained. "Let's have a look inside."

He led the group up to the second floor, where Hoffmann's apartment had been turned into a little museum. They continued on into a little room with a clavichord and a small writing desk looking out through a window in a cramped gable-shaped alcove.

As Emil began to speak to the group, London moved closer to Letitia, who had been known to take small "souvenirs" from places like this. Letitia pretended not to notice, but she clasped her hands together as she listened.

"Hoffmann's years here weren't happy ones," Emil explained in hushed, reverent tones. "But then, little about his short life was happy. He and his wife lived hand-to-mouth during most of their years together, and he spent much of his life working as a lawyer and bureaucrat, scraping together a living in such cities as Berlin, Warsaw, Dresden, and Leipzig without ever quite finding a true home."

Emil peered out the alcove window.

"Here in Bamberg, he gave private music lessons and worked as a stagehand, theater manager, and music critic."

Touching the writing table, Emil added, "Sitting right here, he also wrote his first successful literary work—*Ritter Gluck*, a supernatural story about a man who believes himself to be possessed by a long-dead composer. It was then that he began to call himself E.T.A. Hoffmann, replacing his middle name 'Theodor' with 'Amadeus,' in honor of the composer Wolfgang Amadeus Mozart."

Emil fell silent for a moment, clearly soaking in the history of this room.

Finally he said, "Despite the squalor of his life, Hoffmann truly lived a life immersed in poetry, 'where the sacred harmony of all things is revealed,' as he put it."

London smiled at Emil's display of cultural reverence.

This is the Emil I like, she thought.

As London and Emil led the group back outside back across the *Inselstadt*, they encountered more costumed revelers, including a soldier-shaped nutcracker, dolls, toys, and mice—all characters from the Hoffmann story that became the basis for Tchaikovsky's ballet *The Nutcracker.*

The group soon came to the edge of a broad paved square where a splendid fountain stood adorned with five statues.

Taking her turn at lecturing, London explained, "This is the Maximilian Fountain, built in 1880. The statue on the pedestal in the middle is of King Maximilian I of Bavaria. The four statues around the fountain are of St. Heinrich II, his wife Kunigunde, King Konrad III, and Bishop Otto von Banberg ..."

London's voice faded as she realized she was losing the group's attention.

And small wonder, she thought.

Maximilian Square was clearly the center of the city's festive bustling activity. Stalls and booths with food and beer were set up all around the perimeter, and the middle of the square was filled with tables, chairs, and umbrellas. A curtained makeshift stage stood at the far end of the square. A band was playing nearby, and perhaps hundreds of people were dancing, drinking, eating, and celebrating.

London chuckled and said, "Well, I guess the tour ends here. Enjoy the party."

The group broke up to join the festivities. London turned to look for Emil, but found that he suddenly wasn't there.

Where did he go off to? she wondered.

Before she could go looking for him, she heard a woman's shriek nearby.

"How dare you, sir!"

CHAPTER ELEVEN

London whirled around to see an unexpected confrontation. A very angry-looking Audrey Bolton was standing face to face with a middle-aged man in a three-piece pinstriped suit. The man was holding a nearly empty beer mug in his hand, and he was laughing in the woman's face.

The front of Audrey's dress was drenched with beer.

"Schau dir das an!" roared the man. *"Ein großes nasses Huhn!"*

Audrey looked all around frantically. When her eyes fastened on London, she cried in a voice fierce with anger, "What did he just say?"

London knew the answer to her question.

"Look at this!" the man had said. *"A big wet chicken!"*

But she really didn't want to translate for Audrey.

As she approached the conflicting pair, London noticed that none of the bystanders looked amused by the man's proclamations. Apparently their sympathy was with Audrey.

"American, are you?" the man said to Audrey in accented English. "Is this your first taste of Bavarian lager? How do you like it?"

"This isn't funny," Audrey snapped back.

"My dear, you should learn to watch where you're going."

"I *was* watching where I was going!" Audrey shrieked. "You stumbled and bumped right into me!"

Several bystanders murmured their agreement with Audrey. Even though London had no doubt that the drenched woman was telling the truth, she wanted to defuse the situation before things got a lot worse.

London took Audrey by the arm and said, "Come on, let's go back to the ship and get you dried off."

The man was still laughing heartily.

"You Americans can't hold your beer!" he bellowed.

London turned and stared directly at him with disbelief. The man was wearing a monocle and had a waxed mustache. In other circumstances, she might take him to be a sophisticated gentleman. She thought he certainly should know better than to behave like a boorish drunk.

Wherever she traveled, London made a strict point of not quarreling with locals. But Audrey she was clearly not at fault here. And the woman's enjoyment and well-being were London's primary responsibility at the moment. She decided that she actually had a professional responsibility not to let this incident go.

She spoke to the man in German, telling him, "I think you should apologize to the lady."

The man let out a noisy scoff.

"Apologize?" he said. "For her inexcusable clumsiness? I hardly think so."

London felt her face redden.

Stay cool, she told herself.

The last thing she wanted to do right now was lose her temper. She felt frustrations that had built up over recent days—discovering murders, accusations of guilt, the constant pressures of keeping passengers happy. She knew that those frustrations were in danger of exploding.

She brought her feelings under control and said, "Just say you're sorry, and we'll leave it at that."

The man stopped laughing and frowned at London.

"What business is it of yours, anyway?" he asked.

"Tell her you're sorry," London repeated firmly. She saw heads nodding in the group that surrounded them, and heard expressions of support in several languages.

The man glanced around, then the edge of his lip turned up into a sneer.

"Very well then, *fräulein*," he said. "If you absolutely insist."

Turning toward Audrey, he nodded his head and spoke.

"I sincerely apologize, *Frau Huhn*."

Then, with a casual jerk of his arm, he splashed London with most of his remaining beer.

"Oh, dear," the man said. "Another accident."

London whole body flooded with rage. This was no accident. She stepped directly in front of the man and looked him straight in the eye.

"You are very rude," she snapped at him in German. Stepping closer, she continued, "I did not expect to encounter such behavior in such a charming place as this. You should be ashamed ..."

Before London could say another word or make another move, she felt a strong hand pushing her away from the man.

A uniformed security guard had forcibly separated the two of them.

"Let's have no more of this!" the guard said in German.

Turning to the belligerent man, he added sternly, "Especially from you, sir."

Cursing under his breath, the man turned and stumbled away.

London felt simultaneously relieved and embarrassed—but most of all, grateful to the guard for intervening.

"Thank you, sir," she said to him in German.

"Don't mention it," the guard said with a tip of his cap. "I just hope this unfortunate incident doesn't spoil your visit to our lovely city."

London turned her attention back to Audrey, whose own humiliation seemed so great that she hadn't noticed the rest of the altercation.

"Come on, let's go," she said to Audrey.

The two of them headed back toward the *Nachtmusik*.

Audrey exclaimed, "That man just called me *Frau Huhn*—Mrs. Chicken!"

"Just forget it," London said.

As they continued on their way, London fingered the blouse and vest that were part of her uniform. She wasn't actually drenched with beer—not like Audrey. It would soon dry and be hardly noticeable.

Meanwhile, Audrey was stalking silently along beside her with her arms clutched across her soaked blouse.

"Is there anything I can do for you?" London asked.

Audrey scoffed loudly and said, "*Now* you ask. No, I hardly think so. Not at this point."

London felt a pang of guilt, and then a touch of annoyance.

Audrey clearly thought that London shared some responsibility for her discomfort. But obviously, London couldn't have stopped the man from spilling beer on her. And she felt sure she'd been right to demand an apology from the guy.

But she admitted to herself that things could have gotten worse if the security guard hadn't pulled them apart when he did.

Why did I let him get to me like that? she wondered.

She reminded herself that she'd been through a rough several days, even besides the two recent murders. Other things had been bothering her as well, including Emil's behavior and Amy's secretiveness.

Small wonder that I'm not at my best, she thought.

"I'm very sorry your visit to Bamberg had to end this way," London said to Audrey as they neared the boat.

Audrey let out a burst of harsh, angry laughter.

"Oh, this isn't over," she growled. "Not by a long shot. I'm not one to take an affront like this lying down. No, this is far from over, just you wait and see."

Audrey rushed on ahead of London and headed up the gangway.

Following behind her, London felt uneasy at Audrey's proclamation. Audrey practically radiated hostility at the best of times, and she did have good reason to be angry with the drunk who had splashed her. But would she really pursue some kind of retribution?

As she turned that over in her mind, London looked up and saw that Bryce Yeaton was on his way down the gangway. He was wearing street clothes instead of his chef's outfit.

"Goodness, what happened to you two?" the handsome Australian asked. Without responding, Audrey just hurried past him.

"We just ran into a bit of trouble," London told him, not wanting to explain further. "It's OK, we just need to clean up a little. Where are you off to?"

"I'm taking the rest of the day off," Bryce said. "I've always dreamed of attending Hoffmann Fest, and this is my chance. Why don't you join me? I'll wait here while you get ready."

London thought she might be blushing and looked down to avoid his gray eyes. She had always found this man attractive, with his dimpled chin and carefully groomed stubble of beard. But right now, she wasn't in much of a mood to party.

"I don't think so," she said, shaking her head. "I'm finished with my tour, and I'd better get back to my onboard duties."

Bryce chuckled and said, "I doubt you'll find a lot of work to do here. Just about everybody else is out enjoying themselves. The *Nachtmusik* looks like some kind of a ghost ship. Are you sure you won't come?"

"Thanks, but no," London said. "I think I've seen enough of Bamberg for one trip."

"OK, then. I take it the *Maximiliensplatz* is the hub of festive activities."

"That's right. Most of the action is right next to the fountain."

"That's where you'll find me if you happen to change your mind," Bryce said.

"OK, have a good time."

"I'll do that."

Then with a flirtatious smile he added, "I really hope you'll decide to join me. It would make things much more fun."

Bryce continued on his way into town.

Resisting the urge to call him back. London headed up the gangway. She found no one in the reception area, not even behind the desk. Audrey must have gone on to her room.

London stepped into the nearby Amadeus Lounge, hoping to talk with her friend Elsie. That was when she realized Bryce was right— there wasn't going to be much for her to do on board. The popular recreation area and bar was nearly deserted. The *Nachtmusik* really did seem like a ghost ship.

Elsie wasn't even at the bar. Instead London saw an assistant bartender, who didn't seem to have anything to do except polish the brass rail.

London sighed. The festival hadn't turned out to be very entertaining, at least not for her. But maybe it was a mistake to miss out on it this evening. Especially now that she knew that Bryce would be there, maybe even still hoping for her to join him.

She reminded herself that there was at least one onboard responsibility that she really should attend to.

London checked her list of passenger quarters to find Audrey Bolton's stateroom. Then she took the steps down to the Adagio deck and knocked on Audrey's door. There was no answer. She realized Audrey might well be in the bathroom getting herself cleaned up.

Or maybe she's just sulking.

London knocked again, and this time a voice called back.

"Who is it?"

"It's London Rose. I'm just checking in to see how you're doing."

"Leave me alone."

"Are you all right?"

"Just leave me alone, I said."

Audrey sounded as though she might be crying. London was worried now. Of course she had a master keycard that would open the door in case of an emergency. But was this an emergency? Should she take the liberty of letting herself into the stateroom?

"I just want to make sure you're OK," London said.

"I'm OK," Audrey replied, rather sharply.

"Are you sure?"

"Of course I'm sure! For Pete's sake, Ms. Rose, when are you going to learn to mind your own business?"

London felt stung now. But again she reminded herself of her motto.

"The customer is always the customer."

And if someone in London's charge wanted to be left alone, she had no choice but to comply.

"OK, then," she said. "Call me if you need anything."

London took the stairs down to the Allegro deck. She didn't see another soul as she walked the rest of the way to her own stateroom.

When she went inside, Sir Reggie came running up to her and jumped up into her arms. She plopped herself down on the bed with her dog in her lap.

Reggie immediately started sniffing the damp part of her blouse.

"Like that smell, do you?" London said.

As if in reply, Sir Reggie licked the spot. London gently thumped his nose.

"Stop that. Beer is not for dogs."

Reggie whined and crouched in her lap. London sat there for a moment, relishing the peace and quiet after the noisy fiasco she'd just been through. She thought about calling Amy to check in with her, but decided not to. Amy would probably just find some new way to put London out of sorts.

Anyway, she's probably in town just like everybody else, she figured.

If so, London could hardly blame her.

The words Bryce had said when they'd parted a few minutes ago were still running through her mind.

"I really hope you'll decide join me. It would make things much more fun."

She also remembered his flirtatious smile.

London thought it over as she scratched Sir Reggie's head.

It's really pretty silly for me to stay here.

After all, there seemed to be absolutely nothing for her to do aboard the *Nachtmusik* except maybe sit right here feeling sorry for herself.

She set Sir Reggie down on the floor and headed to the closet. It would feel good to get out of her uniform and put on regular clothes again. She took out one of her basic black mixable pieces, a pair of swingy gaucho pants. She chose a colorful blouse, dangly earrings, and a pair of cute flat-heeled shoes, and went to the bathroom to wash up and change.

When London came out of the bathroom, she found Sir Reggie sitting right next to the room door with his leash in his mouth.

"Sorry, Reggie," she said. "I'm—"

She stopped herself before she said she was going out on a date.

This isn't a date, she told herself.

There surely wasn't much chance of anything romantic happening in the midst of all that revelry. Which she figured was just as well. Surely it was best to stick to her vow to keep things between herself and Bryce Yeaton perfectly professional.

"Come on then, let's go," she told Sir Reggie.

She clipped the leash on Sir Reggie's collar, and they headed out to find out what adventures might be in store for them.

CHAPTER TWELVE

"This is not going to be a date," London said to Sir Reggie as they wended their way through the streets of Bamberg toward the raucous sounds of the Hoffmann Fest in full swing.

Sir Reggie let out a yap that actually sounded sarcastic, as if he were saying, *"Yeah, right."*

London sighed. Of course, she'd been trying to convince herself, not Sir Reggie.

Even my own dog doesn't believe me, she thought.

And the truth was, London more than half wished it did turn out to be a date, unprofessional though that might be. The thought of spending the rest of her time in Bamberg with Bryce certainly put a renewed spring in her step. Reggie had to trot especially fast just to keep up with her.

Soon they arrived at the edge of the broad *Maximiliensplatz,* which was much more crowded than it had been earlier—and much noisier. London looked out over the sea of people with mild dismay. Many of them were still in costume, but some had reverted to more ordinary clothes.

How am I ever going to find Bryce in this crowd? she wondered.

If only she'd accepted his invitation from the start, they could have arranged to meet in a particular spot—the Maximilian Fountain, perhaps.

"Do you think you can find Bryce, pal?" she said to Sir Reggie. "Can you catch his scent, maybe?"

Sir Reggie let out a doubtful growl.

London said, "I guess that's too much expect even from a crack canine detective like you. Come on, let's start looking."

She picked up Sir Reggie to avoid having him trampled by the many moving feet, some of which were already quite unsteady. As soon as they entered the crowd, she bumped into a tall man who made an unexpected turn. Looking upward, she saw a familiar face. It was the security man who had intervened during her rant at the obnoxious man who had splashed both Audrey and her with beer.

London felt herself blush with embarrassment.

"Guten Tag, mein herr," she said.

The tall young man smiled and tipped his cap.

"Guten Tag, fräulein," he replied.

London sputtered a bit as she started to explain herself in German.

"I owe you an apology, sir. You see, I work as Social Director aboard the tour boat that arrived this morning, and that man had just been terribly rude to one of my tourists, and—"

The man laughed as he interrupted.

"No need to apologize, miss. You are not in the least to blame, nor the first to tangle with that man. He has been disturbing people ever since he showed up. He does this every year, I am sorry to say. And every year I wish I could ..."

The guard paused a moment, looking very serious now.

"Well, I wish I could have him arrested, at the very least. But I'm under strict orders not to antagonize him. You see, he's a rather influential gentleman from Munich, and our mayor and town councilors are afraid it would cause a bit of a scandal."

Now London laughed.

"He doesn't strike me as much of a gentleman," she remarked.

"No, I suppose he doesn't. And I am sure he doesn't behave that way in his home city. But he looks down on us Bambergers, thinks we're ignorant provincials, and that he is slumming just to spend time here. I suppose he gets drunk and disagreeable to show his contempt for us."

He shook his head and frowned.

"It really makes me angry," he added. "I wish I could do something to teach him a lesson. But the choice is not mine to make."

The guard offered London his hand.

"My name, by the way, is Willy Oberhauser,"

"Mine is London Rose," London said, shaking his hand.

"You must introduce me to your little friend," Herr Oberhauser said, nodding at the dog.

"Oh, yes," London said. "This is Sir Reggie."

Herr Oberhauser's smile broadened as Sir Reggie let out a yap at the sound of his name.

"We're both pleased to meet you," London said to the guard.

"The pleasure is all mine. Enjoy the rest of your visit."

Herr Oberhauser headed back into the crowd, chatting with people he knew.

Still holding Sir Reggie, London moved on looking for Bryce. As she wove through the gathering crowd, she recognized a few familiar faces from the *Nachtmusik*.

The enigmatic and aloof Cyrus Bannister was making his way along, observing all that he saw with typically cool self-possession.

The same wasn't true for Kirby Oswinkle, who was weaving along a bit unsteadily, clutching an enormous half-full beer stein.

London stifled a sigh. Kirby was obnoxious under the best of circumstances.

Will he be worse after a few beers? she wondered.

Her mind boggled at the thought of most of their one hundred passengers ashore drinking their fill. They wouldn't even have to spend much. Most of the beer vendors were offering free samples in small paper cups.

How much trouble was London going to have corralling them when it came time to set sail later on? And what shape would they be in tomorrow morning?

She hoped that at least some of them would also be eating the enticing snacks the vendors were also offering. She accepted a huge *brezen* herself, a big fresh pretzel that was deliciously crunchy and salty.

Sir Reggie whined, and she broke off a small piece for him.

When she spotted Elsie, her bartender friend waved and nodded her head to indicate the handsome young man at her side. London knew that the multilingual Elsie made friends easily and often managed to find a local date wherever the ship docked. With a laugh, Elsie slipped her hand through the man's arm, and they wandered happily away into the crowd.

London was sure that tomorrow morning Elsie would have the bar in the Amadeus Lounge well supplied with virgin Bloody Marys and other supposedly therapeutic cocktails.

A flash of light on mirrored glasses drew London's attention to two men sitting at a table off at the edge of the festivities. The men were Bob Turner and Stanley Tedrow. It looked as though the security man and the aspiring author had just shifted their conversation from the ship to the shore as they kept discussing how to solve mysteries. Now they both had steins of beer on their table, and the conversation seemed to be more animated. London had to wonder just what would go into

Tedrow's book now.

"Everybody seems to be having a good time," she told Sir Reggie. "But I still can't find who I'm looking for."

Sir Reggie woofed in agreement.

She spotted Walter and Agnes Shick sitting at another little table. She was glad to see the elderly couple out for the festival, but to London's surprise, seemingly unrelated words ran through her mind.

"There's so much going on around here that you don't know about."

For a moment London wondered why she had connected Amy's petulant claim with one of her favorite couples from the ship. Then her heart sank as she realized that Amy could have been taunting her with a secret about these very people. Had Amy found out about the Shicks being in witness protection for decades? Would she make some kind of trouble for them?

But then London's thoughts were interrupted by another sight.

Audrey Bolton was there in the crowd, wearing a nice new dress. At first glance, London was glad to see that Audrey had freshened up and left her room to join the party.

Then she saw that Audrey's expression was quite angry.

The gangly woman seemed to be speaking in a scolding manner while jabbing her finger into someone's face.

Who was Audrey angry with this time?

London could only see that it was a man. As she moved closer, she saw that he was holding a mug of beer in his hand.

Oh no! London gasped as she hastened toward them.

It was the same annoying man who had splashed beer onto her and London—the man that Willy Oberhauser had called "a rather influential gentleman from Munich."

Was the earlier crisis about to get worse?

CHAPTER THIRTEEN

Hoping to prevent another ugly scene, London pushed her way through the crowd toward Audrey.

But a group of revelers momentary blocked her way and obscured her view. By the time she could see where she was going again, the man from Munich was nowhere to be seen.

Audrey was standing there with a self-satisfied expression.

"Is everything OK?" London asked anxiously.

"Oh, everything's just fine!" Audrey said with an uncharacteristically happy smile.

"Was that man bothering you again? Where did he go?"

"He just faded off into the crowd," Audrey replied with a chuckle. "And I'm sure he won't try to bother me again. In fact, I don't think he'll be rude to anyone from now on."

Without another word, Audrey turned away and stalked toward one of the stalls.

London stood there watching her go, wondering what the woman might have said to the obnoxious gentleman,

"At least the crisis seemed to be averted," she told Sir Reggie. "But do you suppose that Bryce has already left?"

Or gone off somewhere with someone else? she added silently.

In response, Sir Reggie let out a yap. He scrambled against her shoulder, staring off at something behind her and wagging his tail.

London turned around and felt her breath quicken. Her dog had spotted the man she was looking for.

Bryce Yeaton was sitting on the edge of the makeshift curtained stage that had been mounted at the end of the square. His arms were crossed, and he was watching the human traffic with a look of amused pleasure.

London made her way over to him, and his smile broadened when he saw her.

"Well, hello, there!" he said. "I was hoping you'd change your mind."

"I decided I just couldn't miss it," London said. She hoped that the warmth she felt in her cheeks wasn't a visible blush.

Pointing to the curtain, she asked, "Is there going to be some kind of performance here later on?"

Bryce let out a peal of hearty laughter.

"Well, in a manner of speaking," he said. "It's going to be the grand finale of the day. I've read about what's supposed to happen. It's pretty crazy."

"What's going to happen?" London asked.

Bryce tugged on the curtain.

"I don't suppose anyone will object if we step back there to have a peek for ourselves," he said.

London put Sir Reggie down on the stage and she and Bryce climbed up on it too. Bryce parted the curtain, and they stepped behind it. London gasped at what she saw—and what she smelled.

"What on earth!" she said.

In the middle of the stage was a staggeringly huge wooden barrel, with a small flight of stairs leading up one side to the top. An odd-looking chair was mounted over of the barrel.

"Is that smell what I think it is?" London asked.

"It sure is. That barrel is entirely full of beer."

"But who's going to drink it?"

"Nobody—I hope. But somebody's going to get a good taste of it, that's for sure."

"I don't understand."

Bryce grinned as he explained.

"At the beginning of every Hoffmann Fest, all of the beer vendors draw lots. The winner—or maybe I should say the loser—is made to wear a cat costume, and is declared to be *Katers Murr*, 'Tomcat Murr.' The tomcat is a comical character from a novel by E.T.A. Hoffmann. Tomcat Murr is enthroned in that chair, but it's hinged and he gets a ritual dunking in the barrel of beer. Tomorrow, he gets to come back in a dry royal robe and reign over all of the continuing festivities."

"Wow," London said, trying to imagine the scene. "But isn't that kind of a waste of good beer?"

"Don't worry, it's not *good* beer—at least not according to the refined tastes of Bambergers. It's just cheap commercial German lager, all kinds of brands just dumped in together. It's sort Bamberg's way of showing their scorn for lagers and any other kinds of beer that aren't made right here in town."

"When is this supposed to happen?" London asked.

"Later this evening. Hopefully we'll have time to catch it before we set sail. Have you had dinner yet?"

"No."

"Me neither. Let's get a sandwich and some brew."

"Yes," London said with a big smile. "Let's do that."

It had just hit her that she was having a good time. The festival was more interesting than she had expected it to be, but her smile was definitely for the man she was with.

As they got down from the stage, she took the hand he offered her—not because she actually needed the help but because she welcomed his humorous display of gallantry.

London and Bryce headed toward the stalls at one edge of the square. At a food vendor, they stopped and each ordered a *Fischbrötchen* sandwich. They set their sandwiches down on a free table and put Sir Reggie in one of the chairs.

Bryce gave the little terrier one of his kitchen-made dog treats, then headed off to a beer stall. He soon came back with beer in two large glasses shaped rather like tulips, wider at the top than at the base, and narrow in the middle.

"I think you're going to like this," Bryce said.

London lifted the glass to take a sip.

"Hey, not so fast!" Bryce said with a laugh. "First savor the bouquet!"

The bouquet? London wondered.

That was a word she'd always heard in reference to wine, not beer. Of course, she knew better than to be surprised that Bryce was something of a beer connoisseur.

She held the foamy head near her nose and breathed in the enchanting aroma.

"Oh, my," she said. "I don't think I've ever had beer that smells like this."

"I'm not surprised," Bryce said. "Not unless you're familiar with *Hefeweizen*—served here in its own specially shaped glass. Can you describe the smell for me?"

"It's very rich," London said, sniffing the beer again. "Almost warm, somehow."

"You know German, right?"

"Pretty well."

"So what does the word *Hefeweizen* mean?"

London was rather amused by the question.

Bryce is quizzing me, she thought.

"Well, *hefe* means yeast and *weizen* means wheat," she said.

Then something clicked in her mind, and she was able to identify the smell.

"Of course!" she said. "It smells yeasty—much more so than beers I'm used to."

Bryce nodded, obviously enjoying himself as he introduced London to this new taste experience.

"Right. That explains why it looks white and foggy. And it's made from different ingredients than you're used to—mostly unfiltered, fermented wheat, and also some barley. Now go ahead and try it."

London took a taste of the foamy head. She found that the beer was every bit as delicious as it smelled—rich and full with an interesting texture and an ever-so-slight and pleasing touch of bitterness.

"It's delicious," she said.

"I'm not surprised," Bryce said.

He took a sip himself, and his face lit up with surprise.

"Oh, my!" he said.

"Is something wrong?"

"Anything but!" Bryce said. "It's just that …"

He took another sip and said, "We've got to go have a chat with this vendor."

London picked up Sir Reggie and followed Bryce over to the stall where he'd purchased the beer. The sign above the stall read *Schutzkeller Brauen*—"Storm Cellar Brew." A hearty-looking man wearing *lederhosen* stood behind the counter.

Bryce set his beer glass on the counter spoke to the vendor in German.

"Sir, this is the most unusual *Hefeweizen* I've ever tasted."

The man smiled and replied, "It is to your liking, I hope."

"Oh, yes. But you've really got to tell me just how you achieved this unique taste."

The German wagged his finger at Bryce impishly.

"Ah, ah, ah! Surely you know that is a secret! I cannot tell you that!"

"Oh, come now, good sir," Bryce said, wagging his own finger at him. "You're not being fair! We're just two visiting foreigners who will be leaving Bamberg this very afternoon. Who would we ever tell? Your secret is safe with us."

The beer vendor glanced back and forth, then leaned toward Bryce and London and whispered.

"It is the hops."

"Hops?" Bryce asked.

"Taste it again."

Bryce did so, and a light seemed to come on in his eyes.

"Of course!" he said. "*Hefeweizen* is normally made with few if any hops. You've blended more hops with the fermented wheat. And maybe some extra barley as well. It produces more carbonation, and also a unique bitter-mellow sort of flavor."

"You are a man of discerning taste. I am glad it meets your approval. My name, by the way, is Helmut Preiss. My family has owned the *Schutzkeller Brauen* for four generations."

Bryce shook hands with him and introduced himself and London and Sir Reggie.

Bryce took another sip of the beer.

"There's something else unique about this beer," he said. "I can't quite put my finger on it."

"Surely you don't expect me to tell you my whole recipe," Preiss said with a smile.

"Fair enough," Bryce said to him. "In any case, I imagine your brewery has won first prize many years at the Hoffmann Fest."

"I am proud to say that is true," Herr Preiss said. "And I have hopes of winning the gold medal again this year."

"I'm sure you will," Bryce said. "But tell me—does anybody know what unfortunate brewer is going to be this year's dunked *Katers Murr*?"

Herr Preiss laughed gleefully.

"Not me, I am relieved to say! The lots have been drawn, and that dubious honor has gone to another brewer. We can only hope he is very thirsty!"

As other customers crowded around his stall, Herr Preiss added, "But I must get back to business. Eat and drink hearty."

Back at their table, Bryce gave Sir Reggie another dog treat, and London and Bryce sipped more of the beer. They began to eat their *Fischbrötchens*, a type of sandwich that was common at food stands. Though hardly a gourmet food, it was still delicious—a slab of grilled mackerel on a bun with a tart, tangy mayonnaise-based sauce flavored with pickles, onions, and horseradish.

And maybe a little curry, London thought.

The sandwich and the beer went perfectly together.

As London looked at the man sitting across the table from her, a thought crossed her mind

Maybe that's not all that's perfect together.

*

After they finished eating, London and Bryce took a tour of the beer vendors, sampling just a small cup of beer at each stall. The lagers ranged from light, crystal-clear pilsners to darker, heavier bock beers with their toasty, ever-so-slight hint of sweetness. There were also various types of *Weißbier*—"white beer" made from wheat—although none of the brands were nearly as delicious as the *Hefeweizen* they'd first tasted.

Although the samples were seldom more than a good mouthful, London kept reminding herself not to overdo it. She was already feeling a little lightheaded and would have to pay attention to the passengers later tonight when the *Nachtmusik* set sail again.

London and Bryce saw more familiar faces as they made their circuit. The captain, who appeared to be drinking something non-alcoholic, seemed nevertheless to be quite jovial, seated as he was with four pretty, *dirndl*-clad young women. The staff and crew seemed to be maintaining a fair degree of sobriety, which could not be said for a good many of the passengers.

London reminded herself that Bryce was the ship's medic as well as its chef.

"You might have to deal with a lot of headaches pretty soon," London said.

"Don't worry," Bryce laughed. "The infirmary is well-stocked with aspirin. And I imagine my own recipe for treating hangovers is going to be quite popular."

Bryce then cocked his ear.

"Listen," he said. "Isn't that sound familiar?"

London listened over the rumble of the crowd.

"Oh, my!" she said. "I do think I recognize that voice."

She and Bryce and Reggie made their way toward the music. Sure enough, they found Letitia Hartzer singing along with a *lederhozen-*clad accordionist. The song was "Lili Marlene," a German love song that became popular all over the world during World War II, sung in those days with equal enthusiasm by Allied and Axis troops alike.

Gus and Honey Jarrett were also here, clad in their faux-traditional costumes and dancing to the music. A crowded circle of local people were watching and listening and singing along with delight.

When "Lili Marlene" came to an end, the audience offered mugs of free beer to Letitia and the Jarretts to ply them to sing and dance some more. The three tourists downed their beers a bit more quickly than they probably should have.

"Oh, dear," London said. "They're not going to be sober for long."

"I'm afraid it's too late to worry about that," Bryce laughed.

Letitia and the accordionist launched into another song, this time in English—"We'll Meet Again," another World War II favorite made famous by the British singer Vera Lynn. Some people in the audience knew those lyrics in English, and they sang along while Gus and Honey started dancing again.

As they walked on, London kept an eye out for Emil. But she soon figured that her moody colleague had skipped the festival altogether. She didn't see any sign of Amy anywhere either. The truth was, London didn't miss either of him.

She and Bryce and Reggie eventually came to a tiny puppet theater, where a marionette performance was in progress in front of an audience of entranced and delighted children.

London explained to Bryce, "This is a performance of *Kasperltheater*, a genre of puppet theater in the German-speaking world. See that character with the big grin and the blue hat and the long nose? That's Kasper, and he's always the hero in *Kasperltheater*."

A number of stock *Kasperltheater* characters paraded through the story—Kasper's wife Gretel, a policeman, a robber, a grandmother, and other colorful personages.

In this particular story, an evil witch has turned Kasper's friend Seppel into a chicken. With the help of a good wizard, Kasper puts things right again and is rewarded by the king for his resourcefulness and bravery, while the witch winds up getting eaten by a crocodile. After this happy, triumphant ending, London and Bryce continued on their way.

Activity in the *Maximiliensplatz* only got more boisterous as evening started to fall and the time grew nearer for the ritual dunking of *Katers Murr.*

Putting his hand lightly on her shoulder Bryce asked, "Tell me the truth, London. Do you really want to spend the rest of our time in Bamberg waiting for some unlucky brewer to get dunked in a huge vat of cheap beer?"

London felt her whole body grow warm as she looked into his smiling gray eyes. Bryce was suggesting that they get away from the crowd, and right now that sounded good to her.

"I'd just as soon miss it, if that's all right with you," she said, smiling as well.

She was sure she must be blushing now, but it didn't matter anymore.

"What do you say we take a little walk, then?" he said.

"I'd like that."

London had a destination in mind as they left the square and began wending through the quaint streets of Bamberg. She looked down at Sir Reggie and wanted to say to him, *"It looks like this is turning out to be a date after all."*

After the din of the festival, the relative quiet was a welcome change. London and Bryce said very little as they walked along, but London realized she was feeling a little giddy—and probably not just from the beer she'd been drinking.

When he took her hand it felt perfectly comfortable, just as she had felt when they'd danced together days ago back in Vienna.

It was getting dark when the two of them arrived at *Schönleinsplatz,* a picturesque square that was now all but vacant due to the revels over at the *Maximiliensplatz.* London and Bryce made their way to a circular fountain partly surrounded by hedges and park benches, where they sat down together. Sir Reggie lay down at London's feet, making himself inconspicuous for once.

It was only when Bryce began to put his arm around her that London's reservations kicked in and she drew back a little.

"I don't know about this, Bryce," she said.

"I know how you feel, but …"

He paused for a moment.

"What's there to know?" he asked.

London smiled and said, "Good question."

Their lips were about to meet when London's phone buzzed.

CHAPTER FOURTEEN

When the phone buzzed, London and Bryce leaned their foreheads together instead of their lips.

"You're going to answer that, aren't you?" he said with a note of wry disappointment.

"Of course I am," London replied with a sigh.

They both laughed and drew apart. Their anticipated first kiss wasn't going to happen. At least, not right then.

When she took the call, London wasn't surprised that it was Amy who had interrupted her romantic moment.

The concierge spoke briskly. "I take it you're rounding up the passengers by now."

London glanced at her watch.

"It might be a little early for that," she said.

"I wouldn't be too sure," Amy said firmly. "You know we have to be absolutely certain that everybody is back on the boat before we can leave."

London stifled a sigh. Of course Amy was being fussy. But maybe she had a point.

Things are pretty crazy over at the Maximiliensplatz, London reminded herself. Maybe she should start encouraging passengers and crew to head back to the boat.

Amy was still talking. "I'm hard at work here checking people in. I can't come out there and get them back myself."

"I'll get on it," London said.

"I don't hear a lot of noise," Amy said. "Are you all right?"

"Of course I am," London said.

"Aren't the festivities in full swing?"

"Yes, they are."

"Then why are things so quiet? Where are you exactly?"

London felt a twinge of annoyance.

Why don't you just mind your business? she wanted to say.

But she resisted the temptation.

"I'm at the *Schönleinsplatz,*" she said instead.

"The *Schönleinsplatz*? What's going on there?"

"Nothing, really." London had to suppress a laugh.

At least nothing's going on now, she thought.

"Who are you there with?"

London cringed at Amy's meddlesome tone. Was it possible that she had some idea of what might be happening between her and Bryce? Was that why Amy was calling her before she really needed to?

London decided to just ignore the question.

"I'll head back over to the *Maximiliensplatz*," she said. "I'll check on our passengers."

She ended the call.

"I take it that was Amy," Bryce said.

"It was."

"And I take it that it's time to get back to work."

"That's right."

"Well, when duty calls …"

They got up from the bench and left the quiet plaza, with Sir Reggie trotting along beside them. As they walked through the streets of Bamberg back to the main festivities, they held hands again.

London felt warm and happy with this new stage of their relationship. True, things hadn't quite ended the way both she and Bryce had expected. But something had definitely changed between them.

Maybe it's best not to rush things, she thought.

As they neared their destination, they wordlessly stopped holding hands. London didn't feel ready to go public with whatever was developing between them, and she was relieved that Bryce apparently didn't either.

When they got back to the *Maximiliensplatz*, London picked up Sir Reggie again to keep him safe from the swarm of human feet. The square was more crowded and boisterous than before.

The people were all gathering in the vicinity of the stage. London realized that the dunking of *Katers Murr* must be coming up soon. Surely everybody would return to the ship soon after that happened. She would just have to make sure there were no stragglers that could delay their departure.

London and Bryce and Reggie squeezed among the throng, reminding any of the *Nachtmusik*'s passengers and crew they met to return to the ship soon, and to spread the word to anybody else they saw. There didn't seem to be many of them still out, and the ones they spoke with were agreeable.

When they reached the far side of the plaza, London paused in her steps with surprise at the music playing there. As before, they heard an accordion, a familiar female singer, and a chorus of tipsy voices. But the song was not at all what she'd expected—although the words were certainly familiar.

Oh, give me a home where the buffalo roam,
Where the deer and the antelope play ...

"They're singing 'Home on the Range,'" she said to Bryce.

"I thought I recognized it," her Australian companion said.

They pushed the rest of the way to where Letitia and the accordionist were still performing. Instead of dancing, Gus and Honey Jarrett were sitting together at one of the tables.

Honey was singing almost as loudly as Letitia—and at the same time, tears were running down her face. Also singing and weeping a little himself, Gus held Honey's hand and kept passing her tissues.

Many of the German listeners were singing along in accented English.

London heard a familiar male voice.

"Tell me, Sir Reggie—what do you think of the performance?"

London turned and saw the dark-clad Cyrus Bannister, who was standing with his arms crossed and taking in the performance with his usual icy detachment. Sir Reggie growled a little, as if in response to Cyrus's question.

Cyrus gave Reggie one of the special treats that he and many other passengers were carrying around and looked at London critically.

"Dogs have very sensitive ears. Sir Reggie shouldn't have to suffer through this."

"But what's going on?" Bryce asked.

"Honey got homesick," Cyrus explained. "So she requested that Letitia and this so-called musician play 'Home on the Range.' She's from Kansas, you see. And 'Home on the Range' is Kansas's state song."

Now London noticed that Cyrus was slurring his words just a little. Even he wasn't entirely sober, but at least he was still in pretty good control of his faculties.

83

Then Cyrus added in a slightly tipsy but authoritative tone, "Although 'Home on the Range' was written during the 1870s, it didn't become the Kansas state song until 1947. It seems to have considerable emotional resonance for native Kansans. Honey got very sentimental about hearing it."

"I can see that," London said, as Honey's blubbering nearly overcame her attempt to sing.

Cyrus said, "There are six verses, each with a chorus, and they're just getting started. They could go on for another few minutes."

London stood there for a moment, wondering just what to do. Surely the song would end before Letitia, Honey, and Gus absolutely had to return to the ship. But somehow, she couldn't bring herself to interrupt the performance. And yet she couldn't stand around waiting for the song to end when there were other passengers to notify.

"Maybe we should split up," she told Bryce. "A lot of our passengers are out here and we really do have to get them back to the ship."

"Okay," he said. "You can work on this bunch. I'll go around them and notify any I find over that way."

"Thanks," she said.

"A temporary separation," he commented with a grin. "Just for the sake of efficiency."

With a light squeeze of her arm, Bryce stepped away and disappeared into the crowd.

As London stood waiting for a break in the performance, Cyrus turned to her and spoke in an uncharacteristically helpful manner.

"I assume it's getting toward time to head back to the ship. Don't worry about these three, I'll make sure they get aboard with time to spare."

London thanked him, then she and Sir Reggie continued on their way. Bob and Mr. Tedrow were still sitting at their table discussing the secrets of detective work. Although they'd obviously had quite a bit to drink, they weren't disagreeable about being told it was getting toward time to leave, and seemed ready to wrap up their conversation.

When they ran across Kirby Oswinkle, London was relieved to find that a considerable intake of beer hadn't exacerbated the man's usually abrasive personality. To the contrary, he seemed to be in quite a jolly mood.

But his expression saddened as he saw London approach him.

"Don't tell me," he said. "It's getting toward time to head back to the ship."

"I'm afraid so," London said.

"Ah, well. All good things must come to an end."

London was amazed as Kirby tottered on his way. This beer festival was the only thing she could remember Kirby wholeheartedly approving of.

London got a glimpse of Elsie some distance off. Fortunately, Elsie seemed to have figured out for herself that their shore leave was ending. London saw Elsie blow her beau-for-a-day a kiss and head on out of the square.

One person London was worried not to see was Audrey Bolton. However the festival might be affecting the troublesome woman's mood, London hoped she'd get back to the ship on time. She also hoped she hadn't had another encounter with her drunken nemesis.

Checking for more passengers had led London and Sir Reggie right up to the stage, where the crowd was dense in anticipation of the impending dunking of the tomcat. A small *oompah*-style band had gathered nearby and was tuning up and getting ready to perform. The stage itself was still dark and the red curtains were still closed.

London spotted something odd on the edge of the stage just in front of the curtain. She leaned over and picked it up, then shuddered a little as she looked at the object more closely.

It was a glass monocle.

London set Sir Reggie down on the edge of the stage and took a closer look at the monocle. She held it up to the light and saw that it was a prescription lens. She couldn't tell for sure whether it was the same one she had seen earlier in the day—but then, how many of these things were likely to be in use?

As she was focused on the monocle, Sir Reggie suddenly jerked away, pulling the leash out of her hands. The little dog ducked under the curtain and disappeared.

"Sir Reggie," London called.

But Sir Reggie didn't reappear.

London climbed the steps onto the stage and pushed her way past the end of the curtain. It had gotten a lot darker around the massive beer barrel than it had been earlier, and it was harder to see.

But there was Sir Reggie, licking at a puddle of liquid on the stage.

What on earth ... ? London wondered.

She stooped down and touched the wet floor and lifted her finger to her nose.

"It's beer," London said.

She pulled Reggie away and gently scolded him.

"Now, now, boy. That's not for dogs."

London could see that quite a bit of beer had been spilled or splashed out of the barrel.

But how?

Her warning tingle turned into a palpable sense of dread. Something felt very wrong here. She straightened up and, leaving Sir Reggie on the stage, she headed up the stairs that led up the side of the barrel.

When she reached the top of the barrel, London could see that the collapsing chair that should be awaiting the arrival of *Katers Murr* was dangling freely, as though it had already dumped someone.

She peered down into the barrel.

Something was floating there.

She couldn't quite see what it was.

Suddenly there was a blast of trumpets, and London was engulfed in blazing light.

The stage curtain opened, the *oompah* band struck up a jaunty tune, and the audience went wild.

She shielded her eyes and looked out into the square.

Sure enough, a man wearing a big cat's costume was being led to the stage, accompanied by blaring music and confetti.

"Who is that?" someone yelled in German.

"Get out of there, lady," another voice complained.

London realized they were talking about her. She wanted to scramble down and get out of sight in a hurry, but she turned and looked again into the barrel.

In the blazing light, she could now see what was inside the huge vat.

Someone was floating face-down in the beer.

CHAPTER FIFTEEN

The shock was stunning when London plunged into the vat. Suddenly she was over her head in chilly, smelly beer.

Paying no heed to the voices from the crowd, she had dropped Sir Reggie and her shoulder bag onto the platform and leaned out over the vat. She had tried to get hold of the floating figure, apparently a man, from the platform. But she couldn't reach him. So she'd kicked off her shoes and gone in feet first after him.

With a strong kick, London bobbed back to the surface, gasping and coughing from swallowing some of the cheap lager. Her eyes and nostrils stung from the pungent carbonated liquid. Paddling furiously to stay afloat, she saw that now the man was within reach.

London took hold of his arm and struggled to turn him over without sinking again herself.

It wasn't working.

Then she heard sounds from above. A familiar voice was calling her name, accompanied by the yapping of her little dog.

She glanced upward, and was flooded with relief to see Bryce's face looking over the top edge of the beer vat. He must have been nearby and seen her plunge inside.

Sir Reggie was also peering into the vat, but Bryce pushed him back with a sharp command to "Stay."

Then Bryce yelled, "I'm coming, London," and scrambled down the ladder attached to the inside of the vat.

He held out a hand toward London.

She grabbed the floating man with one hand and Bryce's hand with the other. Together they maneuvered the man closer to the ladder and got him turned face up.

London gasped when she saw that face.

How very strange, she thought.

It was the very same rude, mustachioed man who had thrown beer on Audrey and on her. He had somehow lost his monocle down on the stage and wound up here, floating in the very same kind of liquid he had been so rudely slinging about.

His eyes were squeezed shut, and his mouth gaped open.

Bryce got his shoulder under one of the man's arms and began to drag him up the ladder. London grasped the ladder and pushed from below. As they struggled, two townspeople arrived to help, leaning down beside Bryce and helping to lift the limp man.

Working together, they all got him up onto the platform and then down the steps to the stage.

As London watched, Bryce checked for breath and pulse, then shook his head and immediately started on chest compressions.

People were now crowding around them on the stage. London pushed them back.

"Gib uns Platz!" she kept saying—"Give us room!"

The two local helpers pushed the stunned spectators back, and they all formed a circle around them.

"I'm afraid he's gone," Bryce said breathlessly as he continued the CPR.

In a matter of seconds, London heard the sound of a siren.

An ambulance, she realized with relief.

Someone in the crowd must have called the official emergency number the moment they realized what was happening.

The crowd parted, and three paramedics with a gurney came rushing onto the stage.

"Are you a doctor?" one asked Bryce.

"Just a ship's medic," Bryce replied. He got out of their way as the professional paramedic team tore the man's clothing loose from his chest, efficiently dried his skin, and applied defibrillator pads.

But even their efforts didn't revive him.

"It's no use," the head paramedic said. "He's dead."

*

Soon a group of police officers was pushing the crowd farther back and setting up a perimeter of red and white police tape printed with the word POLIZEIABSPERUNG—"police cordon." Meanwhile, the paramedics put the body on the gurney, covered it up, lowered it off the stage, and wheeled it to the waiting ambulance.

Overwhelmed with the sensation that she was stuck in what seemed to be a recurring nightmare, London sat down right there on the edge of the stage.

How could this be happening—again?

She had discovered bodies at two earlier stops on the *Nachtmusik*'s European tour, and both of those had been the result of foul play.

At least, she thought, *this one must have been an accident.*

Obviously aware of her concern, Bryce sat down beside her and patted her hand.

"I'd just come within sight of the stage when the curtain opened up," he said. "Imagine my shock when I saw you up there!"

"Thanks for coming to help me," London said.

"What else was I to do?"

Sir Reggie came up on her other side, wriggling anxiously, but the little dog just sniffed them both and decided not to climb into her wet lap.

Then a uniformed policeman approached them.

"Are you the people who found the body?" he asked in German.

London nodded and said, "I found the … the man in the beer vat. Bryce came to help me get him out."

"Kindly wait here for Detektiv Erlich," the policeman said, then walked away.

A paramedic brought London and Bryce blankets to wrap around themselves, but London's blanket didn't make her feel any better. She was still soaked to the skin and shivering and reeking with beer.

She looked out into the crowd on the other side of the police tape. Among the many gawkers she saw several familiar faces, including Letitia, Cyrus, and Gus and Honey.

What must they be thinking? she wondered. *And what will happen now?*

"So much for getting everybody back to the ship on time," she said to Bryce. "I'd better call the captain."

She tapped Captain Hays's contact number and quickly heard his jovial voice.

"Well, hello there, London Rose. Jolly good festival, wasn't it? I certainly thought so. I do hope you're calling to tell me you've got everybody herded up and ready to head back here. We don't have much time to spare."

London replied sadly, "Captain, I … I'm afraid we have a bit of a problem."

Captain Hays let out a hearty chuckle.

"Not another dead body, I hope," he joked.

London fell silent. She simply couldn't make herself say yes.

"Oh, dear," the captain said with a note of realization. "You wouldn't jest about something like this, would you?"

"No, sir. I wouldn't."

"It's not one of our own passengers, I hope."

"No. And it was probably an accident. With some luck …"

London hesitated. She certainly *hoped* luck was on their side.

"It looks like Bryce and I have to stay and answer some questions," she continued. "Hopefully we'll still be able to set sail pretty soon."

"I do hope so," Captain Hays said.

London ended the call and pulled the blanket more tightly around her shoulders. Of course now even the blanket was soggy with beer. She was shivering from more than just being wet. Shock was creeping more deeply into her pores than even the beer. She couldn't shake the image of the dead man out of her mind.

Soon a casually dressed balding man with a well-trimmed beard and mustache ducked under the tape and walked toward them, followed by Willy Oberhauser, the security guard she had met a little while ago.

The newcomer produced a badge and spoke to London and Bryce.

"I am Detektiv Kurt Erlich, with the Bamberg *Kripo*," he said in German.

London knew that *Kripo* was short for *Kriminalpolizei*, which meant "criminal police." She hoped that didn't bode badly for the situation.

"I met the lady earlier," Willy Oberhauser said to Erlich. "She is an American."

London and Bryce introduced themselves, and explained that they worked on the tour boat that was currently docked nearby.

Erlich shook his head and said in accented English, "I'm sorry your enjoyment of our city has been spoiled by this unfortunate event. But I shouldn't have to detain you very long. Accidents will happen."

Then with a chuckle he added, "I suppose it's rather cold-hearted of me to say this, but I doubt that Herr Forstmann will be deeply mourned here in Bamberg."

London remembered Willy Oberhauser telling her that the victim was *"a rather influential gentleman from Munich."*

"You knew the victim?" Bryce asked Erlich.

"Oh, yes," Detektiv Erlich said. "Sigmund Forstmann was well-known throughout Bavaria—and even a bit feared, one might say. He was a food and drink critic for the *Sternenkurier*, a newspaper in Munich. Every year he would come to our little festival, drink too much and behave like a boor, and then go back to Munich and write a feature story about what fools and ignoramuses and savages we provincials are. Now would the two of you kindly tell me how you found the body?"

Before London or Bryce could say anything, the chief paramedic walked up to Erlich and whispered something in his ear.

Erlich's expression darkened a little as he turned back to London and Bryce.

"I'm afraid things just got a bit more complicated," he said. "The paramedics found a rather large bump on the back of his head. They think his skull might actually have been fractured by a rather severe blow. Not that this new development necessarily suggests that Herr Forstmann's death wasn't an accident. But as a matter of procedure, I'm now obliged to approach the situation rather differently."

London's heart sank at Erlich's words.

Is it starting again? she wondered.

Erlich climbed the steps onto the platform. He pointed to the throne-like chair where *Katers Murr* was supposed to have sat.

"I see that the dunking seat is unfastened," he said to Willy Oberhauser, who was standing on the stage. "Has it been like this all afternoon?"

"No, sir," the security guard said. "It's been rigged and ready for the ceremony all day long."

Indeed, London remembered the seat being fastened when she and Bryce had stopped by to look at it earlier that day.

Erlich wiggled the seat with interest.

"So perhaps this is how Herr Forstmann fell into the vat," he mused. Turning to one of the police officers, he asked, "Do you think it could have happened by accident, Polizist Wedekind?"

"Certainly not," Wedekind said as he climbed the steps to join the detective. "I personally inspect the mechanism every year to make sure it's safe."

The policeman fingered a long handle sticking out of the floor several feet away from the chair.

"Someone must have pulled this lever," Wedekind added. "I'm sure the chair couldn't have been triggered by accident. And as you can see, the lever is too far away for someone to reach if they're sitting in the chair."

London tried to imagine how the incident had unfolded.

It all seems so crazy, she thought.

"Might Herr Forstmann have bumped his head on the way down?" Erlich asked the policeman.

"Not a chance," the policeman said. "Look at how well-padded the chair is with foam. This whole thing is rigged up so the unlucky 'tomcat' can't get hurt in any way. Like I said, I make sure of that every year myself."

Erlich shook his head and scratched his chin.

"I don't like the looks of this," he said.

I don't either, London thought with dread.

The situation seemed to be getting worse with every passing moment.

"If only we could know exactly how it happened," Erlich mused.

He walked back and forth along the platform, peering at everything closely.

"First of all, *why* would Herr Forstmann have sat in the chair in the first place? I can only guess that he didn't do so voluntarily. Perhaps someone knocked him unconscious, dragged him up onto the platform, put him in the chair, and pulled the lever, dunking him—as farfetched as all that may sound."

He added with a grim scoff, "Of course, there's no mystery as to *why* someone would want to do that to Herr Forstmann. I suppose there are hundreds of people right here in Bamberg who have fantasized, at least, about doing him some sort of harm. He has no shortage of enemies here. I must admit that *I* am not entirely innocent in that regard."

Erlich turned toward Willy Oberhauser.

"I assume that Herr Forstmann was drunk, as usual," he said.

"Very much so," Herr Oberhauser said.

"And belligerent."

"Absolutely."

"And as usual, I assume he antagonized a fair number of people," Erlich said.

"Of course."

"Did he make anybody especially angry?" Erlich asked Oberhauser.

"As a matter of fact, he did," Oberhauser said.

Pointing to London, he said, "This woman here lost her temper at him. In fact, I had to forcibly separate her from him to keep her from doing him harm."

London was stunned by Oberhauser's accusatory tone.

She was also shaken by a dawning realization.

I'm already a murder suspect.

CHAPTER SIXTEEN

London stared aghast at Willy Oberhauser. She was shocked at the harshness in security guard's voice, so different from the consideration he'd shown to her earlier today.

Did he really think she was guilty of murder?

"Tell me more," Detektiv Erlich said to the security guard. "Be precise."

Pulling out a note pad and pencil, Erlich jotted down brief entries as Oberhauser continued.

"There was another American woman from the ship—a taller woman. It started when Herr Forstmann spilled beer all over her and was his usual obnoxious self about it. The woman was very upset. That is what first attracted my attention to the matter. Then this woman here—London, I believe she said her name is—demanded that he apologize to the other woman. He wound up spilling beer on her also—deliberately, I'm sure. And then she attacked him."

London's mouth dropped open.

"I did not attack him!" she objected.

"Well, you very nearly did," Oberhauser said. "If I hadn't pushed you away from him, I can't imagine what you might have done."

London flashed back to the incident, wondering for a few split seconds whether there was any truth to what the security guard was saying.

It had all started with hearing Audrey's voice shrieking at the man who had poured beer all over her. London had stepped toward Forstmann and snapped at him, *"You should be ashamed."*

London didn't think of herself as an aggressive person, but she remembered being very angry—even feeling that various frustrations from recent days might explode within her. But she was certain she hadn't made any physical contact.

Would she have gotten physically combative if Oberhauser hadn't stepped in to separate her from Forstmann?

She didn't like to think so. And she didn't think she was wrong to have defended a passenger who had been purposely sloshed with beer.

Then she remembered that very same passenger had again exchanged angry words with Forstmann this evening.

And where is Audrey right now? she wondered.

She looked out into the crowd. While she recognized several passengers who hadn't yet returned to the ship, Audrey herself was nowhere in sight.

Detektiv Erlich tapped his pencil against his notebook.

"Let's hear your side of the story," he said to London.

London knew she ought to be relieved at being offered a chance to explain herself. But she'd learned from recent experience that she had to be very careful about what she said. And she wasn't ready to tell the police that Audrey had spoken with the dead man again after that first incident.

"It's true that Herr Forstmann spilled beer on one of our passengers," she said. "It's also true that I intervened and told him to apologize. Then he spilled beer on me, and I got really angry. But I didn't attack him. I don't believe I even touched him."

"How did you happen to find the body?" Erlich asked.

"I noticed something … it was the man's monocle lying on a step next to the stage. I'd guessed that he'd dropped it. I went up onto the stage and saw that some beer had been splashed out of the vat. Then I climbed up onto the platform and …"

London cringed as she continued.

"The curtain opened and the lights came on and there was loud music—and I saw a body in the vat. I … I tried to get him out."

Indicating Bryce, she added, "Then my colleague, Mr. Yeaton, came up onto the platform to help me, and we dragged Herr Forstmann out of the vat. Mr. Yeaton tried to revive him until the ambulance arrived."

Erlich squinted curiously.

"Can you account for your activities during the few minutes before you found the body?" he said.

London said, "I'd been wandering among the crowd, making sure that all our passengers knew that it was time to head back to our ship before we set sail again."

Erlich shrugged and said, "Your story does make sense, I suppose."

"Of course it does," Bryce said, bristling. "What doesn't make sense is the idea that London had anything to do with the man's death. When I got here, she was trying to rescue him. Why would she do that

95

if she meant to kill him?"

While London appreciated Bryce's intercession, she knew that it wasn't a very strong argument in her favor. Indeed, somebody in the nearby crowd spoke up to contradict him.

"We all saw her when the curtain went up. She looked surprised, that's all—as if she didn't know the dunking was about to take place."

Another onlooker agreed. "She didn't start to try to rescue him until we'd all seen her. Maybe trying to save him was just an act."

London was beyond shocked.

Do they seriously think I might have killed him? she wondered.

Bryce seemed to be starting to get really angry.

"That's ridiculous," he said. Pointing to the vat, he added to Detektiv Erlich, "Your own theory is that someone hit the man on the head and hauled him up onto the stage and put him in that chair and dunked him. Do you think London looks strong enough to do all that by herself?"

Detektiv Erlich stroked his chin and stared at London's 5-foot-6-inch slender build.

"Not by *herself*, I suppose," he said.

Bryce stared at him with disbelief. London herself was perplexed for a moment. Did the detective think maybe she and Bryce had committed the crime together? How could Bryce have had anything to do with it, when he'd showed up out of the crowd after London discovered the body?

Then she realized.

Audrey.

After all, both London and her cranky passenger had reason to be angry with Herr Forstmann. But did anybody really believe that she and Audrey had been angry enough to kill him?

London was hardly surprised by the detective's next question.

"Is the woman who he spilled beer on here right now?"

London again scanned the crowd and called out.

"Audrey, are you here? Detektiv Erlich needs to talk to you."

There was no reply, and London couldn't see Audrey anywhere.

"I'll need the name of this woman," Erlich said.

London told him Audrey's name and he wrote it down.

"I also need to know how to get in touch with your captain," Erlich said. "Your boat may not leave port until this matter is settled."

London told Erlich the phone number, and Erlich stepped aside to make the call.

"Poor Captain Hays," London said to Bryce.

"I know," Bryce said. "This is going to be very hard news for him. But then, nobody on the boat is going to be very happy to hear that we're in for yet another delay in another city. Frankly, I'm not happy about it either."

Erlich finished the call and walked back over to London and Bryce.

"You two may leave now," Erlich said to them. "But of course neither the two of you nor any of your passengers or crew may leave Bamberg until we get to the bottom of what happened here."

Of course, London thought, holding back a sigh.

She and Bryce wrapped themselves together in one of the blankets they'd been given, and London tugged on Sir Reggie's leash. As the three of them started to walk back toward the ship, another worrisome matter occurred to her.

She turned and said to Detektiv Erlich, "There's something I need to tell you more privately. Could you walk with us for a moment?"

"Certainly," the detective said.

London spoke to him cautiously as they separated themselves from the crowd.

"Detektiv, I've got something … well, a bit strange to tell you."

"Well?" Erlich asked.

London gulped hard.

"This, uh, isn't the first dead body I've come across during the last few days."

Erlich's eyes widened as he looked at her.

"*Oho!* That does come as rather a surprise."

London continued, "You see, one of our passengers, Lillis Klimowski, was killed in Gyor about a week ago. I found her dead in the Cathedral Basilica of the Assumption of Our Lady. Then a couple of days ago I found a dead tour guide in the House for Mozart in Salzburg."

Erlich nodded.

"I heard something about what happened in Salzburg. I didn't hear many details, except that it was a case of homicide. Was the woman's death a homicide also?"

"I'm afraid so," London said.

Erlich clucked his tongue and spoke with a note of wry understatement.

"Well, that certainly casts an interesting new light on things."

"I thought I should tell you right away," London explained. "Since your investigation will involve me and the *Nachtmusik*, you were sure to find out about these deaths sooner or later. And naturally, you'd be suspicious."

"Naturally."

"So I wanted to set things straight as soon as I could and save you time and confusion. May I jot some information down for you?"

Erlich passed her his pencil and notepad.

London said as she wrote, "These are the names and contact information of the lead investigators in both cases. If you call them, they'll certainly confirm that neither I nor anybody else aboard the *Nachtmusik* were in any way culpable for those deaths."

Erlich took the notepad back, looked at it, and tucked it into his pocket.

"Yes, this should be very helpful," he said. "I will certainly check in with these two investigators. Of course this won't resolve any questions about your role in Herr Forstmann's death. Meanwhile, I expect you to be ready for further questioning tomorrow. The same goes for the other woman who was with you when the beer-spilling incident took place."

Erlich turned and headed back toward the crime scene.

Other straggling passengers joined London and Bryce and Reggie on their way back to the boat. London's shoes squished with her every step, and the weight of her soaked clothes made her slouch. The situation reminded her of Gyor, when she and Bryce jumped into the Danube to rescue Sir Reggie from drowning after the dog had tackled a fleeing criminal.

At least that episode had ended well, with Sir Reggie alive and the criminal in custody. London had no idea how this new adventure was going to end.

Apparently offended by the smell, Sir Reggie kept a few feet of distance from them. Although London and Bryce kept huddling under the same blanket, their physical contact felt anything but romantic.

London found it hard to believe that, just a little while ago, they had been on the verge of sharing their first kiss.

How fast things change, she thought.

The day had certainly taken unexpected turns.

And London was pretty sure the worst was yet to come.

As London, Bryce, and Sir Reggie climbed up the gangway, an anxious group of passengers awaited them in the reception area. They were greeted by a cacophony of voices.

"Is it true what the captain just announced over the PA system?"

"Has there been another murder?"

"Are we not allowed to leave Bamberg?"

"Why does this keep happening to us?"

"When are we going to set sail again?"

London felt dizzy from the barrage of questions—and also from the stench of the beer, which now made her gag. Before she or Bryce could think of anything to say, Captain Hays came striding into the reception area.

"No questions right now, if you please," he demanded of the group. "Give these two good people some room to breathe."

The crowd dispersed somewhat, and Captain Hays looked London and Bryce over.

"You two look rather worse for the wear," he said. "And you don't smell especially good either. Detektiv Erlich told me about your dunking."

Looking down at the dry Sir Reggie, the captain said to the dog, "At least *you* seem to have been spared the worst of it."

Then he added to Bryce and London, "Go to your rooms, get yourselves cleaned up, and try to rest. Take as long as you need to recover your wits. From what Detektiv Erlich told me, we probably won't have to deal with the repercussions of this dreadful episode until tomorrow."

London and Bryce thanked him for his consideration.

With a nod and a shrug, the captain said, "Bit of a run of bad luck we're having, isn't it?"

He turned and headed up the stairs to the bridge. London and Bryce took the elevator down to the Allegro deck. Before they parted in the passageway, they stopped and looked at each other and smiled shyly.

"I hope … sometime soon …" Bryce said, his voice trailing off.

London's smile broadened. She knew what he was leaving unsaid—that he hoped they'd soon pick up where they'd left off.

"I hope so too," she said.

They exchanged chaste, beer-flavored kisses on the cheek and headed off to their staterooms.

Sir Reggie hopped through the doggie door to London's stateroom before London could open the door. Once they were both inside, the dog headed over to his water bowl and drank thirstily, as if trying to wash away the smell.

"Consider yourself lucky, pal," London said as she gave him some fresh dog food. "Not only are you not soaked in beer, nobody suspects you of murder. Or at least Detektiv Erlich didn't say you were. You'd better be on your best behavior until we know for sure."

London stood dripping for a moment. She didn't dare sit down anywhere for fear of soaking the bed or the furniture. She kicked off her shoes, hoping they weren't ruined, and gathered together a bathrobe and slippers, holding them at arm's length as she went into the bathroom.

She didn't bother taking off her clothes until the shower was running. She stepped into the stall and undressed under the water, hanging the clothes on the shower rail for the housekeeper to take care of tomorrow. She scrubbed herself thoroughly and took an especially long time shampooing her hair.

The act of scrubbing her scalp seemed to stir up questions and worries.

She found herself thinking about what Detektiv Erlich had said about whether London herself could possibly have committed the murder.

"Not by herself, I suppose."

Of course he'd been considering the possibility that London and Audrey had killed him together. And given how the victim had angered them both by throwing beer on them, she couldn't exactly blame Erlich for harboring such a suspicion.

And now London found herself wondering something herself.

What about Audrey?

The last time she'd seen her, the woman had just had another altercation with Herr Forstmann. And now London felt a bit unsettled by something Audrey had said about the soon-to-be-victim.

"I don't think he'll be rude to anyone from now on."

At the time she hadn't known what Audrey had meant by that.

And she still didn't know.

Had Audrey been hinting at something worse than a good scolding?

Don't be ridiculous, London told herself as she rinsed the lather out of hair.

But was it so ridiculous?

London couldn't help imagining how things might have unfolded. Detektiv Erlich had suggested that the killer might have hit Herr Forstmann over the head, then hauled his unconscious body up the steps to the platform and put him in the chair and pulled the lever to dunk him.

Could Audrey have done all that on her own?

Audrey was a good bit bigger and taller than London, and she seemed like an exceptionally strong woman. And London knew virtually nothing about her except that she was grouchy and temperamental.

As much as she hated to think that any of her passengers were capable of murder, she couldn't discount the possibility. It also occurred to her that she didn't even know whether Audrey had come back to the ship or not.

London decided she'd better get dressed and find out if the woman was on board. She came out of the bathroom and took out a clean uniform and put it on. But before she headed out the door, her cell phone rang.

Her heart sank as she saw that she'd received a text from none other than Jeremy Lapham, the CEO of Epoch World Cruise Lines. London was sure that Captain Hays must have notified him of the murder by now.

His message was short and terse.

"We must have a video chat. Now."

CHAPTER SEVENTEEN

London's hands were shaking as she opened up her laptop on the table.

"This isn't going to be easy," she said to Sir Reggie, who sat on the floor looking up at her with apparent concern.

She wondered if Mr. Lapham was going to hold her responsible for turning up at the scene of too many murders. That kind of thing couldn't be good for the tourism business.

She took a deep breath and opened the conference program

The CEO of Epoch World Cruise Lines appeared.

Or at least part of him did.

Although London had spoken to her boss on the phone a few times since the *Nachtmusik* had started its journey, this was the first video chat she'd had with him since he'd first offered her the job of social director.

The view of him was the same as she'd had back then— just his neck and his cleft chin and a pair of thin lips. He had tilted his webcam tilted so she couldn't see his eyes, but she again had a clear view of an extremely fluffy black and white cat that lay comfortably in the man's lap.

She could actually hear the sound of purring as Mr. Lapham stroked the animal with long, slender fingers.

She still had no idea why the CEO chose to appear in this peculiar manner. If he was trying to project an aura of mystery, she had to admit he was succeeding.

"Hello, London Rose," he said in a soft voice not unlike the purr of his cat.

"Hello, Mr. Lapham," London said.

"The captain tells me there's been another death," Mr. Lapham said, getting right to the point.

"I'm afraid so, sir," London said.

"Another murder?"

"It looks like it."

"But not another passenger, I'm told. Well, that's a small blessing, I suppose."

He added with a resigned-sounding sigh, "I'm afraid this wasn't entirely unexpected."

London felt a jolt of surprise.

A possible murder—not unexpected? she wondered.

Mr. Lapham continued, "I suppose I should have warned you that there might be more trouble ahead. But I'd kept hoping for the best. And I'm sorry to say, I may have played my own unwitting role in this unfortunate development."

"Uh, Mr. Lapham," London sputtered, "how could you possibly hold yourself in any way responsible for what happened today?"

"Let me try to explain," Mr. Lapham said. "Like you and everybody else, I've been rather—what is the word I'm looking for?—*gobsmacked* by the events of the last few days. Two murders! They came as a complete surprise to me. It forced me into making a major decision."

Uh-oh, London thought. *Maybe the trip is being cut short.*

The thin lips twitched slightly, but were still silent.

Or maybe I am about to be fired.

Finally the CEO spoke again.

"I decided it was time to switch astrologers."

London's eyes widened.

Is he joking? she wondered.

Mr. Lapham continued, "Noelle, my astrologer of some thirty years, has been highly reliable in the past. She even predicted the recent downturn of my ocean cruise line business. And she assured me that now was an opportune time to launch a smaller-scale European river travel enterprise."

He sighed again.

"Alas, Noelle hasn't kept up with the times. She simply didn't take into account the discovery of Eris in 2005, much less the dwarf planet's rather impish influence on my birth sign of Aries. Eris has brought a fair amount of strife and discord into the equation. I'm sure you can understand my concern."

London wondered whether she was expected to reply, but she had no idea what to say.

Then the CEO continued, "Alex, my new astrologer, has brought my chart up to date, but I'm afraid I've got some damage control to attend to."

"Damage control?" London managed to ask.

"I'm talking about business matters. Hopefully I can make some better-informed decisions in the near future. I'll keep you in the loop, I promise. In the meantime ... well, I fear you might have some rather bumpy times. I'm dreadfully sorry."

London didn't know what to say for a few seconds.

"Mr. Lapham, you have nothing to apologize for," she finally said.

"It's kind of you to say so. And I don't want you to think that I'm beating myself up about all this. No one could have precisely anticipated people dying all over the place! Astrology isn't an exact science, after all. But I didn't become the businessman I am by not taking appropriate responsibility for my enterprises. I'm dealing with things in my usual pragmatic, realistic manner."

Mr. Lapham sighed deeply again and continued.

"Meanwhile, I don't want you to worry yourself unduly. The last thing I want you to do is go playing 'Nancy Drew' again, like I ordered you to do back in Gyor. My Lord, I almost got you killed! Let's never make that mistake again. Crime-solving is what I hired Bob Turner to do. And judging from what Bob told me about his cunning detective work solving that murder in Salzburg, I made a wise choice."

London managed to refrain from laughing.

Bob had certainly played a role in capturing the Austrian tour guide's killer, and he'd even come to London's rescue when her life had been in danger. Still, "cunning detective work"? Those weren't the words London would choose. But she was perfectly happy to let Bob claim the credit for solving the mystery. And she'd rather not go playing "Nancy Drew" again if she could possibly help it.

"Keep the passengers happy," Mr. Lapham added. "That's what you're best at. And from what Captain Hays has told me, you are very good at it indeed. I made a wise choice in hiring you."

London felt a flood of relief. Thinking her job might be in danger had reminded her how much she actually loved working on this ship.

"Thank you, sir," she said. "I always do my best not to disappoint you."

The call ended, and London sat staring at the computer screen.

Astrology? she wondered.

It didn't sound like Mr. Lapham was really dealing with the current issues in a "pragmatic, realistic manner."

But what do I know?

She'd really never given astrology a lot of thought or attention, so she figured maybe she shouldn't jump to judgment.

For all I know, maybe there's something to it. Maybe there's a lot to it.

Something else Mr. Lapham said rattled through her mind.

"The last thing I want you to do is go playing 'Nancy Drew' again."

Although she had to admit that she'd gotten some thrills out of investigating two murders, she didn't look forward to plunging into another case. But she wondered—did she have any choice, especially since Detektiv Erlich had reason to suspect her? Surely the police would clear her of suspicion pretty soon …

Or will they?

Could she really leave the investigation entirely to the local police—and to Bob Turner?

She shuddered at the very idea. If Bob got involved, his blundering ways might make things a whole lot worse. She wondered whether he even had any idea what was going on. She hadn't seen him or Mr. Tedrow since well before the murder had happened. She guessed that they'd come aboard the ship before she'd even found the body, and that Bob knew no more about the murder than the passengers who had gotten the captain's announcement over the PA system.

And maybe that was just as well. Bob's investigative skills left a lot to be desired. Her best hope was that the local police would clear things up quickly. Then maybe the *Nachtmusik* could get back on schedule.

Then London reminded herself of what she'd been about to do just before she'd been ordered to video chat.

I've got to check in on Audrey Bolton.

Sir Reggie had apparently gotten bored during the chat. He was curled up on the bed and didn't look interested in going anywhere, so London left the room alone. She walked up the spiral stairs to the Adagio deck and along the passageway to Audrey's apartment.

She knocked on the door but got no reply.

"Audrey, are you in there?" she called out.

"Yes," came a voice from inside.

"May I come in?" London said.

"This is not a convenient time."

London stood there for a moment feeling stymied.

"Uh, Audrey," she finally said. "I assume you know that someone

105

just got killed at the festival."

"Yes, the captain announced it."

Audrey's voice sounded tense and anxious.

"Do you know who got killed?" London asked.

A silence fell.

She doesn't want to know, London realized.

Even so, London knew she had to tell her.

"Audrey, the victim was the man who spilled beer on us. Naturally, the police ... well, they can't help suspecting the two of us. I explained everything I could to Detektiv Erlich. But naturally he's going to want to hear your side of the story."

There was another silence.

"I expect you'll be hearing from him tomorrow," London said.

"That's fine," Audrey said. "I will be prepared."

London stood there wavering for a few moments.

"Audrey, can I come in?" she suggested again. "Maybe we could talk about what happened."

"There's nothing to talk about. I'm really rather busy."

London couldn't think of anything else to say. It was getting late, and she figured she'd better make a final tour of the ship and see how passengers were dealing with this new turn of events.

But as she continued on her way, she kept hearing what Audrey had said about Herr Forstmann.

"I don't think he'll be rude to anyone from now on."

Was it possible ...?

No, London told herself. *Surely not.*

Don't let your imagination run away with you.

She decided she'd pick up a sandwich as she made her rounds and return to her room to eat and settle in for the night.

She had no idea what tomorrow might bring, but she had a bad feeling that things were going to get worse before they got better.

CHAPTER EIGHTEEN

Suddenly, the bottom of the throne-like chair fell out from under London. Her paper crown fell off as she slid down a chute and splashed head over heels into some pungent liquid.

Beer, *she realized as the taste stung her tongue and nostrils.*

She coughed and choked and thrashed her arms, but she was soon completely submerged. She kicked downward, but her feet didn't hit the bottom.

She sensed that she was sinking deeper and deeper.

This isn't the festival vat, *she realized, starting to panic.*

It was something much deeper.

Maybe it's a river ...

... or a lake ...

... or an ocean.

She thrashed harder and more desperately as her throat filled up with beer.

London's eyes snapped open when something cold nudged her cheek.

Sir Reggie had poked her with his nose. Now the little dog was staring into her eyes and whining anxiously.

She was all tangled up in sheets and blankets and had apparently been groaning and thrashing over that strange dream.

The morning light pouring in through her stateroom window was a welcome sight.

"Don't worry," she said to Sir Reggie with a reassuring pat on his head. "I just had a bad dream. Everything's OK."

But is everything really OK? she wondered.

Yesterday a prominent beer critic had drowned in a vat of beer, and London herself was a potential suspect in his murder.

And today ...

Well, she didn't know what might happen next. She could have a really rough day ahead.

Then, as she got out of bed ...

"Ow!" she groaned, discovering that she ached all over.

That was from helping the man out of the beer vat, which had turned out to be a useless effort.

As she dressed in a fresh uniform and got ready to go to work, London couldn't shake off the feeling that she was still soaked in beer. For one thing, the whole stateroom seemed to be full of the smell.

That wasn't surprising. She'd been dripping wet when she came in last night. And her nice festival outfit was still wet and smelly and hanging in the shower stall.

As she pulled a brush through her hair, the smell seemed to get stronger.

Didn't I shampoo all of it out? she wondered.

She even thought she could still smell beer on her hands and arms. Had it gotten so far into her pores that she couldn't get rid of it?

She briefly considered taking another shower—not only to get cleaner, but also to relax her sore muscles. But then she would have to deal with those smelly clothes hanging there and it probably wouldn't do much good.

Anyway, it was time to get her day going.

She poured fresh water and food for Sir Reggie. As she watched him eat eagerly, she realized she was pretty hungry herself.

She asked him, "Do you want to join me for breakfast in the Habsburg Restaurant, boy?"

Sir Reggie let out an affirmative yap.

As they headed out of the room, London felt grateful for the loyal animal's company.

On their way up one flight of stairs to the Adagio deck, London found herself worrying about Audrey again. She remembered the peculiar conversation they'd had through Audrey's stateroom door.

"This is not a convenient time," the woman had said.

Now London wondered—what could Audrey have been doing that was more important than talking about a murder?

I'd better check up on her again, London decided.

Instead of going into the restaurant, she and Sir Reggie headed down the passageway that ran among passenger staterooms on that level.

When she knocked on Audrey's door, there was no reply. Remembering how hard it had been to get the woman's attention yesterday, London wasn't especially surprised.

She knocked again and called out.

"Audrey, it's me, London."

But there was still no reply. She wondered if maybe Audrey wasn't awake yet. After all, she, too, had had a tough day yesterday and was probably tired.

Maybe I shouldn't bother her, she thought. *She could be sleeping late.*

But she reminded herself that Detektiv Erlich was probably going to be here soon, and he was going want to talk to Audrey as well as to London.

"I will be prepared," Audrey had said yesterday when London had mentioned Erlich's impending visit.

But that visit was likely to happen soon, and if Audrey really was still sleeping …

She knocked on the door again.

"Audrey, are you there?" she asked.

There was still no reply.

London felt a tingle of worry. She wondered whether she should use her master key to let herself inside just to make sure …

Make sure of what? she asked herself.

She didn't even know exactly why she was worried. Again she wondered—did a part of her imagine that Audrey had had something to do with Herr Forstmann's death?

What a ridiculous idea, she told herself.

Anyway, she certainly wasn't going to make matters better by entering Audrey's room and invading her privacy, especially if she found her still in bed. And if Audrey wasn't in her room, she was probably somewhere on the boat, perhaps even having breakfast in the restaurant.

She and Sir Reggie went back down the passageway and into the attractive restaurant in the bow of the ship. Sunlight glowed through the Habsburg's big windows, sparkling on clean white tablecloths and silver serving dishes, but only a few passengers were there to enjoy the morning's offerings.

She didn't see Audrey anywhere. She did, however, see Bob Turner sitting alone at a table, wearing his ever-present mirrored glasses and hunched over a red beverage that London was pretty sure must be a virgin Bloody Mary.

London remembered that the ship's security man and his friend the would-be mystery author had seemed to be putting away a lot of beer at the festival yesterday. It looked like the poor guy wasn't feeling too great this morning.

In fact, several other passengers that she'd seen partying quite enthusiastically yesterday also looked pretty haggard.

Things might be kind of subdued on board today, she thought.

Then she saw that at least two of the ship's staff appeared to be unaffected by the hangovers that afflicted others in the room. Captain Hays and Elsie were sitting together at a table with well-loaded breakfast plates. The captain was talking on his cell phone while Elsie was devouring her meal. London knew that the captain had the good sense to exercise moderation and that Elsie was generally unaffected by whatever she chose to imbibe.

When Elsie saw London, she waved her over and then whispered so as not to disturb the captain's phone conversation.

"Hey, London! It's good to see you! Sit down with us!"

Pulling an empty chair up next to Elsie, London sat down and Sir Reggie jumped up in her lap.

Elsie dug around in a pocket and then gave Sir Reggie one of the dog treats that Bryce had specially made, and that everybody seemed to be carrying around these days.

Then Elsie pointed to the captain and whispered to London, "He's talking to the boss."

London nodded uneasily, wondering what Mr. Lapham might be saying this morning. The drift of the conversation was hard to pick out from the captain's minimal statements.

"Yes, sir ... That sounds like an excellent idea, sir ... Yes, I suppose that is a possible consideration ... If you say so, sir ..."

While the captain continued in this mode, Elsie leaned toward London and whispered again.

"I heard about the murder," she said. "Are you holding up OK?"

"I guess," London said. "I'm glad Bryce was there when it happened."

"Was he?" Elsie asked eagerly. "I happened to see you and that Australian hunk heading away from the festival together. So tell me— what happened then?"

London rolled her eyes at Elsie's nosiness.

"Nothing happened," she said.

"Why do I find that hard to believe?"

"It didn't."

Elsie glared at London as if she knew better.

London sighed. She knew that Elsie was remarkably perceptive and usually helpful, but she didn't want to discuss how close she and Bryce had come to sharing their first kiss before disaster had struck. At least, not here at a breakfast table with the captain.

Elsie took one last bite of her breakfast and put her silverware down.

"Well, I don't have time to torture the truth out of you right now," she hissed. My bar staff is flooded with orders for hangover cures."

Before her friend could go, London whispered, "Uh, Elsie ..."

"Well?"

"Do I ... still smell like beer?"

Elsie sniffed and grimaced slightly.

"Now that you mention it ... maybe a little."

London stifled another sigh.

At least I can count on her to be honest, she thought.

Elsie wagged her finger at London and said, "We've still got some talking to do."

Then she got up and left the restaurant.

London sat there, uneasily listening to the captain's side of the conversation with the CEO. The part that she could hear was not particularly encouraging.

Neither was the wrinkled brow on the captain's forehead.

CHAPTER NINETEEN

By the time Captain Hays finished the conversation with CEO Lapham, his expression was one of complete bewilderment. London couldn't remember ever seeing the captain look so mystified.

What had the CEO said to him?

But as the captain put his cell phone back in his pocket, he looked at her and smiled cheerfully.

"Well, hello there, London!" he said. Pulling out a treat of his own and tossing it to Sir Reggie, he added, "And you too, my aristocratic friend."

He asked London, "How are you doing this morning? Yesterday was rather hard for you, I'm sure. Did you get a good night's sleep?"

"It was fine," she replied, not exactly truthfully. She hoped to find out what was on the CEO's mind this morning instead of discussing yesterday's events.

"Excellent," Captain Hays said. "As it happens, I just got off the phone with Jeremy Lapham."

London nodded and looked at him attentively.

The captain added, "He said he talked to you yesterday."

"Yes, he did," London replied, wondering whether she had said something wrong during that odd conversation.

"Well, I'm glad to say he's coming up with excellent ideas concerning how to deal with our run of bad luck. Fortunately he doesn't think we'll need to skip any of our planned destinations. But he's going to offer vouchers and discounts, deals for meals and drinks and services and such, that will sweeten the trip for our passengers. It will cost money, of course, and it will be hard on Epoch World Cruise Lines. But it may help pull our company through—as long as nobody else gets killed, I suppose."

London breathed a sigh of relief. It sounded like the CEO was just busy taking care of everything.

But that still didn't explain the captain's apparent perplexity.

A waiter came up to the table, and she ordered her usual favorite breakfast of Eggs Benedict. She kept glancing around, looking not only for Audrey but also for Bryce. She didn't see either of them.

Then Captain Hays cleared his throat as if preparing to bring up an awkward subject.

"Uh, London ... when you spoke to Mr. Lapham yesterday, did he bring up any ... well, rather unorthodox theories about recent events?"

"Yes, I suppose you could say that, sir," London said.

"And did they pertain to ... celestial influences?"

London nodded as solemnly as she could manage. She had to stifle a giggle at the idea that it was the CEO's unusual interests that had bewildered the captain, not some kind of bad news for the tour.

"Yes, he spoke to me of similar matters," the captain said. "What was your, eh, assessment of his ideas?"

"I honestly don't know," London said. "I guess I've never really given a lot of thought to astrology."

"Neither have I," the captain said. Then he straightened up and continued in his brisk English fashion, "Mustn't be closed-minded, eh? As far as either one of us knows, there might be something to it. Jeremy Lapham surely must know what he's doing. He's been in this business a lot longer than you or me, so he's got a pretty good idea of what works and what doesn't. Perhaps we should get our charts done ourselves one of these days, what do you think?"

"Maybe," London said with a shrug.

The captain leaned across the table toward London.

"But if it's all right with you," he added in a confidential tone, "I'd really rather keep the more *mystical* contents of our conversations with Mr. Lapham to ourselves. People might ... well, misunderstand."

"I agree," London said.

"Excellent," Captain Hays said.

Then he pointed to Bob, who appeared to be asleep, and said, "Meanwhile, Mr. Lapham seems content to leave investigative matters to our master sleuth over there."

Captain Hays shook his head and added, "I wish I could share Mr. Lapham's confidence in Mr. Turner. I sure hope the police here in Bamberg are better at their work. By the way, it's lucky we've met this morning. Detektiv Erlich called me this morning and said he wanted to meet me in my stateroom. He also wants to speak to you, I believe, and one or two other people. Could you come to my quarters as soon as you finish breakfast?"

"I'll do that," London said, hoping her dread didn't show in her face.

"Jolly good," the captain said, wiping his lips and setting down his napkin. "Enjoy your breakfast."

Tossing Sir Reggie another treat, he got up from the table and walked out of the restaurant.

"Reggie, you're going to get fat if people keep spoiling you," London said.

Sir Reggie yapped cheerfully as if he considered this an excellent idea.

When London's breakfast arrived, she savored the cup of rich coffee and the delicious Eggs Benedict. She always enjoyed the taste of eggs with a thick slice of Canadian style bacon, served on an English muffin flavored with rich and buttery Hollandaise sauce. But there was something special about the Eggs Benedict that came out of Bryce's kitchen.

Maybe it was something about the spices in the recipe—perhaps a substitute for the usual touch of cayenne pepper, or just the right touch of real paprika.

Maybe I should ask Bryce about it sometime.

Or maybe she shouldn't.

Maybe some mysteries are best left unsolved, she thought as she savored another taste.

Soon she heard a familiar voice speaking over the PA system.

"This is your captain speaking. Would Audrey Bolton kindly come to my stateroom? It's rather urgent. Thank you."

London realized she should have expected this announcement. Apparently Detektiv Erlich had just told Captain Hays that one of the "other people" he wanted to talk to was Audrey.

I just hope Audrey shows up, London thought.

Meanwhile, more and more customers were showing up, and many of them looked pretty haggard. Bob was still slouched alone at his table.

When she finished eating, she and Reggie walked over to where Bob was sitting. Because of his sunglasses, London couldn't tell for sure if he was awake. He certainly didn't seem to be aware of her presence.

Maybe I should just leave him alone, she thought.

But Sir Reggie apparently had different ideas. The dog barked, and Bob jerked sharply in his chair.

114

"London!" he said with surprise. "I'm sorry ... I didn't quite catch what you said."

Sir Reggie barked again.

"Oh, it's *you*, eh?" he said to Sir Reggie. "I'm glad to see you, little partner."

Tossing Sir Reggie yet another treat, he said to the dog, "I hope you're ready to tackle a new murder case, partner. I've got a feeling this new one is going to be a doozy."

Looking at his watch, Bob said to London, "Have you seen Stanley Tedrow? I was expecting him for breakfast by now."

"I'm afraid not," London said.

"He's probably hard at work on his book," Bob said. "He's a sharp guy, that Stanley—a real quick learner. A great listener, too. It's a good thing he came to me for advice, though. He really had a lot of goofy ideas about criminal investigation. Fortunately I've been able to clear him about a few things."

London couldn't imagine what sort of tips Bob might be giving Mr. Tedrow.

Bob continued, "Well, maybe it's just as well that he didn't show for breakfast. I've got a lot of mental work to do today, with a new murder to solve."

London thought back to those moments when she'd discovered the body. Looking out over the crowd, she'd recognized several passengers and crewmembers. But she hadn't seen Bob among them. She was sure he hadn't even been there.

Did he even have any real idea what had happened?

She asked cautiously, "Uh ... do you have any theories?"

"Nope," Bob said. "But these things can't be rushed."

London suspected that the police took a less leisurely attitude.

"What kind of investigating do you plan to do?" she asked.

Bob's lips twitched a little.

"From what I know so far, this is a rather different sort of case than the one I solved back in Salzburg. It'll make different demands on my crime-solving faculties. Normally I've got to get out in the field, interrogate lots of people, scrounge around for physical evidence. But this time ..."

Suddenly he couldn't hold back a yawn.

He said, "I think this case calls for a more *cerebral* approach. It wouldn't be wise to go ashore and meander around and get

115

overstimulated with a lot of needless detail. I've got to sit still and focus my mind, apply abstract reasoning to the problem, use pure logic and nothing else …"

His voice faded away.

After a moment, his mouth dropped open and he let out a snore.

London tried not to laugh.

Obviously, Bob was too hungover to do any serious investigating today.

And that's probably just as well, she thought.

His efforts tended to result in some pretty crazy theories that did little except distract from any real investigation others might be doing. It did concern her a little, though, that Mr. Lapham was expecting so much from him. She kind of liked Bob and didn't want to see him fail at his job.

She just hoped that the police would wrap up this case as soon as possible.

Thinking of the police reminded her that Detektiv Erlich was probably in the captain's quarters right now waiting to talk to her. She and Sir Reggie left the restaurant and headed back down to the Allegro deck.

The door to the captain's stateroom opened as London and Sir Reggie approached. To London's surprise, Bryce stepped into the passageway.

"Bryce!" London said.

Before she could ask what he was doing here, he was followed by Detektiv Erlich himself. London again remembered the captain mentioning that Erlich wanted to talk to "one or two other people."

One of them was obviously Audrey.

I guess the other one was Bryce, London figured.

Erlich said to Bryce, "Thank you for your cooperation, sir. I will be in touch if I have any more questions."

"Of course," Bryce said.

As Bryce continued on his way, he and London exchanged sheepish glances. London found herself wondering what Bryce and the detective had discussed.

"Come on inside," Detektiv Erlich said.

London and Sir Reggie walked into the captain's stateroom, and Erlich shut the door behind them. The captain sat at his desk looking quite concerned. Although London didn't quite know why, she suddenly felt a lot more nervous and worried than she'd already been.

CHAPTER TWENTY

When London stepped into Captain Hays's office, she wasn't encouraged by the atmosphere. Detektiv Erlich was frowning darkly, and the usually amiable captain also appeared annoyed. London guessed that the captain hadn't liked some of the questions the detective had asked Bryce just now.

And where was Audrey? Surely she must be one of the people they wanted to question. Had she already come in and answered Detektiv Erlich's questions and left? Had she been cleared of all suspicion?

London took a seat to wait for whatever was taking place. Sir Reggie crouched on the floor beside her, tucking his head between his paws and looking as uneasy as she felt.

Erlich paced silently in front of her for a moment, thumbing through his notepad.

The captain remained seated at his desk and spoke first.

"Detektiv Erlich, you seem to be quite convinced that Herr Forstmann's death was a murder, and neither an accident nor a prank gone wrong. But so far, you've said nothing to convince me of that fact. Since you insist on questioning my staff and keeping my ship from leaving Bamberg, I think you owe me more of an explanation."

The edges of Erlich's lips turned into a slight smile.

"You are correct, Captain," he said. "I am glad you asked."

He took out his cell phone and brought up an image and showed it to the captain, and then to London.

He explained, "This is a forensic drawing made by the *gerichtsmediziner*—our medical examiner—of the wound to Herr Forstmann's head. This is the wound he apparently suffered before he was submerged. You can see that the indentation has a distinctive shape. It was made by a hard, cylindrical object. There is nothing at the crime scene that could have made this precise wound, much less accidentally. The injury definitely came from a deliberate blow."

Erlich seemed to take particular care to give London a close look at the drawing, which was very detailed, including measurements.

He asked her, "Do you have any idea what this object might have been?"

London could tell by his tone of voice that he was gauging her reaction. If she was guilty, he surely thought, she might respond with alarm to the sight of this drawing. Of course, the image meant nothing to her. She could only guess that it was caused by a smooth hard, rounded object—a metal pipe, maybe.

"I have no idea what caused the injury," she said, quite truthfully.

Apparently pleased by her answer, the captain let out a grunt of approval.

It's a good thing he's here, London thought. She realized she wouldn't like to be questioned like this without an authority figure from the ship also present.

Finally Erlich stopped pacing and looked at her sternly.

"Fräulein Rose, I want to clarify a few things you said yesterday and get more details."

"Of course," London said, gulping hard.

Erlich tapped his pencil against his notepad.

"You told me you'd gone up onto the stage after finding Herr Forstmann's monocle."

London replayed the moment in her mind.

She said, "Actually, my dog ducked under the curtain, and I followed him to see what interested him."

"You didn't mention earlier that you'd been following your dog," Erlich said.

London's eyes widened.

"Does it matter?" she asked.

"Everything matters," Erlich said.

London was shocked by the suspicion in his voice. He seemed to be looking for even the smallest inconsistencies in her account.

Erlich then said, "And after you went onto the stage, you climbed up onto platform above the vat."

"That's right."

"Why did you do that?"

London's head swam for a moment as she tried to remember. She glanced down at Sir Reggie and remembered the dog sniffing around on the stage floor. Then it came back to her.

"I saw beer splashed on the floor. I wondered how it got there."

"And you thought maybe someone was in the vat?"

"I didn't know what to think. I ... guess I went up onto the platform

119

to find out."

Erlich looked at her as if he didn't quite believe her. Indeed, London half-wondered whether she was telling the exact truth.

What was *I thinking right then?* she wondered.

She couldn't really remember *thinking* anything at all. To the best of her memory, she'd simply acted on reflex.

Jotting down notes, Erlich said, "And you only saw the body when the curtain opened and the lights came up?"

"Yes."

Erlich paused and scratched his chin.

"I've talked to a fair number of witnesses," he said. "None of them remembers hearing you call for help at that moment."

London felt a tingle of rising anxiety.

"Well, I don't believe I *did* call for help," she said.

"No?" Erlich said.

"No, I just jumped into the vat myself to see if I could help him."

Erlich gazed at her skeptically for a moment. London was starting to feel unnerved now.

Captain Hays growled with disapproval.

"Now see here," the captain said to Erlich. "I can't imagine why it should concern you whether she called for help or not. Why would she? A whole crowd was watching. They could see there was trouble. London's first instinct was to jump in herself and see what she could do. Can anybody fault her for that?"

Erlich turned his gaze on the captain.

"I didn't say I faulted her for anything. But I would like to hear *her* answer to my question."

He looked at London again, waiting for an answer. The truth was, London was sure the captain had just explained the matter as well as she could. But she knew it wouldn't do to repeat his words.

"I don't know why I didn't call for help," she said. "I just didn't think of it at the time."

Erlich nodded, then paced a bit more before speaking again.

"I have talked with your colleague, Bryce Yeaton," he said. "It appears that you were with him shortly before the incident."

London felt her heart quicken as she remembered the sheepish look she and Bryce had exchanged just before she'd come into the stateroom. Now she realized the situation was even more fraught than she'd feared. Her own answers had to be consistent with whatever

Bryce had just told Erlich.

She tried to convince herself that that shouldn't be a problem. Bryce had surely just told Erlich the truth. All London had to do was do the same.

So why do I feel so flustered? she wondered.

She couldn't help feeling as though Detektiv Erlich was deliberately trying to catch her off guard. And she couldn't be sure how much Bryce had told them or exactly how he had described everything.

Erlich asked, "Could you tell us exactly what you were doing just before you found the monocle?"

"I was wandering through the crowd looking around for passengers and crew members," London said. "It was getting toward time for our departure, and everybody needed to return to the boat."

"Where was Herr Yeaton at the time?"

"He was doing the same thing elsewhere."

"And what were the two of you doing before that? Before you started searching for passengers and crew?"

"Um, Bryce and I took a little walk."

"Where did you go?"

"To the *Schönleinsplatz.*"

"Why did you go there?"

"We just wanted to get away from the festivities for a little while," she said.

"And what did you do at the *Schönleinsplatz?*"

London felt her face redden with both embarrassment and irritation. *Why on earth does that matter?* she wondered.

London sensed more and more that Erlich was trying to throw her off balance by asking some questions that were surely irrelevant to his investigation. Doubtless he had asked Bryce the same question. But how had Bryce answered it? Had he told him about their would-be romantic moment?

She didn't know, and she cringed at the idea of saying anything about it in front of the captain. But she thought that the safest thing was to be as forthright as possible.

Her jaw tightened as she said, "If you must know, we almost kissed."

She glanced warily over at the captain. She thought he looked even more irritated, but couldn't tell whether he was annoyed with her or with Detektiv Erlich.

London added, "But we were interrupted by a phone call."

"A phone call from whom?"

"The ship's concierge. She told us it was time for us to start rounding up passengers."

Erlich thumbed through his notes again, then looked at the captain.

"Audrey Bolton hasn't responded to your call," he said.

"No, sir. She has not," the captain said.

Erlich tapped his pencil against his notepad again.

"Fräulein Rose, you told me yesterday that Herr Forstmann splashed you and this other woman—Audrey Bolton is her name—with beer."

"That's right."

He turned a few pages back in his notebook.

"I don't believe you've been completely forthright with me," he said. "I talked to some witnesses who say that you and Audrey Bolton had a second altercation with Herr Forstmann."

London felt suddenly puzzled.

"Uh, I don't think so," she said.

"Are you quite sure?"

London thought for a moment, then realized something.

"Actually, I happened to encounter Audrey after she'd run into Herr Forstmann again. I only saw him walking away from her and I didn't speak with him. She didn't tell me what had happened, but she said everything was fine. Whatever had happened between them was apparently over with."

The detective shook his head critically.

"Why didn't you tell me about this second encounter when we spoke yesterday?"

London was startled and a little angry.

"Well, it didn't occur to me to mention it, and frankly …"

"Well?"

"You didn't ask."

London was a little shocked by her own sharp tone of voice. She hadn't meant to be rude. She just thought there was something truly unfair about the question. But judging by Erlich's frown, he didn't like her tone.

Even so, she didn't feel like apologizing.

Finally Erlich said, "I mentioned yesterday that I would want to talk to this Audrey Bolton."

London's stomach sank as she remembered knocking on Audrey's door a little while ago and getting no reply. Apparently Audrey hadn't even responded to the captain's announcement requesting her to come to his stateroom.

None of that boded well.

"I'll try to reach her," London said.

She found Audrey's number on her cell phone and made the call. After a couple of rings, she heard a familiar cheerless voice.

"Hello. You know who you've reached. And you know what to do when you hear the tone."

After the beep, London stepped aside and said in a low voice, "Audrey, you need to call me. I told you yesterday a detective wants to talk to you today. He's here in the captain's stateroom right now. You've got to get back to me right away."

She ended the call and looked at the detective.

"You couldn't reach her, I take it," Erlich said.

"I left a message," London said.

"I'm afraid we need to do better than that," Erlich said. "Take me to her room."

London stifled a groan of despair.

"I knocked on her door this morning," London said. "No one answered."

"We will try again," Erlich said firmly.

London, Captain Hays, Detektiv Erlich, and Sir Reggie walked up a flight of stairs to the Adagio deck, and London knocked on Audrey's door again.

"Audrey, it's London," she called out. "The police detective is here with me. If you're there, please come to the door."

The group waited for a moment for a reply.

"Audrey, it's important," London said.

There was still no reply.

"I like this less and less," Detektiv Erlich said in a tone of ironic understatement.

London felt the same way, although she didn't say so.

Where is that woman? she wondered.

"I'm sure she'll turn up soon," Captain Hays said.

"I wish I shared your naïve faith in human nature," Erlich said, stroking his well-kept beard. "In my experience, people seldom avoid talking to the police unless they are guilty of something. And in this case, we're talking about something very dire."

Detektiv Erlich stood staring at the door silently for a moment.

"I want you to open the door," he finally said to London and the captain.

The captain snapped, "You've got no business invading my passengers' privacy."

"My business is to solve a murder," Erlich said dryly. "I have no intention of conducting a thorough search the woman's room. I only want to know whether she is in there or not. I don't think that's too much to ask. Of course, if you want me to go through legal channels, this whole thing could become much more difficult than necessary. And a lot less pleasant."

As London looked at the captain, he nodded his head in reluctant approval.

London took out her master keycard and opened the door.

The window curtains were open, and morning sunlight poured inside. The room was neat and clean, and the bathroom door was open. As London and the others went inside, they could easily see that no one was here. Even so, the detective checked the closet and glanced under the bed.

Detektiv Erlich's lips twisted into a smirk.

"Well, it appears that our suspect has—what is the American idiom?—'given us the slip.'"

"I wouldn't jump to conclusions, Detektiv," the captain said sternly.

"What other conclusions are there to come to?" Erlich asked.

London wondered that herself. But she figured there was one way to find out. She went to the still-open closet, which was visibly full of Audrey's clothes and shoes.

Pointing out a couple of empty suitcases, London said, "Wherever she went, it doesn't look like she plans to go very far or for very long."

"Indeed, it does not," the captain said with a snort of satisfaction.

Detektiv Erlich frowned again.

"I want you to give me a full description of the woman," he said to London and the captain. "I'll order a team to search for her. If she is anywhere in Bamberg, we'll find her."

The captain scoffed indignantly.

"See here, now you're just being melodramatic. What do you plan to do, set up some kind of police dragnet?"

"Do you have another suggestion?" Erlich said.

"Not at all, if you don't mind this turning into a nasty international incident. Which I assure you is what will happen if you push things too far. Regarding your murder case, I've come up with one or two theories of my own. Would you care to hear them?"

The detective nodded.

In a knowing tone, Captain Hays said, "From what you've told me already, Herr Forstmann was almost universally disliked here in Bamberg. Which means that just about everybody in your lovely town is a viable suspect. That's rather inconvenient for you, isn't it? Especially since Herr Forstmann was a prominent personage from Munich."

Captain Hays's manner grew more daunting as he continued.

"I imagine you're under rather a lot of political pressure, aren't you? You'd like this whole case to just go away without a lot of fuss—and certainly without accusing anyone locally. That makes the *Nachtmusik*'s arrival here rather convenient. You don't even have to *prove* that one of my passengers committed the murder. All you have to do is buy some time by casting suspicion upon us. Eventually the case will sort of magically disappear. Or so you hope."

Erlich's face had turned red—partly out of anger, London was sure, but also out of frustration that the captain had stated the situation pretty accurately.

The captain's expression suddenly changed to one of mock apology.

"But—oh, dear, I am being rather harsh, aren't I?" he said. "I'm dreadfully sorry. Let's both take a bit of a pause to cool our heads, shall we? Have you had breakfast?"

"No," Erlich replied, looking a bit startled.

"Then come on over to our wonderful Habsburg Restaurant. We'll sit down and talk this over like civilized gentlemen, and I'm sure you'll enjoy the rather sumptuous repast."

The detective looked undecided for a moment. Then he nodded abruptly and said, "I shall accept your kind invitation."

"Marvelous," the captain said. "The restaurant is just up one deck, in the bow of our ship. Please go ahead and I'll join you there in a moment. We can talk about these matters further."

Erlich looked back and forth from Captain Hays to London. Then he apparently decided that having accepted the invitation he should be agreeable.

125

"I look forward to your company and to any aid you can offer me," Erlich said. Then he made a stiff bow and left the room.

As soon as the detective was out the door, the captain whispered to London, "We need to take care of this ourselves. As promptly as possible."

"I agree," London replied.

In fact, she was relieved to hear the captain say so. Things had gotten way out of hand.

"What do you want me to do?" London asked the captain.

"Go ashore and head right into town. Find Ms. Bolton, wherever she is."

Then he straightened his uniform and went out the door

London looked down at Sir Reggie, who had been watching the proceedings with interest.

"You heard the captain's orders," she said. "We've got work to do."

She and Reggie left the captain's office stateroom. They stopped by London's stateroom for her bag and a leash, then hurried up to the reception area. As they headed toward the gangway, London realized that she felt a little uncertain about her mission.

She could only hope that her assumption was correct, and Audrey Bolton hadn't intentionally "given them the slip."

Because for all London really knew, Audrey might actually be the killer.

CHAPTER TWENTY ONE

Hia hia hia ho
Hia hia hia ho
Hia hia ho ...

The raucous yodeling chorus startled London as she and Sir Reggie stepped out onto the gangway. A group of men dressed in *lederhosen* and women in *dirndls* were clustered at the base of the gangway. They were singing, yodeling, and some were also dancing. The same small *oompah* band was also there again, playing more cheerfully than ever.

After yesterday's events, London had expected Bamberg to be more subdued.

As she and her little dog walked down the gangway, she was even more surprised to spot Emil Waldmüller standing nearby listening to the band. Hadn't the ship's historian mocked this same group a day ago?

With an oddly melancholy smile on his face, Emil was tapping one foot and mouthing the words of the song.

London focused on the words the group was singing, trying to make sense of the lyrics.

Ein   esel   wolte   nicht   nach   hause   gehen,
Nicht nach hause gehen.

Something to do with a donkey that won't go home, she thought, wondering why that would ever appeal to Emil.

When she and Sir Reggie set foot on the shore, she made her way over to Emil and spoke loudly enough to be heard over the music.

"I thought you didn't like *oompah* music."

Emil's eyes widened with surprise. London seemed to have caught him completely off guard.

"Eh? I—I do not like it at all," he stammered. "I believe I made that perfectly clear yesterday. Whatever gave you the idea that I felt differently?"

London smiled and thought, *Well, maybe the fact that you're standing here singing along.*

But she decided not to say so aloud. Emil seemed rattled enough by her arrival. She didn't want to spoil his mood altogether—although judging from his sudden frown, maybe she'd unintentionally done so already. And he wasn't tapping his foot anymore.

Instead she said, "I'm surprised that things seem so festive today."

"Surprised?" Emil said. "Why on earth would you be surprised?"

London crinkled her brow.

"Well, after what happened yesterday ..." she began.

"Oh, yes, another murder," Emil said. "It is why we are staying an extra day here in Bamberg, is it not?"

London couldn't imagine why he was talking about it so casually, almost as if he was barely aware of what had been going on. This wasn't like him at all. To the contrary, the *Nachtmusik*'s past delays in port had positively infuriated him.

Why is he acting this way? she wondered.

Emil continued with what struck London as an air of forced haughtiness.

"Well, you certainly would not expect a little thing like that to upset the festivities, would you? Especially when there is beer involved. These are Bavarians, after all."

London guessed that he was right. The Hoffmann Fest seemed to be far too much of a tradition here in Bamberg to get canceled on account of a beer critic's murder. She stood listening to the band, which seemed to be playing the same tune over and over again.

"What is this song?" she asked Emil.

"I certainly would not know," Emil said with a scoff.

London was baffled. A moment ago she'd caught him singing along with the music. Now he was pretending he didn't even know it.

She listened again and picked out some more lyrics.

Da   kam   die   esel   liebe   Veronika   ...

London did her best to translate in her head.

Then came a donkey, dear Veronica ...

She mused aloud to Emil, "The song seems to be about two donkeys—one that won't go home, and another..."

Suddenly the lyrics came clearer to her.

"It's about a lovesick donkey, isn't it?" she said. "He's standing around waiting for a female donkey, 'dear Veronica,' to show up, and when she does, he winds up going away with her."

Emil's scowl deepened, and his face got red.

"As I said, I would not know," he said gruffly. "Now if you will excuse me, I have … eh, some business to attend to."

He turned and made his way past the costumed revelers, who were again yodeling the song's chorus.

Hia hia hia ho
Hia hia hia ho
Hia hia ho …

London was truly taken aback now. She'd never known the usually rather staid historian to have such odd mood swings.

She picked up Sir Reggie and asked him, "Was it something I said?"

Sir Reggie let out an uncertain little whine.

The revelers here on the waterfront walkway were growing more numerous and festive by the minute. As the band struck up yet another tune, London reminded herself of the orders the captain had given her a few moments ago.

"Go ashore and head right into town. Find Ms. Bolton, wherever she is."

Now her mind boggled at the task. It would have been hard enough to go looking for Audrey if the town were quiet and peaceful. How was she going to find her in the midst of this chaos?

London was troubled by an even more worrisome question.

What if she doesn't want to be found?

Surely then the task would be impossible.

"Where do you think we should start looking, boy?" she asked her dog.

Sir Reggie looked at her as if she were crazy for asking him.

"I guess it's up to me, huh?" she said with a sigh. "Well, it's not like we can go searching house to house. I guess the *Maximiliensplatz* is as good a place to get started as any. Come on, let's get going."

Still carrying Sir Reggie, London made her way through the crowded waterfront walkway and into a short street leading up into the city. Before she got far along, she turned and looked back at the people gathered near she ship.

From here, she could see that Emil hadn't gone away after all. He had come right back and was standing where she had first found him, listening to the band. He even appeared to be again tapping his feet and mouthing the words to the song.

What's going on? London wondered

Why had he lied to her just now by telling her he had "business to attend to"? And why was he behaving so oddly?

She remembered again what Amy had said to her just a couple of days ago.

"Honestly, London, there's so much going on around here that you don't know about."

It certainly seemed that Amy was right. Not that the ship's concierge had been willing to tell London anything helpful. She'd actually blamed London for not knowing more about what was going on.

"Don't you ever look right under your nose?"

London sighed again.

"If only it were that easy," she murmured aloud.

As she made her way along the stone-paved street into the plaza that was central to the celebration, London mused on the mysteries that confounded her.

Too many unanswered questions, she thought.

Why were Amy and Emil both being so furtive? It would certainly be more helpful if they could be simple and straightforward about things.

Where was Audrey, and why had she disappeared? Could she be hiding her own guilt, or at least not talking to London about something she knew?

And then there was the most worrisome question …

Who killed Sigmund Forstmann?

As she and Sir Reggie neared the *Maximiliensplatz*, London could hear announcements over a loudspeaker. The words were garbled but she gathered that the winner of the beer competition would be announced later that afternoon.

London's spirits sank a little at the sound. She knew that the brewer's awards were a big part of the celebration. She needed to find Audrey right away, before the big plaza became even more crowded and hectic than usual. Although Audrey was exceptionally tall and might stand out in a crowd, it was likely to become harder and harder to find her.

Besides, back on the ship Captain Hays was keeping Detektiv Erlich occupied so she could bring their missing passenger back without submitting her to a police roundup. How long could the captain ply the detective with food and conversation before the local *Kriminalpolizei* went into action?

When she reached the *Maximiliensplatz*, London was relieved to see that it was still open enough to walk about freely. She put Sir Reggie down, and the two of them began to wend their way along the stalls where one could buy, among other things, masks and costumes.

Like yesterday, many of the revelers were costumed as fanciful characters—fairies, owls, flowers, nutcrackers, and so forth. A gigantic flea and a snowflake appeared to be carrying on a conversation, and their words caught her attention.

London heard the snowflake say in German with a chuckle, "Now, now. Let's not gloat. And let's not speak ill of the dead."

The flea replied in German as well. "Well, I'm not sure how else to talk about him."

"I know what you mean," the snowflake said.

"And anyway, it's just one more reason to celebrate," the flea said. "Do you really think he was murdered by somebody on that cruise boat?"

The snowflake replied, "I'm not sure why any of those people would have done it. None of them knew him like we do. But I can tell you who is the happiest man in town to have him dead."

London stopped in her tracks and leaned forward to hear the next words.

CHAPTER TWENTY TWO

As London stood listening, she gasped at what she heard.

The snowflake paused for effect, and then finished the sentence.

"… the *Katers Murr* himself."

The flea scoffed. "Surely you're not saying that Rolf Schilder killed anybody."

The snowflake chuckled. "Schilder? A murderer? I hardly think so. But Schilder *is* going around telling people how happy he is that Forstmann is dead. And he's got good reason to be happy. Forstmann always wrote terrible reviews of his beer."

London's mind was racing. So the *Katers Murr* was a brewer, and the murdered man had given him bad reviews.

Could it be possible …?

"Those bad reviews were well deserved," the flea said. "That beer of his is terrible! But anyway, we all know that Schilder is no killer. He's more like a mouse than a cat. He wouldn't hurt anybody. Besides, he wouldn't be gloating if he'd really killed someone. He'd be keeping quiet about it."

"That's true," the snowflake replied with a laugh. "And I guess that if Forstmann's bad reviews were really a reason for murder, he'd have been dead long ago."

The flea also laughed. "Whoever did kill him, I'd like to shake his hand."

A costumed mouse approached and wagged his finger.

"The two of you should be ashamed, talking like this."

"Don't tell me you're going to miss him," the snowflake said.

"No, I couldn't stand him, but even so …"

The costumed characters moved out of earshot.

They're not exactly grief-stricken, she thought.

Nor did she suppose she had any reason to be surprised. It was like Captain Hays had said to Detektiv Erlich a little while ago.

"Just about everybody in your lovely town is a viable suspect."

London could understand why Detektiv Erlich would prefer that someone aboard the *Nachtmusik* had killed Forstmann. Bamberg's festival would suffer bad publicity if someone who lived in Bamberg had killed Forstmann out of spite. By contrast, the last thing London wanted was for the murderer to be somebody aboard the *Nachtmusik*.

But what if that turned out to be the case?

As she moved on around the plaza, London caught sight of a couple of familiar faces. Bob Turner had come ashore after all, and so had Stanley Tedrow. Bob appeared to be circulating among the crowd asking people questions, presumably about Forstmann's death. Tedrow was following him around, dutifully taking notes about his investigative mentor's methods.

London wondered—was there even the slightest possibility that Bob might turn up some clues or evidence? From past experience she doubted it, but she hoped she was wrong. More than that, she hoped Bob's efforts weren't going to do more harm than good.

The crowd was beginning to build up now, so she picked up Sir Reggie again. Just a few moments later, she was truly startled when the air suddenly filled up with what looked at first like large pieces of confetti.

She reached out and grabbed one of the floating papers. It wasn't confetti, but what appeared to be paper currency—various denominations of German Deutsche Mark. The people around her were laughing and grabbing the bills for themselves.

What on earth ...? London wondered.

Then it occurred to her—the Deutsche Mark hadn't been Germany's official currency since 2002, when the country had adopted the euro. She looked more closely at the two-hundred-mark bill in her hand, and sure enough, the portrait on it wasn't of some historical figure but a comical make-believe cat.

Katers Murr, she realized. Tomcat Murr.

It was pretend money, printed especially for the festival.

The revelers, of course, knew this, and were having a great time seizing gobs of the phony money and throwing it around to each other. Before London could figure out exactly what was going on or why, she heard a voice calling out in German from the direction of the stage.

"All this and more can be yours! Just vote for *Zenitbrauen* for this year's first prize! There is plenty of money where this came from!"

London pushed toward the stage. Pacing about in an open area in front of the stage was a man in the same enormous cat costume she'd glimpsed in the crowd at the moment when she'd discovered

133

Forstmann's drowned body. This time he was also wearing an ermine robe and a paper crown.

He was carrying a bag of the phony money and throwing it everywhere among the laughing crowd.

London turned to a pair of delighted bystanders.

"What's going on?" she asked them in German over the din.

"You must be from the ship," said one of the bystanders.

"I guess you wouldn't know," said the other. "The *Katers Murr* is pretending to bribe the crowd into voting for *Zenitbrauen*, his own brewery, to win the beer competition. Whoever is chosen to be the cat does this every year."

"It's a joke, of course," said the other. "The voting is already done and over with, and the ballots are being counted right now. Later on, the master of ceremonies will announce the real winner of the brewers prize."

London and Sir Reggie watched for a few moments as *Katers Murr* continued his antics. She remembered the name the costumed figures had said—Rolf Schilder.

"More like a mouse," they'd said.

Mouse or cat, the man was being appropriately silly. She watched for a few moments, then forced her attention back to the reason why she was here.

She'd made her way all the way across the *Maximiliensplatz* without seeing Audrey anywhere. She dreaded the thought of going back to the ship without her. But was she really going to spend the rest of the day wandering among the growing crowd? After all, she had no way of knowing whether Audrey was even anywhere nearby.

While she tried to make up her mind, she found herself eyeing the closed red curtain, wondering what might still be behind it. The dunking of *Katers Murr* had been scheduled for yesterday. Surely it had been canceled altogether. So had the huge vat of beer and the dunking device been removed? And where was the police tape she'd seen yesterday?

London walked around behind the edge of the makeshift proscenium arch that framed the stage. Sure enough, the stage itself was still surrounded by police tape. And the vat, the steps and platform, and the trick chair were all still in place.

London looked around. Despite all the noise just a few feet away, she saw that she was truly alone. The edge of the proscenium masked her from the view of the crowd.

She started to feel her curiosity get the better of her.

As if sensing this, Sir Reggie let out what sounded like a whine of protest.

"You're probably right, pal," London said as she set him down on the edge of the stage. "I know this is still a crime scene. But I can't help myself. I guess I'm just having a 'Nancy Drew' moment."

She ducked under the police tape to join Sir Reggie on the stage. The dog sniffed the floor, taking an interest in the dried stains where beer had been puddled yesterday after Sigmund Forstmann's fall into the vat.

The whole stage smelled strongly of stale beer. As she and Sir Reggie climbed the steps, she wasn't surprised to see that the vat was still full, with an unhealthy-looking filmy layer of froth and grime spread across the top. London guessed that the beer would have been removed by now under normal circumstances.

The last time she'd been here, she'd been soaked with beer and too badly shaken to really try to work out logically what had happened here. She hoped maybe she could do better now.

First she looked carefully at the chair itself. Its bottom still hung loose from having been triggered into dropping Herr Forstmann. London remembered Polizist Wedekind saying he'd personally inspected the machinery for safety. It certainly looked safe enough to London.

London could also see that the chair and the entire drop into the vat were well-padded. There really was no way Herr Forstmann could have hurt his head accidentally, let alone have received such a distinctively shaped wound.

So what really happened here? she asked herself.

She knew that Detektiv Erlich had been considering a theory that London and Audrey had clubbed the beer critic unconscious, then dragged him up onto the platform, placed him in the chair, and fatally dunked him.

Of course London knew that she herself had done nothing of the kind.

But what about Audrey? she wondered.

Could the quarrelsome passenger have done something like this alone?

Audrey was an unusually tall woman, and for all London knew, she

135

might be quite strong as well. Herr Forstmann, by contrast, had been about London's own height and build.

Maybe it's possible, London thought.

But was it really plausible?

London tried to imagine how the events might have unfolded. Maybe Audrey and Herr Forstmann had quarreled on the stage behind the curtain—or maybe right here where London was standing, on the platform. Maybe Audrey had hit him over the head ...

But with what?

Not her purse, surely.

It had to be something hard and cylindrical ...

London's thoughts were interrupted by a man's voice speaking in German.

"I see you've returned to the scene of the crime."

CHAPTER TWENTY THREE

London whirled around in alarm. The man who had spoken so harshly was standing on the stage below her. His arms were crossed and his stare was baleful.

It was Willy Oberhauser, the security guard.

Now I'm in real trouble, she thought.

"You Americans," Oberhauser said with a smirk. "I guess you have never heard of police tape, eh? It is supposed to keep you out of active crime scenes."

He was being sarcastic, of course. London almost said that, yes, Americans had police tape just like the Germans, and she knew all about it, if only from watching cop shows on TV. But the last thing she wanted was to come across as the least bit snarky.

After all, she really had just broken the law.

"I'm sorry," she said, picking up Sir Reggie and climbing back down the stairs to the stage. "I should have asked for permission."

"Permission for what?" Oberhauser asked.

"Well ... to have a look around here for myself."

"And why would you want to do that?"

The little dog in London's arms was grumbling as though he might break out into a growl and she didn't think that would help the situation at all. She patted Sir Reggie and told him *shhhh.*

Finally she said, "Well, since I'm suspected of murder, you can't blame me for wanting to check out the evidence. I might have to clear myself."

"Leave all that to the police," he said. "They'll find evidence to clear you ... *if* you are innocent."

Startled by his accusatory tone, London realized that this security guard certainly seemed to be prone to mood swings. She remembered how he'd changed yesterday when he'd broken up her altercation with Herr Forstmann. After he'd sternly separated the two of them, he'd been remarkably pleasant toward her—and actually rather sympathetic. He'd even been eager to make Sir Reggie's acquaintance.

She also remembered his cheerful parting words on that occasion.

"Enjoy the rest of your visit."

But his attitude toward her had taken a dark turn again as soon as Herr Forstmann's body was found. He'd been the first person to name London and Audrey as suspects in the murder.

And now London wondered ...

Why?

Did he really suspect her? Or was he anxious to be the one who solved the crime?

Or ... could he be trying to deflect any possible suspicion ...?

As calmly as she could manage, she said, "Surely you don't really think I had anything to do with Forstmann's death."

"It's not my job to make any such assumptions."

London felt her composure slipping away.

"Well, it's certainly what you did yesterday," she told him, "when you pointed me out to Detektiv Erlich. And isn't it what you're doing now? Why are you so anxious to blame me? You said yourself that lots of people in Bamberg got angry about Herr Forstmann's behavior at the festival every year—including yourself."

The security guard didn't move from his spot.

Is he going to arrest me? London wondered with dread.

"Like I said, I'm sorry," she said, trying to sound more repentant than she felt. "I'll leave right now. But first maybe you could help me with something. I'm looking for that tall woman I was with yesterday. The one Herr Forstmann spilled beer all over."

"You mean the one who might have helped you kill Forstmann?" Oberhauser said.

London fought down the urge to answer him sharply.

"Have you seen her today?" she said instead.

"No, and I hope I don't. I'm having enough trouble with all of you nosy Americans today."

London's forehead crinkled with interest.

"Who do you mean?" she asked.

Oberhauser said, "There's a man wearing sunglasses who keeps telling people he's a detective who is going to solve the case all by himself."

Bob Turner, London realized.

The security guard continued, "I've told him more than once to mind his own business, but he never listens. And I'm telling you the same thing—to mind your own business, or else. It's time you both took heed."

His expression was grim as stepped toward her, and his hand reached menacingly toward a holster on his hip.

"Otherwise, I promise there will be consequences," he said, glaring directly into her eyes.

London shuddered sharply.

Is he threatening me with deadly force? she wondered.

And maybe threatening Bob as well?

It seemed like an absolutely crazy idea. Here she was in a lovely city where a celebration was taking place. In fact, she could hear the sounds of the Hoffmann Fest in progress nearby. She knew that people in clever costumes from E.T.A. Hoffman stories were celebrating right there in the plaza in front of the stage. It even sounded like the *Katers Murr* might still be clowning around on the front side of that closed red curtain, perhaps no more than twenty feet away. But here behind the curtain and further hidden by the edge of the proscenium, both she and Oberhauser were masked from sight.

Would anyone hear her if she cried out?

And what would happen if they did?

Oberhauser was an official security guard. He was a local authority, and she was just on tour from a faraway country.

What if he did something really rash, then made up his own story about what had happened? Might he claim to have acted in self-defense?

Who would believe her? Surely they would take his word over hers.

And of course, if he did something truly extreme, maybe she wouldn't even be able to contradict him.

London shushed another soft growl from Sir Reggie.

She stood frozen with alarm, unable to think of anything to say.

To her relief, the guard seemed to have second thoughts about what he was doing.

He hesitated with his hand on the holster.

London's mind raced. What could she do?

She managed to speak in a nearly normal tone of voice.

"I should get back to my errand," she told him. "The captain will be expecting me back at the ship. And Detektiv Erlich is there with him. They're waiting for me to find another passenger and come right back. I wouldn't want them to send out anyone looking for me."

"Yes, you should go on back," the security guard said, letting his hand fall away from the holster. "Do your job and go back to your ship immediately. And you must stay there. All of you Americans. Stay put aboard until you leave Bamberg."

London was sure Oberhauser had no authority to give such a command. Even Detektiv Erlich hadn't ordered her or anyone else to stay aboard the *Nachtmusik* and not come into Bamberg. But the last thing she wanted to do right now was to argue.

Even so, she wasn't going to make any promises about staying aboard the *Nachtmusik*.

"I'm sorry to have troubled you," she said instead.

London turned away from the confrontation, and the security guard actually held up the tape for her as she ducked under it and climbed down from the stage.

When she walked by the front of the stage, she saw that the *Katers Murr* was indeed still there, begging the surrounding spectators to vote for his beer. The crowd was still grabbing at fake money floating through the air.

As far as any of them knew, nothing at all had happened.

Hurrying away with her dog still in her arms, London didn't look back, but she thought she could feel Oberhauser's eyes following her.

She felt a wave of discouragement. She'd come ashore with one simple purpose, to find Audrey Bolton. She had circled the festival area before going to look at the crime scene and hadn't seen Audrey anywhere. She had only picked up some useless gossip and managed to annoy the security guard, who was clearly suspicious of her. She really had no idea who to ask or where else to look.

The *Maximiliensplatz* was getting more crowded now, and London realized that she wasn't likely to run into Audrey even if she were here somewhere.

She figured she'd make one more pass amid the revelers …

And then what?

If Audrey wasn't anywhere near here, where might she be?

And how could London possibly hope to find her?

As she tried to consider her options, she was stopped by the sound of a familiar voice speaking loudly.

CHAPTER TWENTY FOUR

"I am a detective ..." the man was saying in deliberately over-simplified English. "That means, uh, I solve mysteries ... Catch criminals ... A man died here yesterday ..."

The confused-looking German woman he was speaking to shrugged and said, *"Entschuldigung, ich verstehe dich nicht."*

Although the woman had just told him, "Sorry, I don't understand you," the man clearly wasn't able to manage the translation.

He was nearly yelling, "Do you understand what I'm saying?"

Some members of the small crowd that had gathered around them looked quite amused, but a few looked annoyed.

London sighed.

"I guess I'd better help with that," she told Sir Reggie.

She headed toward Bob Turner, who was for some reason still trying to describe his qualifications to the uncomprehending woman.

Stanley Tedrow was standing beside Turner, holding his notebook in his hand. London was sure that the would-be mystery author was just as inept with the local language as Bob was.

What kind of notes could he be taking? she wondered.

Just as London reached them, the woman said, *"Warum sprichst du mit mir auf Englisch?"*

When Bob just stared at her without replying, she shrugged and walked away. The small group of people who had been standing around and listening also dispersed.

"What did she say?" Mr. Tedrow asked Bob Turner.

"I couldn't catch all of it," Bob said, scratching his head. "But she says she doesn't have any information."

London couldn't hide a giggle at Bob's less-than-forthright reply. Of course he didn't know what the woman had really said. But London had understood her final question perfectly.

"Why are you speaking to me in English?"

Bob gazed all around, as if looking for someone else to question.

London quickened her step toward him. The ship's overconfident security man had obviously been wandering around for a while now, struggling to make himself understood as he carried out his idea of an investigation. She knew that his German was limited to a few touristy words and phrases, so how could he really hope to solve the mystery of Sigmund Forstmann's death? Still, he seemed to be valiantly trying. And Bamberg was a very multilingual town, so it was even possible that he had run into some Germans who happened to speak English and actually tried to answer his questions.

As London approached, Bob turned and spotted her.

He said to Mr. Tedrow, "Hey, Stanley! Look who's joining us."

"Hi, London," Mr. Tedrow said, barely looking up at her. He appeared completely absorbed by whatever he was scribbling in his notebook.

Bob said to London, "How're you doing, missy?"

London cringed. She hated it when Bob called her "missy," which he tended to do when he felt overconfident.

Then Bob scratched Sir Reggie under the chin.

"I'm sure glad you brought along Sir Reggie the wonder dog," he said. "Stanley and I could use his help right now."

He peered into Sir Reggie's face and added, "So what do you say, pal? D'you feel riled and raring for the hunt? Yep, you've got that ferocious wild animal vibe about you, I can feel it. Practically frothing at the mouth, aren't you? Come on, I could use a snout for crime like yours. Let's go sniff ourselves out a killer."

Apparently not interested in Bob's invitation, Sir Reggie nestled back down into London's arms. Meanwhile, Mr. Tedrow kept right on taking notes—although London couldn't imagine why, at this particular moment.

London knew she'd better get right to the point.

"Bob, you've got to stop this," she said.

"Stop what?"

"Whatever you're doing. Running around questioning people. You could get yourself in serious trouble."

"Trouble is my middle name, missy," Bob scoffed.

"I'm serious, Bob. I just talked to a security guard who said he'd tried to stop you from asking so many questions."

"So he did," Bob said.

"He wasn't kidding, Bob. And I think he might ..."

London paused as she remembered how Oberhauser had reached for his holster.

How *did* she think he might react if Bob didn't start minding his own business?

She knew that as a retired New York City police detective, Bob was able to handle a physical threat. But if the local security guard was armed …

But surely, she thought, *he wouldn't shoot anyone right out here in the open. Not with so many people around.*

And yet …

She really didn't know what Oberhauser might do. His behavior was inconsistent—and it scared her.

Not that Bob was exactly predictable either.

London knew that she needed to get Bob away from any possible encounter. Maybe she could cajole him into going back to the ship.

"Bob, have you found out anything at all?" she asked, feeling all but sure that the true answer was no.

"Maybe," Bob said instead. "Just maybe."

"What is it, then?" London asked.

Bob scratched his chin.

"I'm not ready to say just yet," he said. "The idea is just starting to take shape in my mind."

London doubted that Bob had a single useful idea in his head right now. But she felt a flash of hope as she realized she might just be able to get through to him.

"Well, then," she said. "Maybe this is one of those times for … you know, a more *cerebral* approach. Surely all this activity is overstimulating your brain. Maybe you need to work in a more tranquil setting. The Amadeus Lounge, maybe. Or better yet, your own stateroom. Give yourself a chance to do some abstract reasoning, exercise some pure logic. What do you think?"

Bob scratched his chin for a moment, then spoke to Mr. Tedrow.

"What do you think, Stanley? You're starting to understand my methods."

Mr. Tedrow finally looked up from his notebook.

"I think maybe the girl is onto something," he said to Bob.

London cringed again.

Girl! Missy!

It was all she could do not to tell them both to knock it off.

Another time, maybe.

But she was relieved when Tedrow kept on agreeing with her.

"And we could have a nice brunch while we're at it," he said to Bob. "Or maybe relax a little by the pool. I didn't even know there was a pool on the boat until you got me out learning all about investigations. We've got to get some use out of the facilities. We *are* paying for them, after all."

"It's settled, then," Bob said, nodding to both London and Mr. Tedrow. "I'll head right back to the ship and put the full weight of my mighty noggin to the problem. I'll be able to crack the case in an hour or so. Before those grand ceremonies get started, I'm sure."

He patted Mr. Tedrow on the shoulder and added, "Then later you and me and maybe Sir Reggie here will come back here to *par-TAY* like the kids we are at heart. What do you say?"

"It sounds like a plan," Mr. Tedrow said with an admiring grin.

London breathed a little easier as she watched the two men toddle away.

That's one problem solved, she thought. *At least for the time being.*

She looked around the *Maximiliensplatz*, which was quite full of people now. As before, some were in costume, some in basic native dress, and others just wore their everyday clothes. She saw a large chicken and several other farm animals, which she didn't think were from Hoffmann stories but were costumes she had seen for sale. She didn't see Audrey Bolton anywhere.

London still hadn't accomplished what she'd come here to do. And now it seemed less and less likely that she was going to succeed.

Worse, she was sure that some of the people in the crowd were staring at her.

She looked at Sir Reggie sadly.

"What do you think I should do now?" she asked the dog.

Sir Reggie let out a slight growl that seemed to ask, *"What are you asking me for?"*

London sighed and said, "I guess it's up to me, huh? Well, we'd better head back to the ship and admit to Captain Hays and Detektiv Erlich that we've failed in our mission."

Feeling rather depressed, she headed back toward the boat.

Then a movement in the crowd caught her eye.

A hearty-looking man clad in *lederhosen* was waving his arm energetically, trying to get her attention.

CHAPTER TWENTY FIVE

Who is that waving to me? London wondered.

In her anxiety about finding Audrey Bolton, she didn't immediately recognize him. Then she realized that it was Helmut Preiss, the robust-looking brewer of the *Hefeweisen* that had so impressed both Bryce and her yesterday.

At least this was a friendly face. And since he was neither a co-worker nor a passenger, speaking with him should be free of complications. Surely she could take a minute to be friendly before returning to the ship.

She made her way toward Preiss, still carrying Sir Reggie.

"*Guten tag,* Herr Preiss," she said.

"*Guten tag.*" Still speaking German, he added, "Do call me Helmut, please."

"I will," she replied in German. "You may call me London."

Sir Reggie leaned forward and sniffed at the brewer, then gave a snort of apparent approval and settled down into London's arms again.

Helmut told her, "I'm sorry for the terrible thing that has happened during your visit."

"Yes, it … was terrible," London replied.

Gazing at her with an expression of concern, he said, "I hear that you've fallen under some suspicion."

"I'm afraid so."

Word certainly gets around, London thought with dismay.

As she glanced around, she again got the distinct impression that people were staring at her.

She wondered how many people in Bamberg thought the worst of her.

"Well, I share no such suspicion," Helmut said. "I think Detektiv Erlich and his team are being very unfair to you."

London felt a surge of gratitude.

"Thank you for saying that," she said.

"*Nichts zu danken,*" he said. London recognized the German phrase for "Don't mention it."

Helmut continued, "I have already talked to the detective about it, stating my opinion in no uncertain terms. Not that Erlich is likely to heed anything I say. Having Americans to blame is very convenient for him—politically, I mean."

"So I gather," London said.

Helmut's expression darkened.

"It's really quite infuriating," he said in a voice tight with anger. "A man has been murdered by somebody who lives right here in Bamberg. And does anybody seem to care? No, they just try to shift the blame to Americans. Before long they will let the case go cold—that is their goal after all."

He shook his head and added, "Poor Sigmund Forstmann. He deserved better."

London was startled by his words.

"Excuse me for saying so," she said, "but you're the first person in Bamberg I've heard say anything really sympathetic about him."

Helmut chuckled sadly.

"Yes, well—he didn't make a lot of friends in this town. And I'll be the first to admit that he could behave like a boor, and he definitely looked down upon us Bavarians and wrote some pretty terrible things about us in his Munich newspaper, the *Sternenkurier*, over the years. But ..."

Helmut paused for a moment.

"But I liked him, and he liked me. In fact, he was a great champion of my brewery, *Schutzkeller Brauen*—and especially the quality of my *Hefeweisen*. For all the ill he said about Bambergers, he sang my praises far and wide every year after he came here. He appreciated my work like no one else did. Also, he was, like me, a student and scholar of the history of German beer. We used to talk at great length about it. I don't know anybody else who has that kind of knowledge."

In a voice choked with emotion, he added, "I will miss him."

"I'm sorry for your loss," London said.

"Danke schein," Helmut said. "It just makes me angry that whoever killed him may never be brought to justice. I only wish ..."

Helmut was interrupted by a flurry of phony money flying into his face. *Katers Murr* had walked right up to them and tossed wads of fake money at the brewer. The man's voice that came from within the enormous cat headdress was broken up by laughter.

"Why are you so gloomy, Helmut, old fellow? This is supposed to

146

be a happy day, after all! I know that *I'm* very happy."

Helmut brushed a few fake bills aside and replied, "Yes, I suppose you would be, Rolf. No more bad reviews from Sigmund Forstmann."

"Indeed," the man inside the cat suit said. "But of course I'll be sad about not ever getting the chance to ask him why he had it in for my beer in particular. Do you have any idea why he chose my beer to denounce so strongly?"

"I can't imagine," Helmut said.

From the note of sarcasm in Helmut's voice, London guessed that the reason must be perfectly obvious—that Rolf Schilder's beer was simply terrible.

"Oh well, I've got other reasons to be happy," Schilder said, tossing more bills into the air. "I get to enjoy the glory of being *Katers Murr*, the King of the Hoffmann Fest, without the inconvenience of getting dunked in cheap lager! Sigmund Forstmann was kind enough to get dunked in my place. It's too bad I'll never get a chance to thank him."

"Who knows?" Helmut said. "Maybe you'll be seeing him sooner than you think."

The giant cat drew back a bit.

"Why, Helmut, old friend—was that a threat?"

Helmut smiled a less-than-sincere smile.

"Not at all," he said. "Why ever would you take it that way? But you'd better get back to work giving away all that money. I suspect you still don't have enough votes to win this year's award. You've got some serious bribing to do."

Now Helmut's sarcasm was quite overt. London remembered being told a little while ago that the votes were already being counted, if they hadn't been counted already. And judging from everything she'd heard, Schilder's beer didn't stand a chance of winning any awards on its own merits—and certainly not with the help of useless money.

The cat glared at Helmut for a moment, then turned away and danced away through the crowd, calling out to his followers and throwing money in all directions.

London said to Helmut cautiously, "He seems so happy about Herr Forstmann's death. Do you think it's possible ...?"

"That he might be a viable suspect?" Helmut said with a laugh. "Oh, hardly think so. He's nothing more than a cowardly, untalented *großmaul*—the English word is 'loudmouth,' I believe. Don't give him a second thought."

147

London thought for a moment, then said, "Helmut, have you seen a tall woman with wild curly hair? An American woman, not from Bamberg. She kind of stands out in a crowd."

"I can't say I have," Helmut said. "Is she the one Detektiv Erlich told me about—the woman he imagines to be your accomplice?"

"I'm afraid so," London said. "And he wants to speak with her. I'm trying to find her."

"If you'll tell me how to contact you, I'll let you know if I happen to see her."

Then with a sly wink, he added, "Before I say anything about her to Detektiv Erlich, if you know what I mean."

London couldn't help smiling at his playfully conspiratorial tone. Given everything she was dealing with, she was glad to have an ally right here in Bamberg. She took out a business card with her cell phone number and gave it to him.

Helmut looked at the card, then at London, then spoke rather shyly.

"Before you go, I was wondering … Would you like to join me for the awards ceremony? It'll be two hours from now, and there will be a tasty buffet, to say nothing of excellent beer."

London blushed as she realized …

He's asking me for a date.

She certainly felt flattered. With his cheerful eyes and ruddy complexion, Helmut wasn't at all bad-looking—although London couldn't help thinking that the *lederhosen* and feathered Alpine hat looked a little silly.

But of course, she immediately thought about Bryce and the thwarted kiss, and especially what they had said to each other when they returned to the ship.

"I hope … sometime soon …" Bryce had begun.

"I hope so too," London had replied.

The last thing she was interested in right now was a date with a reasonably handsome German she barely knew. And yet, it didn't look as though the *Nachtmusik* would set sail soon. And the idea of being here for the awards ceremony really appealed to her.

"Um, thanks for the invitation, but …" she began.

"But?" Helmut said.

"Could I … bring a date?" she asked with a sheepish smile.

Helmut let out a good-natured chuckle.

"A date? Well, yes, of course!"

London was glad that he wasn't taking her gentle rebuff at all badly.

"Great," London said. "We'll see you then."

As London and Sir Reggie wended their way back through the crowd, London found herself wondering—how would she have reacted to Helmut's invitation if Bryce weren't in the picture?

She doubted that she would have accepted. Carrying on flirtations with locals was more Elsie's style than hers. She preferred to keep her interactions on shore as uncomplicated as possible.

As she again headed for the ship, she almost ran into a person wearing a giant chicken costume, complete with a beaked headdress and a yellow body with stubby wings and cartoonish bird feet.

"Engtschuldingung," she said politely to the chicken—"Pardon me."

But as she tried to step past the chicken, the creature stepped right in front of her and blocked her way.

London stepped the other way, and the same thing happened again.

And then the chicken spoke to her in English.

"We've got to talk."

CHAPTER TWENTY SIX

London stared up into the face of the giant chicken that blocked her way. A small jagged red comb and red wattles were nestled into fluffy white feathers that completely covered the head of whoever was wearing the costume. The large round eyes were glassy and obviously artificial. The giant yellow beak was open, and actually looked rather threatening.

She could see no sign of a human being inside that headdress.

Taking a few steps backward, London saw that the body of the costume was made of white fabric, printed to look like feathers. The sleeves were decorated with fake feathers to resemble wings.

She was about to ask the chicken to get out of her way when the creature spoke again.

"We've got to talk, London."

London's mouth dropped open when she heard the chicken speak her name. Then she recognized that strident voice.

"Audrey?"

"Shhh," Audrey replied, her voice muffled by the mask. "I don't want anyone to know."

The chicken moved closer again, and now London spotted the two eyeholes at the base of the huge yellow beak. That was where Audrey was looking out. And she was doubtless breathing and speaking through the open beak.

"You don't want anyone to know what?" London asked.

"That it's me. That I'm out and around."

With a soft *woof*, Sir Reggie squirmed in London's arms, then dropped down to the ground. He began to sniff curiously around the chicken's big yellow feet.

Then the chicken looked down and noticed Sir Reggie.

"Oh, hello, little doggie!" she said, reaching to pet him with a feathery hand. "It's nice to see you again!"

What on earth ...? London wondered.

She remembered a couple of days ago, when Audrey had called Sir Reggie a "horrid little beast."

Is this really the same person?

London waved her arms with agitation, but she managed to keep her voice down.

"You're right about one thing, we've got to talk! What are you *doing* out and around, and dressed like … like this?"

"I'm incognito. "

London glared at the big chicken in exasperation.

"I told you yesterday that the head detective would want to speak with you and me this morning. He came to the ship and questioned me. The man is obviously suspicious of both of us, and it didn't help that we couldn't find you in your room."

"Oh," Audrey said. "I must have forgotten all about that."

London found that hard to believe.

She shook her head and said, "I even phoned you, but I only got your voice mail."

"Of course I set my phone on silent," Audrey replied curtly. "I didn't want to be distracted from my mission."

London sighed. "Everything you did just made Detektiv Erlich certain that you have something to hide. He even said so. 'Our suspect has given us the slip,' he said."

This time the chicken made no response, although London thought she heard an actual giggle from within the mask.

Annoyed, she kept trying to make Audrey understand what was going on.

"I promised Captain Hays that I would find you so Erlich could talk to you. You've got to come back to the ship with me right away."

"Oh, no," Audrey said. "I'm not ready to do that. I'm conducting my own investigation."

"Your own *what*?"

"I'm going to find out who really killed the monocle guy. That's why I wanted to talk with you."

London stifled a groan of despair. Sometimes it seemed like everybody wanted to be a detective—or at least everyone except London herself. And yet for some reason, she always seemed to get stuck with the job.

"Your 'investigation' can wait," she replied firmly. "We've really got to get back to the ship. Captain Hays is expecting me to bring you back so you can talk to Detektiv Erlich. And if you don't come back

151

right now, we'll both be in real trouble."

"What kind of trouble?"

"The kind of trouble *I* don't want to be in. And believe me, you don't either. Erlich is eager to arrest somebody."

"Why would he arrest me?" Audrey protested. "I didn't kill that awful man. I might have wanted to, but I'm actually not a hostile person."

London just stared at her, remembering the distinct hostility of her earlier encounters with Audrey Bolton. Nothing on the *Nachtmusik* had satisfied this woman, and she had always been extremely condescending to London.

And now she had to wonder why Audrey was suddenly interested in investigating the crime. Could this helpful-hen behavior just be an act?

London quickly decided that those questions really didn't matter. She had to get this woman back to the boat.

"Come on," she said, grabbing the chicken by one wing and starting to escort her through the crowd. Audrey issued a rather hen-like squawk, but at first she didn't resist being tugged along with London. As they headed in the direction of the ship, Sir Reggie trotted along beside them, gazing up at the feathered creature with fascination.

When Audrey seemed to be moving along willingly enough, London let go of the wing. She took out her cell phone and called the captain.

"I've found her," she told him. "I've found Audrey Bolton."

"Oh, thank goodness!" Captain Hays said, sounding as if he was trying to keep his voice low. "I've just about run out of means of detaining Detektiv Erlich in the Habsburg Restaurant. He's been eating everything on the menu. I'll try to get him to finish up this latest course, and I'll take him back to my stateroom."

"Audrey and I will meet you there," London said, ending the call.

As they continued on their way, London looked up at the beaked face and said, "Audrey, would you please take that headdress off?"

"Why do you want me to do that?"

London couldn't help rolling her eyes.

"Well, like you said, we've got to talk. And I'm not going to try having a conversation with a gigantic chicken."

"Sorry, but I can't do that. After all that trouble yesterday, I don't want anybody to know it's me. When I came into town, I found one of

152

those stalls that sell festival costumes. I picked out this one."

She chuckled through the mask.

"Appropriate choice, eh? That awful monocle man—may he rest in peace—called me *Frau Huhn*, 'Mrs. Chicken.' It seemed like a suitable disguise—kind of ironic, if you know what I mean. Almost poetic, when you stop to think about it."

Poetic? London thought.

Again, the change in Audrey struck London.

Poetic? Ironic?

Still chuckling, Audrey said, "I figured this disguise was the best way not to draw attention to myself."

London almost guffawed at the absurdity of the statement. But now it even sounded like Audrey might actually have a sense of humor.

She even likes dogs now!

Where had this version of their cranky passenger been hiding?

Besides, she realized—in a weird way, there was actually some truth to Audrey's rationale. If she hadn't been in costume, at least some people in the crowd might have recognized the unusually tall American with wild curly hair. And some of those people probably suspected the humiliated woman of being involved in Forstmann's death.

But in the midst of a festival filled with people wearing all kinds of costumes, a gigantic chicken was likely to go unnoticed.

London suddenly wished she had at least put on a mask herself. Ever since she'd arrived at the *Maximiliensplatz* today, she'd realized that some people were giving her odd looks. She knew that many of them must have seen her up on that huge beer vat when the curtains opened and the spotlights fell directly on her. They would remember seeing her plunge into the vat. They could even have been in the crowd watching when Oberhauser had all but accused London of being Forstmann's killer.

Suddenly feeling terribly self-conscious, London started to move along faster, heading out of *Maximiliensplatz* into a street where the crowds were less dense. But she only got a few steps along when the chicken walking beside her came to a halt.

Planting the big yellow feet firmly in place, Audrey said, "London, I'm sorry, but I'm not going back to the ship."

"What?" London said.

"I've gone to a lot of trouble to go on this mission."

"You certainly *are* going back."

153

"No, I'm not. I won't stop what I'm doing on account of some German policeman."

Impatiently, London grabbed the chicken's wing again.

When Audrey gave a loud squawk, Sir Reggie barked back at her.

London was horrified to see that all the people nearby had turned to stare at them.

Was she about to have a public altercation with a gigantic chicken?

CHAPTER TWENTY SEVEN

It seemed to London that everything froze in place for a long moment. She knew that she was part of a weird spectacle—standing in a stone-paved street in a historic German town, hanging onto one wing of a large chicken while her little dog yapped and a lot of strangers stood staring at them.

She couldn't help breaking into a laugh at the ridiculousness of the situation.

When she did, she was relieved to see that the people watching them relaxed and went on their ways, apparently satisfied that whatever London and Audrey were doing was par for the course during the Hoffmann Fest.

London pleaded with the chicken, "Audrey, *please* take off the mask."

"But—"

"Trust me. It's really not helping."

Audrey reached up and pulled off the headdress, then shook her hair loose as she tucked the object under her arm. She was sweating from the heat inside the costume, and she actually looked a bit relieved as she took a deep breath.

For some reason, London felt able to breathe more easily as well.

"Maybe we should start over," she told Audrey. "Will you *please* explain to me why you came ashore?"

"Like I said, I was trying to investigate."

"Why not leave it to the police?"

"That's kind of hard to explain."

"Just try."

Audrey looked down at the ground as she shambled along in her yellow claw-shaped boots and didn't reply for a couple of moments.

"My therapist says I have issues," she finally said.

London felt a flash of sympathy. She was hardly surprised, of course. Audrey's therapist was obviously right.

It can't be easy being Audrey, she realized.

But even so, London had no idea what those issues could possibly have to do with her onshore excursion.

Audrey added with a sigh, "I guess you've noticed, I'm not exactly a people person."

Yes, I've noticed, London thought.

Audrey continued, "My therapist says it's because I have trouble with gratitude. I don't know how to *appreciate* things. And people. I know he's right, of course. And it's not like I don't have things in my life to be grateful for. True, I don't exactly have any friends, and nobody in my family can stand to be around me. But hey, I've got a good job and a place to live, and there are three or four TV shows I like, and I read a good book now and then, and there are even some kinds of food I enjoy. I've got to admit, life is good."

London was starting to feel sad for Audrey now.

"I'm really sorry to hear that," she said. "What does your therapist think you should do about it?"

"He keeps telling me I need to learn to *feel gratitude.* And it's like I keep telling him, that's great advice, but how do I do it? I mean, how do I *decide* to *feel* something? I mean, either you feel something or you don't, right? You can't *decide* to fall in love with somebody or really like broccoli, can you? It's something that happens or it doesn't. So what am I supposed to *do* about it?"

"Yeah, I can understand your problem," London said.

She was feeling more and more sympathy with Audrey. She was also feeling more and more anxious for her to get to the point—if she actually had one.

"Well, yesterday, something happened," Audrey said. "It started when you came over to take my side against that awful man—and like I keep saying, may he rest in peace, but he really was an awful man. You really stood up for me, and you told him off, and you wound up getting splashed with beer on account of me, and then the man was killed and now you're in trouble with the law because you tried to help me ..."

We're both in trouble with the law, London thought, but she didn't want to interrupt Audrey's tortuous flow of thoughts. She clung to a shred of hope that Audrey would finally say what she needed to say.

"And the truth is, I haven't been very nice to you, have I? I've been complaining about everything nonstop and blaming you for things that aren't your fault."

"It's OK," London said, and she actually meant it. After all, it was her job to deal with customer complaints, even when they didn't make

156

much sense—because *the customer is always the customer."*

"No, it's not OK," Audrey said. "And last night, alone in my room, I started feeling kind of bad about that, and I was even thinking about giving you a call, but then I started feeling something else …"

Audrey gulped audibly, and her voice grew tighter.

"It was kind of like bubbles inside, all light and airy, and it was a nice feeling, but strange. And so I called my therapist in the U.S. without really thinking what a crazy hour of the morning it was there at the time, and I asked him what I was feeling, and he told me …"

Audrey inhaled sharply.

"He said, 'It's gratitude, you idiot. Go act on it. And let me get back to sleep.'"

London felt an unexpected lump of emotion in her throat. It suddenly seemed brave and kind of Audrey to share her feelings like this.

"So you've really helped me, London," Audrey said, wiping her eye with the feathery tip of a wing. "You helped me feel something really important. And I'm grateful."

London fell silent as Audrey's words sank in.

"That's a very nice thing to say, Audrey," she said.

"Is it?" Audrey said with a surprised-sounding laugh. "It hadn't occurred to me. I guess I'm not used to saying nice things."

"Well, that *was* a nice thing."

"I'm glad to hear it. You know, it actually feels good to say nice things. I could learn to like it. Meanwhile, I really owe you for it. So I decided I'd do whatever I could to help you. I came into town this morning to try to clear your name—well, and my name too, I guess, since we're pretty much in this together."

London felt truly touched to have had such a positive impact an Audrey, however inadvertently.

And yet at the same time, her mind was reeling

All this does sound pretty crazy.

Still, she couldn't help feeling there was some method to Audrey's craziness.

"So Audrey, tell me," London asked cautiously, "have you had any luck in your, uh, investigation?"

Audrey laughed again.

"Well, you'd be surprised the stuff I've overheard people saying. Being dressed like a gigantic chicken is sort of like being the proverbial fly on the wall. People forget you're human, I guess. So they just talk away to each other as if you weren't there. It tells you something about human nature, doesn't it?"

"Like what?" London asked.

"I don't know yet. I'm working on it. Anyway, I picked up on some interesting stuff while going incognito. For example, I've noticed that nobody seems to be all broken up about the awful monocle man's death—may he rest in peace."

"Yes, I've noticed that too," London said.

"The brewers and vendors all hated his guts," Audrey continued. "And it's hardly any wonder. After each year's festival, he trashed just about all of them in his newspaper column—and pretty much the whole town of Bamberg, for that matter."

Yes, I know that already, London thought.

She kept listening in hope that Audrey might say something she didn't know.

Audrey went on, "And every year he got drunk, and the brewers had to decide whether to cut him off, or keep giving him beer in hopes that he wouldn't write anything too terrible about them. He got especially bad this year. Yesterday one of the vendors almost came to blows with him. I'll bet you can't guess which vendor that was."

London felt a sharp intuitive tingle.

"Rolf Schilder!" she said.

"That's right—the guy in the cat suit. The awful monocle guy—"

"His name was Sigmund Forstmann," London put in.

"That's right, Herr Forstmann, may he rest in peace. He was completely plastered by the time he got to Herr Schilder's stall. Schilder refused to serve him any beer. Then Forstmann started saying awful things about Schilder's beer—I mean really gross and disgusting things, referring to body functions and such."

From what she'd heard about Forstmann's beer, London wasn't surprised to hear this.

Audrey continued, "Then Schilder came out from behind the counter of his stall and tried to act threatening, raising his fist and all. But people say Schilder always looks ridiculous whenever he tries to act tough like that. So Forstmann laughed at him, and so did everybody else watching. Schilder snuck back behind his counter, and Forstmann lurched and staggered away to find other people to annoy. Do you think it means anything? Isn't it possible that Schilder is the killer?"

London's brain clicked away trying to process what she was hearing. She found it easy to imagine getting angry enough at Forstmann to want to kill him.

After all, she didn't see herself as the least bit aggressive or hostile. But even so, yesterday Forstmann had goaded her into nearly losing her temper, maybe almost coming to blows with him. From what Audrey had just said, Forstmann had humiliated Schilder in a worse and very public way.

Had this year's *Katers Murr* done something very rash?

And yet she remembered what she'd heard others say about him—for example, what Helmut had said just a few minutes ago.

"He's nothing more than a cowardly, untalented großmaul—*the English word is 'loudmouth,' I believe."*

Then Helmut had added, *"Don't give him a second thought."*

"So what do you think?" Audrey asked.

"I don't know, Audrey. I've overheard people saying Schilder is more like a mouse than a cat."

"Maybe even a mouse can be pushed too far," Audrey said.

London shook her head and said, "I find it hard to imagine a murderous mouse. And we don't know Schilder as well as anyone else in town. He seems to be pretty far from anyone else's suspicions."

Meanwhile, as they neared the ship, Audrey asked London, "What happens now?"

"I'm taking you right to the captain's stateroom," London said. "Detektiv Erlich is waiting to meet you there. You should mention to him the stuff you overheard, just in case he thinks it's important."

"OK, but only after I go to my room and change out of this ridiculous outfit."

London felt a prickle of worry.

"Um, Audrey, I'm not sure that's such a good idea."

"Why not?"

London didn't know how to reply. The truth was, she wasn't sure just why she was worried about giving Audrey a chance go to her room to change out of her costume. Maybe, after going to so much trouble to find her, she was afraid to let her out of her sight even for a few minutes.

But then, maybe London wouldn't have to lose sight of Audrey for long. Maybe Audrey would let her come into her room while she changed.

While London was trying to think of some way of broaching this topic, her phone buzzed.

She took the call and heard Captain Hays's voice again.

"Are you and Ms. Bolton on your way?"

"We're almost there," London said.

"Good," the captain said. "Detektiv Erlich is getting impatient. We mustn't keep him waiting a moment longer than necessary. Come directly to my stateroom. No detours, please."

Captain Hays ended the call.

London said to Audrey, "We don't have time for you to change. We've got to go to the captain's stateroom immediately."

"But London—"

"I'm sorry, I really am," London said firmly. "But we really have no choice."

They went up the gangway to the reception area, where other passengers stared at Audrey with understandable curiosity. Then they took the elevator down to the Allegro deck and headed directly to the captain's stateroom.

Captain Hays opened the door to let them in, and Detektiv Erlich rose from his chair.

Standing there with the chicken headdress under her arm, Audrey stood as if at attention as she spoke to the detective with all the dignity she could muster.

"Sir, I assume that you are the investigating detective. My name is Audrey Bolton, and I believe you wish to speak to me about the unfortunate events of yesterday. I apologize for keeping you waiting. And I don't want to give you the impression that this is my normal state of dress."

With an understated tilt of an eyebrow, Detektiv Erlich said, "I make no such assumption. Please sit down."

The detective then gave London a silent look, which clearly signaled that she should leave. London nodded obediently and left.

She and Sir Reggie headed straight to her stateroom, where she plopped herself down on her bed with the dog on her lap.

"Reggie, my head is spinning," London said. "What am I supposed to think about that woman?"

Reggie tilted his head as if he wondered the same thing.

London continued, "Don't get me wrong, I'm really touched that she trusted me enough to talk so openly about her … well, her issues,

160

but …"

She paused and scratched Sir Reggie on the top of his head.

"Do you suppose it's possible … that she's simply out of her mind?"

Reggie tilted his head the other way.

"I just don't know, pal," London said. "I hate to even consider the possibility, but … how can I be sure that she didn't kill Herr Forstmann? Maybe even she doesn't know what she really did. I mean, suppose she's simply insane? What do you think?"

Sir Reggie, of course, didn't reply.

"But no, I just can't see it," London said. "She's got personality problems, and it sounds like she's doing everything she can do to get over them, which is actually kind of brave of her. I'm even starting to like her."

She squinted thoughtfully and added, "But if she didn't do it, I can't imagine that anybody else aboard the *Nachtmusik* did. What would they have had against him, anyway? Which means the killer is somebody who lives right here in Bamberg."

Sir Reggie let out a little grunt of apparent agreement.

"But since just about everybody here hates his guts, how can anybody narrow down the number of suspects? Detektiv Erlich sure has his work cut out for him. But then, I guess I do too. I don't know how I keep getting stuck doing the 'Nancy Drew' thing, but that's the way it seems to go."

Sir Reggie sighed as she kept scratching his head.

"There must be a way of finding out who really hated him most …"

London's voice trailed off as a plan started to take shape in her head. She tilted up Sir Reggie's chin and looked him in the eye.

"I think I know what to do, pal," she said. "What do you say—do you feel up to some more sleuthing?"

Sir Reggie yapped affirmatively.

"Good," she said. "Let's go."

Sir Reggie trotted after her as she headed out of her stateroom.

161

CHAPTER TWENTY EIGHT

For the investigation she had in mind, London wanted better equipment than the cell phone she normally used for searches. With Sir Reggie trotting at her side, she strode down the passageway and took the elevator up to the Menuetto deck. She knew that Emil's workspace in the ship's library was equipped with an especially fast and powerful large-screen computer.

But when she got there, she found that the door was closed. She turned the doorknob and was surprised to realize that the door was actually locked. The library was supposed to be open all day for free use by passengers.

She glanced down at Sir Reggie and saw that the little dog was staring at the door with interest.

"Has our historian shut himself up in there?" she asked him.

Sir Reggie sniffed at the door and gave a soft *woof.*

London knew that Emil occasionally shut himself up inside the library to be alone with his books—or sometimes, she thought, just to brood in silence. At the moment, she was in no mood to indulge the ship's historian in his scholarly hermit mode.

She knocked on the door sharply.

London was sure that she heard a muffled, whispering sound inside. She thought it sounded like Emil, but she couldn't make out any words and no one came to the door.

Still staring at the closed door, Sir Reggie let out a bark.

The sounds inside the room stopped immediately.

London knocked again and called out.

"Emil, please come to the door. I've got something urgent I need to do in there. And I could use your help doing it."

This time London heard only silence.

"Emil, I know you're in there," she said impatiently. "Don't try to pretend you're not."

After another silence, London looked down at her dog and said, "Maybe I should use my master key."

But now Sir Reggie was looking as though he had lost interest and would just as soon head off elsewhere. He'd never taken much interest in Emil, after all, and the feeling had been mutual.

"Great help you are," London told him.

Then she again considered the conundrum of the locked door. Her master keycard could open any door on the ship, including this one. But what if she went into the library only to find Emil in the sort of foul mood that he'd generally been in lately? He'd surely be angry with her for intruding. And given how exasperated London herself had been feeling lately, they could easily lose their tempers at each other.

She really didn't want to ignite an open battle with Emil. Especially not one that would be so public. The ship's library was situated at one end of the Amadeus Lounge, and a few passengers were scattered about at tables in the big room. London could see the assistant bartender waiting on several who were lined up at the bar on the far side of the lounge.

Thinking that it could be helpful talk things over with someone with a sympathetic ear, she hoped that Elsie might also be there. But when she and Reggie walked across the big room, she didn't see her friend anywhere.

"Is Elsie around?" she asked the young man behind the bar.

He grinned and replied, "Sorry, she went out again to enjoy the festival. Is there anything I can do to help you?"

"Thanks, but I don't think so," London said.

She noticed that business in the lounge today seemed to be scant and slow. Doubtless a lot of passengers and even crew were going ashore to have a good time.

London felt a twinge of envy. Elsie was surely out there having a good time, she figured. Why shouldn't she do the same?

But she had set out to do a certain investigation, and she was going to carry that out before she could even think about joining the party. Maybe later, Bryce would be able to get away from work and they could …

"You sure you don't want a drink?" the assistant bartender asked.

London realized she'd been standing there at the bar trying to make a decision about what to do next.

"No thanks," she told him, and she walked back across the lounge, past that closed library door, and out into the elevator area.

I'll just have to do my research by cell phone after all, she decided. For that, she might as well go back to her room.

Then, as she stepped onto the elevator, her phone buzzed.

She was startled to see that she'd received a text message from Audrey.

Come to my room right away.

She read it aloud to Sir Reggie and said, "I guess Audrey's interview is finished."

It seemed a short time since she had delivered the chicken-costumed woman to the captain and Detektiv Erlich. At least they apparently weren't holding her in custody.

Curious to find out how the questioning had gone and what Audrey wanted with her now, she punched the button for the Adagio deck instead of going all the way down to her own stateroom.

Sir Reggie trotted along beside her as they got off the elevator and made their way to Audrey's room. When London knocked on the door, she heard Audrey's voice shouting out, "Is that you, London?"

"Yes," London replied. "It's just Reggie and me."

"Good. Let yourself in."

London took out her master keycard and opened the door. As she and Sir Reggie stepped inside, she heard Audrey's voice through the bathroom door, which stood slightly ajar.

"I'm changing. I'll be right out."

"Did you talk to Detektiv Erlich?" London called through the bathroom door.

"Yes, I answered all his questions," Audrey called back. "He asked a lot of them. Are police detectives always so nosy?"

London felt a bit jarred by the question.

That's kind of their job, she almost said.

"Pretty much," she replied instead.

"Well, you'd know a lot more about it than I do. You're kind of getting to be an expert about this sort of thing, aren't you?"

London stifled a sigh.

Yeah, I guess I kind of am, she thought.

She tried to imagine how the interview must have gone. How had Detektiv Erlich reacted to Audrey's peculiar and sometimes off-putting manner? Had she convinced him of her innocence, or had she made him more suspicious of her guilt—and of London's guilt as well?

For that matter, London was still struggling to make sense of

Audrey's mercurial personality. She couldn't help wondering …

How sure am I that she didn't have anything to do with Forstmann's death?

Audrey came out of the bathroom wearing an ordinary outfit. London could see the chicken suit hanging inside the bathroom, looking ridiculously oversized even without a human being in it.

"So," Audrey said, "what brings you here?"

"Uh. You texted me. You told me to come."

"Did I? Oh, that's right," Audrey said with a snap of her fingers. "Well, obviously, I was wondering—what do we do next? About solving the case, I mean. I mean, we are working as a team, right?"

London didn't know what to say. She didn't remember Audrey and herself agreeing to work as investigative partners.

And yet …

If there was even the slightest possibility that Audrey herself was some kind of homicidal maniac, wouldn't it be a good idea for London to keep a close watch on her?

Audrey sat down at the table in front of her big window and gestured for London to take a seat on the other side.

"Where do we start?" she asked eagerly.

London sat down and said, "Well, I wish I knew more about who in particular might have some motive to kill Sigmund Forstmann. I thought one way to find out was to read some of the stuff he's written about people here in Bamberg. I was hoping to use a computer to go online to do some research, but the library was closed and—"

Audrey interrupted with a squeal of delight.

"No problem! I've got a computer with a great Internet connection!"

She rushed to her closet and pulled out a laptop computer. London sat down at the table with Audrey as she opened it up on her table and went online.

"So what do you want to go looking for?" Audrey asked.

"Let's check out the newspaper in Munich that Forstmann wrote for—the *Sternenkurier*, I think it's called."

Audrey took them straight to the *Sternenkurier*'s webpage. But they ran into a pay wall as soon as they tried searching for any articles.

"I guess we need a subscription," London said.

"I'll take care of that," Audrey said.

As Audrey set up the account, London was relieved that she was perfectly willing to use her own credit card. It wasn't an account that London would want to show up on the card she used for Epoch World Cruise Lines business expenses, and she didn't have her own card with her.

Audrey sat down at the keyboard to type in searches and commands. Since Audrey seemed to like dogs all of a sudden, London set Sir Reggie on a neighboring chair so he could watch and listen. Then London stood looking at the screen over Audrey's shoulder.

"What next?" Audrey said, cracking her knuckles.

London thought for a couple of seconds.

"Search for the column Sigmund Forstmann wrote last year after the Hoffmann Fest."

Audrey made the search with remarkably quick and agile fingers. The headline in German shouted from the electronic news page.

Your Beloved Critic Survives Another Bamberg Bacchanal

Just a glance at the rest of the article was enough to assure her that plenty of people had good reason to hate Sigmund Forstmann.

CHAPTER TWENTY NINE

The opening paragraph of Forstmann's column confirmed London's suspicions. She told Audrey, "It's pretty much what I'd expect him to write, judging from what I've heard people say about him. He was a big-city snob who looked down on provincial Bavarians and their customs."

"Not a nice guy, then," Audrey observed.

"Not at all."

She translated the passage aloud for Audrey:

Poor E.T.A. Hoffmann! Every year his memory has to endure a public calamity held in his supposed honor. And this year was no different. Costumed and rowdy Bambergers poured into the streets to guzzle mediocre beer and pretend to be characters in stories I doubt very much they have ever read ...

As London glanced a bit farther down the column, it occurred to her that Herr Forstmann reminded her of Emil at his haughty worst.

Except I'll bet Forstmann didn't even like jazz, she guessed.

Skimming a bit more, London said to Audrey, "Run a search on the name Rolf Schilder."

"You mean the Cat King himself?"

"That's right."

"I thought you said he was too mousy to be a killer."

"Maybe, but let's check anyway."

Sure enough, Audrey brought up a whole paragraph about him. Again, London translated aloud.

Rolf Schilder, heir and owner of the once-prestigious Zenitbrauen brand, has committed his yearly crime against taste. He seems to have derived his latest lager recipe from some truly exotic foreign sources. Although I've never tasted water from a Louisiana swamp, I suspect that the taste is remarkably similar—and perhaps not accidentally so, since Schilder seems to always seek out the vilest ingredients he can possibly find. I was surprised not to have to pluck dead mosquitoes out of the murky froth on top.

Audrey said, "From what I've heard, this review is pretty mild in comparison to the stuff he said to Schilder's face yesterday. If I were Schilder, I'd sure want to kill Forstmann. Do you think maybe that's what he did?"

London squinted carefully at the words on the screen.

"That's what I'd like to know," she said. "Everybody in Bamberg seems to think Schilder was just a harmless *großmaul*—a loudmouth. They say he wouldn't hurt a fly. But I wonder. After all, Forstmann has been writing awful things about Schilder's beer for years."

Audrey added, "But I guess he didn't hate Schilder's beer enough to stop guzzling it down, at least when it was free. I already told you about how Schilder cut Forstmann off, and they had a big argument about it."

"Which ended with Schilder's public humiliation," London added, remembering what Audrey had said.

She flashed back to something Schilder had said to Helmut a while ago about one special reason he was happy that Forstmann was dead—that Schilder had escaped the ritual dunking of *Katers Murr*.

"Sigmund Forstmann was kind enough to get dunked in my place. It's too bad I'll never get a chance to thank him."

"He sure had plenty of motive," London observed.

"It's kind of weird, isn't it?" Audrey said. "I mean, the way that *detektiv* is treating you and me like prime suspects, when somebody else had a lot more motivation against him. Do you suppose he's not even the least bit suspicious of Herr Schilder?"

London wondered the same thing. If Detektiv Erlich were here right now, she'd probably flat-out ask him about it.

Reaching over to scratch Sir Reggie's head, Audrey asked, "Do you think Forstmann ever had anything good to say about anybody?"

London felt a prickle of interest.

"That's a good question," she thought. "And I think I know the answer. Search the article for the name Helmut Preiss."

Sure enough, Audrey found a paragraph about Helmut, which London translated aloud.

I don't know how I'd survive this ordeal every year if it weren't for the exquisite Weizenbier—*"wheat beer"*—*that always comes out of Schutzkeller Brauen. That revered brewery is now in the masterful hands of its family heir, Helmut Preiss, who maintains its always-extraordinary level of quality.*

"Well, it sure sounds like Herr Forstmann liked Herr Preiss," Audrey said. "Who is he, anyway?"

"Somebody I've talked to a couple of times," London said. "A really nice guy."

She kept reading.

In my not-so-humble opinion, Preiss positively outdoes all his prior efforts with this year's gold medal-winning Weizenbier, *in which a light taste of vanilla doesn't overwhelm the overall sweetness and roundness of this product's complex, multilayered flavoring. Helmut Preiss is nothing less than a Bavarian treasure.*

London felt a pang of sadness as she kept translating aloud.

Of course, in the interest of full disclosure, I should mention that Helmut Preiss and I are old and dear friends. More than just the finest of brewers, I consider him to be a scholar and conversationalist of the first rank—and a true kindred spirit in every way. As much as I may dread everything else about the Hoffmann Fest, it is a pleasure to visit with Helmut every year.

Audrey observed, "He sounds almost human all of a sudden."

He certainly does, London thought.

There was clearly a respectful and considerate aspect of Forstmann's personality that he rarely showed and few people in Bamberg ever got to know. Helmut Preiss was obviously very much an exception.

She remembered how Helmut had choked up when talking about the deceased critic.

"I will miss him," he'd said.

Only now did London sense the depth of Helmut's grief. She made a mental note to offer him her condolences when she met him later this evening.

Audrey asked, "So do you see anything revealing?"

London skimmed over the rest of the article. While Helmut Preiss's *Schutzkeller Brauen* was the only brand Forstmann had anything good to say about, Rolf Schilder's *Zenitbrauen* product was far from the only beer that he savagely attacked. And London sensed from Forstmann's tone that many of these attacks were personal and utterly unfair.

"There's no shortage of suspects," London said. "But Schilder seems to really stand out of the crowd."

Audrey asked, "Do you want to go back a few years, check and see what Forstmann wrote about Schilder in the past? And maybe about other people too?"

London stared at the screen thoughtfully for a moment.

Then she said, "I'd much rather know what he would have written today—if he hadn't been killed."

Audrey scoffed. "Good luck finding *that* out! Dead people tend not to be very forthcoming about that kind of thing. Or about anything else, for that matter. They mostly keep their thoughts to themselves."

London smiled as an idea occurred to her.

Sometimes even dead people might tell us something important.

CHAPTER THIRTY

London felt certain she was on the right track. The answer to the mystery might well be hidden in whatever the murdered man had been about to write.

She just had to find out what that was.

"Let's look at the masthead for contact information," she said to Audrey.

Audrey brought up the *Sternenkurier* masthead, and London looked over the list of names and contacts. She took out her cell phone and called the phone number for the editorial department. When she got a secretary on the line, she asked to speak to Werner Mannheim, the newspaper's arts, foods, and leisure editor.

When Herr Mannheim answered, she asked if they could speak in English. When he was agreeable, she put the call on speakerphone.

"My name is London Rose," she said, "and I'm an American traveling in Germany who is currently visiting Bamberg. There's another American on this call—Audrey Bolton."

"How can I help you?" Herr Mannheim asked.

London hesitated. She didn't know exactly how to put her question into words. Fortunately, Herr Mannheim spoke.

"Does this have something to do with Sigmund Forstmann's death?"

London figured her best option was to be reasonably truthful, without actually admitting that she herself was a murder suspect.

"Yes, it does," she said. "I was unlucky enough to have discovered his body."

"I'm very sorry," Mannheim said with a note of genuine sympathy. "That must have been very hard for you."

"Thank you, it was very upsetting," London said. "And naturally I'm very curious about the murdered man."

Mannheim chuckled a little.

"Well, he was quite a character," he said. "He was abrasive, and he made enemies very easily, but ... I happened to like him. And I thought he was a fine journalist. I'm sorry that his career had to end this way."

London was relieved to hear Mannheim speaking so openly.

"Do you happen to have any idea about what he planned to write about this year's Hoffmann Fest?"

Mannheim laughed outright.

"His usual diatribe, I suppose," he said. "He didn't tell me anything about that article in particular. But he did plan to write a feature article in addition to his yearly screed. In fact, the last thing he sent me was an email about what he had in mind."

"Could you tell me what the article was going to be about?" London asked.

Mannheim fell silent again.

"Who did you say you were again?" he asked.

Again, London saw no harm in being reasonably truthful.

"I'm London Rose, and I'm the social director aboard the river cruise boat called the *Nachtmusik*. I work for Epoch World Cruise Lines."

"Oh, yes, I've heard of it. A very reputable company."

Another short silence followed.

"I'm looking at his email right now. It's really rather innocuous, and of course nothing's going to come of the story now, so ... I suppose it would all right for me to forward it to you."

London felt a tingle of interest.

"Thank you, I'd really appreciate that," she said.

She gave him her email address, and they ended the call.

"What do you expect to find out?" Audrey asked.

"I really don't know," London said.

But she had to admit to herself, Mannheim's description of the email as "rather innocuous" didn't sound very promising.

The email arrived in just a few seconds, and London opened it on her cell phone.

Dear Werner—

Well, I'm off to Bamberg tomorrow, and I plan to get spectacularly drunk as usual, so wish me a mild hangover. Also as usual, I expect to stay there an extra day and rummage through the archives of Bamberg's Bayerische Biermuseum *[Bavarian Beer Museum]. I'm hoping to collect material for a feature story about lost beer recipes.*

For example, last year I came across the files of Bamberg's Braunbärenbier *brewery, which was owned by the legendary Leitner beer dynasty until it went defunct during World War I. I'm attaching a PDF facsimile of an especially interesting recipe which was never manufactured due to the brewery's untimely demise.*

The beer was to be named Illicium, *which is the Latin word for "enticement" and also the proper name of the spice called star anise. Star anise is a common enough beer ingredient, but the Leitner family found an innovative way to use it—one, I think, that's well worth reviving.*

That's all for now. I'll send in my yearly tantrum the day after tomorrow. Expect the good citizens of Bamberg to lodge numerous complaints about my behavior, which I fully intend to be perfectly abominable.

Freundliche Grüße *[kind regards],*
Sigmund

When London finished translating the email aloud, Audrey looked at her skeptically.

"Doesn't sound very helpful, does it?"

"I suppose not," London said, feeling disappointed. She had felt so sure that she was following a good lead, but the email didn't express anything that might lead to the man's murderer.

"Is there anything else we can do?" Audrey asked. "Do you want to keep searching past articles?"

"No," London said with a sigh. "I don't guess we'll find anything except Forstmann's yearly rants and tirades. We won't learn anything except how many people really hated him. Thanks for your help, though."

"Don't mention it," Audrey said.

As London and Sir Reggie left Audrey's stateroom, she glanced at the unopened PDF attachment she'd just received.

A beer recipe, she reminded herself.

Alas, it was hardly what she'd hoped to find, and it wasn't of any real interest to her personally, although it might be interesting to Bryce …

"Bryce!" she exclaimed aloud as she and Sir Reggie continued down the passageway.

She'd almost forgotten Preiss's invitation, and the ceremony was only a couple of hours off.

She called Bryce's phone number, and he answered right away.

"London! I've been thinking about you. How are you? The last time I saw you was … well, when we both had to talk to that detective. What have you been doing since?"

London's mind boggled at the thought of trying to tell him.

"It's a long story," she said. "How about you?"

"I'm back at work, and glad of it."

"I'll bet you are."

"I can't say I much like Detektiv Erlich."

Me neither, London thought.

"Listen, Bryce," she said. "I got an invitation for two excellent seats at the awards ceremony in a little while. Do you want to come?"

Bryce stammered a little, "Um, sure, I'd love to come, but …"

London waited for him to finish his thought.

"In, uh, what capacity?" he said.

London instantly understood the significance of his question. And she, too, found herself stammering shyly.

"As a date … if that's OK," she said.

Bryce let out a relieved-sounding laugh.

"Count me in," Bryce said.

"Let's meet in the reception area."

"I'll be there."

London and Bryce ended the call. She and Sir Reggie headed down the spiral stairs toward the Allegro deck.

London gulped worriedly when they ran into Detektiv Erlich in the passageway.

"Good afternoon, Fräulein Rose," he said rather stiffly.

"The same to you, Detektiv Erlich," London said. Remembering Captain Hays's diversionary tactics, she added, "I hope you had a good breakfast."

Detektiv Erlich smiled ever so slightly.

"As a matter of fact, I did," he said. "If I didn't know better, I'd say the captain was trying to distract me."

Patting his stomach, he added, "Well, it was a pleasant distraction. And I appreciate how you managed to find the, uh, chicken woman without my team and I having to go to a lot of trouble."

"Do you feel any closer to solving the murder?" London asked.

"That's hard to say," Erlich said with an enigmatic look.

As London and Sir Reggie stood facing him, she remembered something she and Audrey had both wanted to ask him.

"Detektiv Erlich, Audrey Bolton and I were just doing a bit of online research concerning Sigmund Forstmann."

Erlich cocked an eyebrow suspiciously.

"Indeed?" he said. "And why would you want to do that?"

London shrugged and said, "Well, since you seem to suspect us both of murder, naturally we'd like to clear our names. We found and read the article Herr Forstmann wrote after last year's Hoffmann Fest. He seems to have had a particular dislike for Rolf Schilder. And judging from things I've heard Herr Schilder himself say, the feeling seems to have been mutual."

Erlich frowned grimly.

"Your point being?" he asked.

London swallowed hard, daunted by the smoldering look in Erlich's eyes.

"Well, Audrey and I are wondering whether—"

Erlich interrupted her sharply.

"Whether I consider Herr Schilder to be a viable suspect?"

London nodded.

"It's a rather impertinent question, Fräulein Rose," Erlich said. "But I will tell you quite bluntly, Rolf Schilder did not commit the murder. I've looked into the matter myself, and he's got a perfect alibi. Not that I seriously suspected him from the start. I've known him for years, and he's simply incapable of any act of serious violence. I only bothered to check his alibi as a matter of procedure. He's quite innocent, believe me."

Drawing himself up indignantly, Erlich added, "And that's all I intend to discuss with you. You must never speak ill of our *Katers Murr* during one of our most important festivals of the year. From now until you leave Bamberg—whenever that may be—I hope you will be so kind as to mind your own business."

Stepping toward her, he added, "And be assured, I *will* be keeping an eye on you."

Erlich angrily continued on his way up to the Menuetto deck to leave the ship.

As she and Sir Reggie continued on their way to her stateroom, London felt a little weak-kneed over Erlich's palpable hostility.

She was also more worried than ever. Until the crime was solved, the *Nachtmusik* couldn't leave Bamberg. The entire European tour might well be cancelled if it got too far behind, and that could mean that Epoch Cruise Lines would close down, and that would mean that London and a lot of other people would be out of their jobs.

London really couldn't just mind her own business.

If I only knew what to do next, she thought.

CHAPTER THIRTY ONE

Later that evening, London took a deep breath and let it out slowly as she and Sir Reggie rode the elevator up to the reception area. She had felt her whole body tense up at the prospect of returning to the Hoffmann Fest. But without any clues to Forstmann's murder, the only thing left to do was to try to enjoy this enforced stay over in Bamberg.

What's so hard about that? she wondered

After all, she was getting together with Bryce this evening.

So why was her whole body tense with worry?

And why did Sir Reggie let out a half-whine, half-growl that seemed to indicate that he felt uneasy too?

"Let's both try to remember," she said to her dog, "we're going back to the *Maximiliensplatz* to enjoy the end of the festival. Nothing awful or traumatic is going to happen this time. No more German newspapermen drowned in cheap lager! That's not too much to expect, is it?"

Sir Reggie grumbled under his breath as if he wasn't so sure. London waved her finger at him.

"You go ahead and worry if you want to," she said. "I'm going to have a good time, and that's that."

Sir Reggie let out another growl that almost sounded sarcastic.

"Oh, what's the point in arguing?" London replied with a sigh. "You're right, of course. Try as I might to enjoy tonight's outing with Bryce, I'm sure to get into some sort of trouble. I just can't stop looking for answers."

London shuddered again as she remembered the hostility in Detektiv Erlich's voice a while earlier.

"I hope you will be so kind as to mind your own business."

Even Oberhauser had given her the same advice when he'd caught her looking at "the scene of the crime."

Well, she was minding her own business, but not really by choice. She simply hadn't thought of any other way to track down a killer.

The afternoon had passed pleasantly enough. After the *detektiv* had left, things were remarkably normal on the aboard the Nachtmusik. She had busied herself implementing the vouchers, discounts, and deals for meals and drinks and services that Mr. Lapham had proposed to keep passengers happy despite all the troubles and delays.

Of course, passengers were thoroughly delighted. And it made London happy to see them happy. She had also realized that many of them were perfectly content to have another evening to enjoy the festival.

Wanting to wear something cheerful-looking, she had put on her blue dress with the big white polka dots and thought it looked just fine with her flat blue shoes. She had even found a brightly multicolored collar and leash set for Sir Reggie among the collection left by the dog's previous owner. So far, none of those choices had made her feel relaxed or at all festive.

When the elevator door opened into the reception area, a sight met London's eyes that instantly lifted her spirits. Bryce Yeaton stood waiting for her, and when he saw her his face lit up in a smile. She thought his casual gray Henley shirt and dark slacks looked perfect for the occasion.

This is a date, she reminded herself in a moment of giddiness. Maybe she could relax and have some fun after all.

Reggie's mood also lifted, and he tugged on his leash as he scampered about in front of Bryce.

"What is it, boy?" Bryce asked mischievously. "What do you want?"

Sir Reggie yapped impatiently as if the answer was obvious—which of course, it actually was.

Bryce held out his empty right hand.

"Is this what you're looking for?" Bryce asked.

Sir Reggie barked huffily.

Bryce held out his left hand, which was also empty.

"What about this?" Bryce asked.

This time Sir Reggie growled a little.

Bryce clapped his hands, and one of his specially made dog treats appeared between his fingertips.

"What about this?" he asked.

Sir Reggie sat up and waved his front legs and barked. Bryce tossed the treat to him, and Sir Reggie caught the treat in mid-air.

London laughed and said to Bryce, "I never knew you were an illusionist."

"Hey, who said anything about illusion?" Bryce said with a chuckle. "We master chefs can make *anything* appear out of thin air, as long as it's tasty."

Bryce offered London his arm, and they continued down the gangway, with Sir Reggie trotting on his leash in front of them. Other passengers were also headed off the ship to enjoy the rest of the festival.

"So should I ask you about your day?" Bryce asked. "I mean, do you want to talk about it?"

For a moment, London wasn't sure.

She remembered what she'd told him about it on the phone a while ago.

"It's a long story."

But did it really have to be such a long story?

There's no need to go into details, London thought.

"Well, I talked to Detektiv Erlich right after you did," she said. "I'm afraid it didn't go very well. He just seemed to become more and more convinced that Audrey and I killed the critic together. Worse, he also wanted to talk to Audrey, but she'd gone AWOL, we had no idea where. So I went back to the *Maximiliensplatz* to find her—which I eventually did. I brought her back to talk to him."

Of course, she was skipping over her scary confrontation with Willy Oberhauser and also Audrey's chicken suit and lots of other details. But she felt as though she was telling him all that really mattered.

She continued, "Then Audrey and I tried to do a little investigating on our own, using the Internet."

"Did you find anything important?" Bryce said.

"Not really," London said.

Then with a laugh, she added, "Oh—I did run across a long-lost beer recipe you might be interested in. I'll send it to you later."

Laughing as well, Bryce said, "Well, your Internet search was hardly in vain."

It was night now, and Bamberg looked even more festive than by day, with lots of bright, colored lights falling upon brightly colored costumes. London and Bryce paused to listen to an accordionist playing a polka, then continued on their way to the *Maximiliensplatz.*

"Did I happen to mention that I don't like Detektiv Erlich?" Bryce said.

"Yes, I believe you did. What sorts of questions did he ask you?"

"I'm sorry to say, he kept trying to get me to tell him something that would incriminate you—and Audrey Bolton as well."

"I'm not surprised," London said. "I do hope you answered his questions truthfully."

"Of course. And it wasn't hard to do. I saw absolutely nothing that made me even consider the possibility that you might be a murderer."

"I'm relieved to hear that!" London laughed.

As they entered the boisterous *Maximiliensplatz*, London, Bryce, and Sir Reggie followed the sound of an *oompah* band. They soon found themselves in a large circle of spectators watching a dozen folk dancers cheerfully dressed in *dirndls* and *lederhosen*. The crowd was clapping and singing and yodeling along to the music.

Looking among the spectators, London glimpsed several familiar faces, including Gus and Honey Jarrett, Walter and Agnes Shick, Kirby Oswinkle, Letitia, and even Audrey, all of them obviously having a great time.

On the far side of the dancers, London recognized two other people—Bob Turner and Stanley Tedrow.

London smiled as she remembered something Bob had said to Stanley this afternoon before they had headed back to the ship—that they would come back and *"par-TAY like the kids we are at heart."*

Apparently, that was exactly what they were doing.

Or are they?

As London peered among the dancers more carefully, she could see that Mr. Tedrow had out his pencil and notebook. Then she craned forward and was alarmed to see who Bob was talking to.

It was the security guard, Willy Oberhauser.

Oh, no, she thought. *This isn't going to end well.*

Sure enough, Oberhauser's face turned red with rage.

Then he gave Bob a vicious shove that sent him staggering amid the dancers, who scattered in all directions.

CHAPTER THIRTY TWO

Without stopping to think, London dropped Sir Reggie's leash and dashed toward the two belligerent men. The folk dancers had immediately given up on their performance and joined the watching crowd as Oberhauser approached Bob with clenched fists. The ship's security man was lurching backward, guarding his face with his hands.

London threw herself right between the two would-be brawlers, spreading her arms to push them apart.

"Hör jetzt auf!" she yelled at Oberhauser.

Then she repeated her command to Bob in English.

"Stop it now!"

She thought that Bob was too drunk and looked too confused to make more trouble. But before London could turn back to Oberhauser, his heavy hand grabbed hold of her collar and spun her around.

"I told you to mind your own business!" he snarled at her through clenched teeth. "And I said there would be consequences if you didn't!"

London froze with fear as he reached for his holster.

Is he going to shoot me? she wondered.

Right here in front of all these people?

But to her surprise, it wasn't a gun he pulled out of his holster. It was a black cylinder of some kind. With a snap of his wrist and a loud crack, the cylinder suddenly extended to the size of a short club.

A nightstick, London realized.

Suddenly a new theory was trying to crowd its way into her dazed brain. She had seen a drawing ... someone had described "a hard, cylindrical object" ...

Before she could make sense of it, Oberhauser had raised the nightstick high, poised to smash it into London's head.

She didn't have time to avoid the blow.

Then a hand shot into view and grabbed Oberhauser's wrist.

It was Bryce, who had dashed after London into the fray, stopping Oberhauser's intended blow with his own muscular grip.

London gasped with relief, but before she could thank Bryce she

181

was distracted by Sir Reggie's furious barking and a man's yelling voice.

"Let's take him down, Sir Reggie!"

Like a human-sized bowling ball, Bob Turner lunged in a crouch headfirst into Oberhauser's abdomen. The barking dog charged right behind him.

Bryce lost his grip on Oberhauser's wrist, and the security guard hurtled backward to the ground. The nightstick flew out of his hand, twirling through the air.

London surprised herself by catching it as it descended.

By then, Sir Reggie had pounced upon the prone security guard and was snarling furiously right in his face.

London picked up his leash and tugged her angry dog away.

"That's enough, boy," she said.

Looking rather pleased with himself, Sir Reggie obediently came to her side.

With both Bob Turner and Oberhauser still on the ground in front of them, Bryce stepped back from the confrontation.

Just then, two uniformed police officers appeared as if out of nowhere and roughly yanked Oberhauser to his feet. Before London knew it, Detektiv Erlich had joined the two policemen.

It's almost as if they were waiting and ready, she thought.

Erlich scowled at Oberhauser.

"Would you care to explain yourself, Willy?" he demanded.

Oberhauser pointed at Bob and said, "That man attacked me!"

Erlich let out a snarl of laughter.

"So it was self-defense, was it?" he asked.

"Yes!"

"So why were you going to strike this woman with your nightstick? Did she attack you too?"

Before Oberhauser could stammer out an answer, a woman in the crowd called out, "He's lying."

A man agreed, "The American man didn't attack him at all. And the woman certainly didn't either."

"He just went crazy all of a sudden," said yet another spectator. "Just like he always does."

Erlich nodded with a smirk.

"I thought as much," he said to Oberhauser. "In fact, I more than half expected something like this to happen. I ordered my men to keep an eye on you, which they've been doing for a while now."

London struggled to make sense of what she was hearing. Why, she wondered, had Detektiv Erlich given such an order to his men?

"Consider yourself under arrest," Erlich said to Oberhauser.

"But Detektiv—" Oberhauser began.

"No arguments," Erlich snapped. "You've been caught in an act of assault. And I think that you are also guilty of something considerably more dire than that."

As the police put Oberhauser in restraints, something started making sense to London. For quite some time, Erlich had actually suspected Oberhauser of killing Sigmund Forstmann.

And now ...

She took a look at the nightstick that she still held in her hand.

The theory her brain had been struggling to hatch suddenly came clear. She remembered the forensic drawing of the head wound that she had thought might have been delivered by some kind of metal pipe.

"I'm sure you're right about his guilt," she said to Erlich. "Show me that drawing you showed me earlier—the one of the victim's head wound."

Erlich squinted with surprise for a moment. Then he reached for his cell phone and brought up the picture.

"Look at that shape," she said, pointing to the wound. "Now look at this," she said, holding up the nightstick.

Erlich's eyes widened with interest.

The wound and the nightstick looked like a perfect fit.

"That doesn't prove anything!" Oberhauser yelped frantically. "There's no trace of evidence on it!"

Erlich looked at the stick closely. Meanwhile, Sir Reggie seemed to be intensely interested in the object. He stood up on his back legs and sniffed it with palpable curiosity.

Erlich chuckled at the dog's interest.

"As a matter of fact, you're right," Erlich said to Oberhauser. "I don't happen to see any evidence. But this animal certainly has his suspicions."

He took the nightstick out of London's hand and sniffed it.

"Yes, I smell something myself. There's much more than a trace of detergent here. And disinfectant—bleach, I believe."

Looking closely at the object, Bryce pointed and said, "Look here. The black surface is actually faded a little from bleach."

Erlich stared at Oberhauser for a moment.

"Tell me, Willy," he said. "Is it your daily habit to scrub your nightstick spotless and sterile? That's rather damning evidence in itself. It's fairly obvious you were trying to erase any trace of how you used it to bash Forstmann across the head."

Oberhauser's eyes bulged desperately. He was beginning to look like a cornered animal.

He stammered in a guilty voice, "Detektiv Erlich, sir, you—you don't understand ..."

"Not yet, I don't suppose," Erlich said with a sardonic grin. "But I'm sure you'll be glad to explain it to me at the *Bundenspolizeirevier."*

London recognized the word for federal police station.

"You may take him away," Erlich said to the two officers. "I'll join you shortly to get the questioning underway."

As the policemen led Oberhauser from the scene, London could hear Oberhauser muttering.

"You don't understand ... You don't understand ... You don't understand ..."

Then Erlich turned toward London.

"I've got good news, Fräulein Rose," he said in English. "I'm very nearly ready to eliminate you and the tall woman as suspects."

London's mouth dropped open.

"*Nearly* ready?" she gasped.

"I am a meticulous man by nature," Erlich said with a nod. "Don't worry, I'm sure Willy's confession will soon clear you of suspicion altogether. Meanwhile, I feel that I must always—how do you say it in English?—cross all the i's and dot all the t's."

London smiled without bothering to correct his little idiomatic error. She glanced at the crowd and saw that the "tall woman"— Audrey Bolton—was watching the proceedings with wide-eyed amazement.

Bryce scratched his head and said to Detektiv Erlich, "So you've suspected Oberhauser for some time now?"

Erlich shook his head.

"Whenever there's trouble, I'm inclined to suspect Willy," he said. "He's unpredictably moody. There's no way to guess how he's going to behave in a given situation. He can be charming one moment, quite vicious the next. He is—how again do you say in English?—a loose cannon, a ticking bomb."

Erlich paused for a moment as he watched the flashing lights of the police vehicle that was taking Oberhauser away.

Then he added, "You see, Willy was a policeman here in Bamberg until just last year—and good a policeman at that. Over the years he was promoted to the rank of *Polizeihaupmeister mit Amtszulage*—a staff sergeant."

Erlich sighed bitterly and added, "Sadly, his temper got worse and worse, and he had to be suspended over just the sort of behavior you've just experienced. Last year he finally got fired for good. I had hoped that this job as a lowly security guard who is not usually faced with serious situations might work out for him. But as you can clearly see, it has not. And unfortunately, he also had a particular hostility toward Sigmund Forstmann—more even than most of the people in Bamberg."

London flashed back to yesterday, when Oberhauser had actually been quite pleasant toward her.

Unpredictably moody, she thought. *Yes, that describes him perfectly.*

She also remembered what he'd said about Sigmund Forstmann.

"I wish I could do something to teach him a lesson."

Apparently he'd finally given in to that urge—with fatal results.

"For now," Erlich said to London, "I still must insist that you stay in Bamberg until further notice."

"But the *Nachtmusik*—" London began to protest.

Erlich interrupted her, "Your ship shouldn't be detained for very long. Meanwhile, you are under strict orders to enjoy the rest of our Hoffmann Fest."

With a wave, he headed away through the crowd. The *oompah* band began to tune again, and the costumed men and women gathered to resume their dancing.

Meanwhile, Bob had gotten to his feet and brushed himself off. He stooped down to pet Sir Reggie.

"We've done it again, haven't we, boy?" he said. "We've taken down another bad guy. By the way, excellent work sniffing that stick, pal. It really tied the case into a nice little bow."

Then he stood up and said to Mr. Tedrow, "What do you say we head back to the boat, get all this written down in a full report we can turn in to Mr. Lapham?"

Mr. Tedrow replied with a courteous nod.

"I'm honored to serve as your amanuensis," he said.

"My what?" Bob asked.

Mr. Tedrow said, "Uh, that means somebody who writes about your, uh adventures."

"Oh. Good."

Bob pointed to Mr. Tedrow and said to London and Bryce, "I don't know what I'd do without this guy."

Bryce chuckled as the two men ambled away.

"Are you OK with letting him take all the credit?" he said to London.

"I'm getting used to it," London said with a chuckle.

"Can we go to the festival now?" Bryce asked.

"I just have a phone call to make," London told him.

She dialed Captain Hays's number, and she could hear the relief in his voice as she told him over the phone about Willy Oberhauser's arrest.

"Oh, thank goodness it's over!" the captain said. "How soon did Detektiv Erlich say we could set sail?"

"It shouldn't be long," London said. "He expects Oberhauser to tell him the whole truth pretty quickly. Once that's settled, we'll be free to go."

"Excellent! And a job well done, my dear! So you have some time to spare. Go celebrate to your heart's content. You've earned it."

"I'll try to do that," London said, ending the call.

It's over, London kept thinking as she and Bryce and Sir Reggie continued on their way across the crowded square. *There's nothing else to worry about.*

So why did she still feel … well, worried?

Some things that hadn't made sense a little while ago made sense at last—for example, Willy Oberhauser's hostility toward her, and even his not-so-veiled threats. Naturally, he didn't want London to find out … what?

That he killed Forstmann, obviously, she told herself.

But something seemed wrong, and London couldn't quite put her finger on it.

Just put it out of your mind, she told herself.

Surely she deserved to enjoy her remaining hours here in Bamberg.

In fact, surely it was time to celebrate.

But she kept thinking about Oberhauser's words as the policemen led him away.

"You don't understand ... You don't understand ... You don't understand ..."

She had a queasy feeling that the man might be right, that there was still something she didn't understand.

CHAPTER THIRTY THREE

As she, Sir Reggie, and Bryce approached the Hoffmann Fest stage, London saw that it was undergoing a rapid transformation. As she, Bryce, and Sir Reggie approached, London could see both police and civilian workers rushing about, dashing onto and off the stage and carrying things as they went. A man toting a huge bundle of wadded up police tape hurried past them.

Sir Reggie watched the activity with interest, occasionally woofing at someone who dashed by.

"I guess the festival stage is no longer a crime scene," London said to Bryce. She shuddered slightly at the memory of everything that had happened there.

"That's all over now," he replied, squeezing her hand. "Now we can relax right out front, while they announce finalists in the beer competition."

A row of long picnic tables had been set up in front of the stage, apparently for the competition winners. The nearest part of the plaza was filled with smaller tables and chairs for the audience, and most of those were already occupied by an animated crowd of people.

Just as London was wondering whether she and Bryce actually had any seats, a man dressed in *lederhosen* stood up and waved at them.

Bryce nudged London.

"You didn't tell me we were getting together with Helmut Preiss," he said with a grin.

"He's the one who offered us ringside seats," London said, smiling back at him. "I hope you don't mind."

"Oh, not at all."

Helmut's table was indeed quite near the stage, and he had saved chairs for them. As they approached, Helmut shook hands warmly with Bryce and greeted him in a hearty voice.

"Ah, we meet again, Mr. Yeaton! I am always pleased to reacquaint myself with a man of such discerning taste buds."

"And I'm always eager to spend time with a master brewer," Bryce said.

188

London chuckled to herself as they took seats at the table and Sir Reggie jumped up into her lap. She realized the two men were going to have a lot to talk about.

This might not turn out to be much of a date, she realized.

Or at least not the kind I'd expected.

Helmut leaned over and said to Bryce and London, "Word is getting around that there's been a break in the murder case. Do you happen to know if it's true?"

"The police just made an arrest," Bryce explained.

"Who is the suspect?" Helmut asked.

"Willy Oberhauser, the security guard," London said.

"Oh, my!" Helmut said. "Is Detektiv Erlich sure of it?"

"Quite sure," Bryce said.

"Well, I don't suppose I should be surprised," Helmut said. "Willy has a terrible temper. And his hatred of poor Sigmund was always extreme."

He breathed a long sigh of relief.

"That puts my mind at ease, in any case," he added. "I dreaded the possibility that Sigmund's killer might never be brought to justice."

London remembered something she'd wanted to say to Helmut.

"Helmut, I was doing a bit of research this afternoon, and I looked up Herr Forstmann's review of last year's festival. I realized you must have been very fond of him—and he of you. I'm sorry for your loss."

"Thank you, that's a very kind thing to say," Helmut said, his voice choking a little. "And now, let's get something to eat, shall we?"

Leaving a reserved sign in view on their table, Helmut escorted London, Bryce, and Sir Reggie over to a row of steam tables from which wafted a mind-boggling array of delicious aromas.

"I don't even know where to begin," London said.

"Allow me to recommend the *Bayrisches Schweinebraten,*" Helmut said in a gallant tone. "It is always excellent."

Following Helmut's instructions, London put together a delicious meal that included the Bavarian pork dish called *Schweinebraten,* potato dumplings, sauerkraut, and a salad.

After they'd filled their plates, she and her companions headed back over to their table, where Bryce put Sir Reggie in a separate chair and gave him an enormous hot pretzel called a *Brezen.* It was more than big enough to be an entire meal for the little dog, and London hoped he wouldn't eat too much of it too fast.

Three bottles of beer awaited London and her human companions on the tabletop, and Helmut suggested that they try each of them.

"I believe these three beers will be the medal winners in tonight's award," he said.

From one bottle he poured some clear, brownish beer into a glass.

"This is a *bock* beer from Otto Laube's *Seltzames Bier* brewery," he said. "I can't yet tell you its name, because I don't yet know it, and nobody else does except for Otto himself. It is a tradition to announce the names of our beers when the awards are given."

London and Bryce each took a taste of the beer, which had a rich, toasty flavor—with a hint of caramel, as Bryce observed.

Pouring from another bottle into another glass, Helmut said, "This is a *Märzen* from the *Eroberer Brauen* brewery, owned by Lothar Mencken."

Again, London and Bryce each took a taste of the amber-colored *Märzen*, which had a full, malty flavor and a yeasty smell that reminded London of freshly baked bread.

Helmut chuckled as he poured from the last of the three bottles.

"And this is one you tasted yesterday—an innovative new *Hefeweizen* of my own creation. You shall hear its name shortly—*when I win one of the three medals!*"

Bryce and London laughed at Helmut's good-natured boastfulness as they chose his slightly foggy, enigmatically flavorful *Hefeweizen* to drink with their meal.

And a delicious meal it was. London's *Bayrisches Schweinebraten* was a delicious pork roast drenched with dark beer sauce. Bryce gave her a taste of his *Kässpatzen*, a kind of *Spätzle*—egg pasta—flavored with creamy cheese sauce and fried onion. Helmut invited her to try his cabbage rolls, which were stuffed with lamb filling seasoned with garlic and onion and various spices.

London listened with interest as Bryce and Helmut discussed both fine foods and beer recipes, speaking some of the time in German, some of the time in English. The surroundings were so pleasant and the company so charming that London felt herself relaxing and enjoying herself.

But why did Willy Oberhauser's words run through her head again?

"You don't understand ... You don't understand ... You don't understand ..."

Ignoring that refrain, she followed her friends back to the buffet for desserts and strong and delicious hot coffee. London enjoyed tasting Bryce's Bavarian apple strudel and Helmut's apple rings, as well as her own cream-filled éclair garnished with fruit and chocolate sauce.

By then, Sir Reggie had only eaten about half of his enormous pretzel and given up on the rest. So London wrapped what remained in a napkin to take back to their stateroom.

As London and her companions finished up their desserts, the red curtain opened to reveal the altered stage. A huge *Hoffmann Fest* sign hid the gigantic vat and its darker associations completely from view. A podium was placed in front of the sign for the final awards ceremony.

Helmut chuckled as a portly gentleman stepped up to the podium, a tuft of unruly gray hair rising from the top of his head like a puff of smoke.

"Our beloved Lord Mayor, Ulrich Haas," he said to London and Bryce with a wink. "I believe I will take a short nap. Wake me up when he has finished talking."

London laughed as Helmut closed his eyes and ducked his head and pretended to snore. Of course he immediately reopened his eyes and actually listened. But the speech was every bit as dull as Helmut had predicted—the sort of speech London had heard at countless awards ceremonies, an interminable litany of names of people to thank and announcements of upcoming events.

When the Lord Mayor left the podium, a dapperly dressed, small-chinned man took his place and spoke into the microphone.

"Meine Damen und Herren," he began—"Ladies and gentlemen…"

London was startled at the sound of his voice.

Where have I heard that voice before?

"… it is my distinct honor—and also, if I may say so, my disappointment—as the king of this year's Hoffmann Fest to announce the winners of this year's competition."

With those words, he put a familiar paper crown on his head and grinned as the crowd laughed and applauded.

Of course! London realized. *It's this year's* Katers Murr *himself!*

She'd simply never seen Rolf Schilder's face before.

Dressed as a gigantic cat, he'd cut a more formidable appearance. His personality had seemed abrasive and even a bit threatening. But now he was playing his allotted role with self-effacing good humor.

More like a mouse than a cat, indeed, she thought, remembering what she'd heard others say about him.

He spoke again to the crowd.

"Since my bribery money seemed not to have had its intended effect ..."

His voice was interrupted by laughter from the crowd.

"... I must sadly assume that the citizens of Bamberg are incorruptible. Too bad for me, I suppose, but I will find the courage to go on. And now let's get down to the business at hand."

He opened a large envelope and took out a certificate with a medal.

"This year's Bronze Medal goes Otto Laube and his *Seltzames Bier* brewery."

As the audience applauded and Otto Laube climbed up onto the stage, London and Bryce exchanged laughing glances with Helmut. Sure enough, the bronze was going to the delicious bock beer they'd tasted before dinner, and that Helmut had predicted to be a medal winner.

Otto Laube spoke shyly and almost inaudibly—he seemed to have no idea how to speak into a microphone or to a large crowd. But London was able to catch words of thanks and the gist of the rest of his acceptance speech.

Just as Helmut had said the prizewinners would, Herr Laube took the occasion to announce the name of his prize-winning beer—*Wahl des Tänzers*, "Dancer's Choice." He also said something about his recipe that London couldn't entirely catch. The secret of the beer's fine taste apparently had to something do with how the temperature of the fermentation process had been slowly and carefully controlled.

Herr Laube thanked everybody and climbed down from the stage to another round of applause. Then Rolf Schilder returned to the podium, opened another envelope, and took out another certificate with a medal.

He announced, "This year's Silver Medal goes to Lothar Mencken's *Eroberer Brauen* product."

The crowd applauded, and London and her companions smiled over the fact that Helmut had made yet another accurate prediction. Lothar Mencken was the maker of the full-bodied *Märzen* they'd tasted a little while ago.

Lothar Mencken was short but broad, with an enormous toothy smile and a gigantic, cheerful face riddled with what appeared to be acne scars.

Mencken began to speak in such a boisterous tone that most of his words were drowned out by the feedback his booming voice created. But when London wasn't covering her ears because of the screeching noise, she was again able to make out the gist of what was said.

He announced that the name of his new *Märzen* recipe was *Wiesenbrise*—"Meadow Breeze"—and that the key to its fine taste was its unique blend of malts. He thanked everybody, and he stepped back into the crowd to the sound of applause.

Herr Schilder stepped back to the podium and held up the final envelope, looking straight at Helmut with a mischievous, teasing expression.

"Meine Damen und Herren," he said. "I don't suppose there's any real need to open this last envelope ..."

London remembered something Helmut had said to her and Bryce yesterday.

"I have hopes of winning the gold medal again this year."

Herr Schilder obviously expected exactly that outcome, and so did most of the crowd, who cried out to him.

"Open the envelope! Open the envelope!"

With a knowing laugh, Herr Schilder opened the envelope and produced the final certificate and medal.

He announced, "This year's Gold Medal goes to Helmut Preiss and his latest creation from his *Schutzkeller Brauen.*"

Unsurprised but obviously very happy, the crowd broke into an even louder round of applause. London and Bryce gave Helmut congratulatory pats on the back, then he mounted the stage, walked to the podium, and accepted the medal and certificate. Unlike the other speakers, Helmut's words through the microphone were perfectly clear.

"Danke schein, Meine Damen und Herren. As always, this is a great honor, and I never fail to be humbled by it."

He lowered his head for a moment and spoke in a quieter voice.

"I know that many of you do not share my sentiments ... but I only wish Sigmund Forstmann could be here right now. I ... I will miss him."

A vague murmur passed through the crowd.

Helmut managed to smile as he spoke again.

"But enough of sad matters. Allow me to announce the name of the beer that you have chosen to win this medal."

He paused for a moment, then said, "I call it *Illicium.*"

London was jolted by the sound of that name.

Where have I heard that word before? she wondered.

Then Helmut added, "It is a Latin word meaning 'enticement'—and it is also the name of the spice better known as 'star anise.'"

London's breath froze in her lungs as an awful possibility dawned on her.

CHAPTER THIRTY FOUR

"No," London murmured aloud. "It can't be true."

"What's the matter?" Bryce asked.

London's heart was beating hard and fast.

Instead of answering, she grabbed her cell phone and hunted for the email that Forstmann had written to Werner Mannheim, his editor at the *Sternenkurier*.

When she opened it, her eyes immediately fell upon a certain sentence.

"The beer was to be named Illicium, *which is the Latin word for 'enticement' and also the proper name of the spice called star anise."*

Forstmann had written that about a long-lost beer recipe. And Helmut Preiss had just very nearly the same thing.

Helmut kept speaking, "Brewers often make use of star anise, but rather vulgarly, in my opinion ..."

London opened the PDF file that had been attached to Forstmann's email—*"an especially interesting recipe,"* he had called it. The file was a facsimile of a yellowed old document composed in elegant handwriting.

She felt dizzy as she read the opening words.

"Brewers often make use of star anise, but rather vulgarly, in my opinion ..."

Those were exactly the same words Helmut had spoken just now.

Things got worse as Helmut kept talking.

"How does one keep star anise from overwhelming the recipe, creating beer reminiscent of licorice candy?"

Glancing along the document, London found exactly that same sentence written there.

She got up from her chair.

"London, what are you doing?" Bryce asked as he reached out and stopped Sir Reggie from following her.

She began to read loudly from her cell phone, in exact unison with what Helmut was telling his audience.

"The secret, I believe, is for west to meet east, so to speak—through

195

a judicious use of spice combinations common to Chinese cooking ... "

The crowd murmured with surprise, looking back and forth at London and Helmut as they continued to speak exactly the same words.

"The spices I speak of are, like anise, common to Chinese 'five spice' ... "

Helmut fell silent, staring at London in horror. But as London mounted the steps to the stage, she kept right on reading.

"... fennel, cinnamon, Szechuan peppercorns, and cloves. "

London was standing on the stage now, staring at Helmut with an accusing expression.

"Would you like to continue?" she said to him. "Or would you like for me to say the rest of it for you?"

Helmut's face had gone white, and he seemed to be in a state of shock.

London said to him, "Can you deny that your new beer is stolen from a hundred-year-old recipe created by the Leitner beer dynasty?"

Helmut silently turned and walked down the steps off the stage.

London called after him in a trembling voice.

"And can you deny that you yourself are the murderer of Sigmund Forstmann?"

The crowd gasped loudly.

Helmut staggered for a moment, then began to push his way into the crowd.

The Lord Mayor leaped up from his chair and pointed to Helmut and yelled out.

"Police! Somebody! Stop him before he gets away!"

Helmut broke into a run, pushing people aside and even knocking some of them down. London charged after him, weaving her way through the scattering crowd.

Yapping ferociously, Sir Reggie broke away from Bryce and plunged on ahead of her, his leash flapping behind him.

Up ahead, London saw the brassy gleam of an enormous musical instrument. It was the tuba player from the *oompah* band that had been playing in the square a little while ago. Helmut collided with the musician, sending him spinning around.

Barely able to skid to a halt in time, London managed not to collide with the tuba player herself. But her momentary delay was costly. She no longer saw Helmut anywhere.

He must be out of the square by now, she realized.

196

How could she possibly find the man in Bamberg's maze of narrow streets? But then she heard the unmistakable racket of Reggie's barking somewhere up ahead and realized that her little dog was still hot on Helmut's trail.

Following the sound of barking, London kept running through the narrow, crooked streets. She could tell that she was on the right track by the trail of dazed pedestrians Helmut left in his wake. Dashing past fallen nutcrackers, mice, fairies, and owls gave her the weird feeling that she was running through some bizarre dream. She was glad to see the most of the characters were getting back to their feet, not badly harmed.

Finally, Reggie's barking led London to the river, not far from where the *Nachtmusik* was docked. London could see Helmut running along the riverfront walk as Reggie kept barking and snipping at his heels.

Obviously winded, Helmut was moving more slowly now, which came as a relief to London. Her lungs were burning painfully from the chase.

Gasping for breath, she managed to call out to the man, "Helmut, why are you running? Do you really think you can get away?"

Helmut staggered to a halt at the river's edge and turned toward London. Sir Reggie took up a post in front of the man, as if daring him to move.

Helmut called back to her in a hoarse, panting voice that expressed a feeling of utter defeat.

"You're right. It's no use. The time has come for me to …"

But before he could finish his sentence, a gangly figure flew like a blur out of a side street. The tall, gangly newcomer smashed right into him, sending him hurtling off the sidewalk all the way into the river, where he fell with a mighty splash.

"Oh, dear!" Audrey Bolton exclaimed, looking down into the water. "I hope I didn't hurt him!"

"So do I," London said, as she trotted up to Audrey and Sir Reggie, then looked down at Helmut. Fortunately, a couple of police officers had already arrived and were dragging him out of the water. He appeared to be limp but fully conscious.

Audrey plopped down on a nearby bench, and London sat beside her. A bit winded himself, Sir Reggie jumped up between them.

"Where did you come from, anyway?" London asked Audrey.

Audrey looked at her with an irritated expression.

"Well, that's a fine greeting," she huffed. "I was only trying to help."

London felt slightly amused to hear a bit of Audrey's former crankiness creep back into her voice.

"You did help ... I guess," London said.

Although the truth was, Helmut seemed to have given up his escape at the very moment before the collision.

"I just want to know how you got here," London asked again.

For a moment, Audrey got a faraway look in her eye, as if she didn't quite know the answer to that question.

Finally she said, "Oh, I remember. I was back there in the audience watching the awards ceremony when ... well, the *thing* happened. You know what I mean. That whole weirdness about the beer recipe."

"Yes, I know."

"I understood right away. Obviously, Herr Preiss was the real murderer. And as soon as you gave chase, so did I. I stayed pretty close behind you for a block or two. Then I saw a side street that I thought might make a good short cut and I ran that way and ..."

Audrey shrugged.

"I guess I headed him off," she said.

"I guess you did," London said with a chuckle. "And thanks."

"You're welcome."

Meanwhile, a police van arrived, and Detektiv Erlich himself got out. The officers who had pulled Helmut out of the river had also put him into restraints, and they now escorted him toward the vehicle.

"Well, London Rose," Erlich said, crossing his arms. "You seem to still be up to your old tricks." He glanced at Audrey and asked, "How many culprits are you ladies planning to bring to justice today?"

Sir Reggie let out a soft woof as if he didn't want to be ignored, but Audrey was being uncharacteristically silent.

"Uh, I don't know," London began.

"You don't know?"

"I mean ... I still don't understand. We thought Willy Oberhauser was guilty, and you even arrested him, and ..."

Her voice faded away into uncertainty.

"Oh, Willy was guilty, all right," Erlich said with a scoff. "At least of part of the crime. He told me his story when I questioned him at the *Bundenspolizeirevier*. He found Forstmann prowling around the beer vat on the stage. Forstmann was drunk, of course, and when Willy asked him what he was doing there, he got belligerent—no surprise."

Erlich put his hands in his pockets.

"They got into an altercation, and Willy lost his temper and whacked Forstmann on the head with his nightstick—unfortunately, hitting him much harder than he'd intended, although he had no idea how serious an injury he'd caused. Willy said he left the scene quickly. He was alarmed by his actions and still very angry, and he was afraid of what he might do next."

Erlich tilted his head and added, "Willy swore to me that he'd done Forstmann no further harm. He'd just left him there on the stage, looking dazed but still very much alive."

Erlich shrugged and said, "Well, I had no idea whether to believe him—at least not until my men called to tell me what took place between you and Helmut Preiss. I came out right away, and here I am."

Erlich sat down on the bench next to London.

"I must admit, though," he said, scratching his chin, "I still don't understand exactly what happened—at least not all of it."

At that moment, one of Erlich's officers came back from the van.

"Detektiv Erlich," he said. "Herr Preiss says he'd like to talk."

"Excellent," Erlich said, getting up from the bench. "The sooner he makes a full confession, the sooner I'll be able to put my mind at ease."

Turning again to London, he added, "You ladies stay right here. I'll come back and fill you in."

"Excuse me, sir," the officer interrupted, "but Herr Preiss especially wants to talk to Fräulein Rose."

Erlich drew back with surprise.

"Well, come on, then," he said to London.

London handed Sir Reggie's leash to Audrey and left the two of them on the bench as she followed Erlich over to the back of the van.

A very wet Herr Preiss sat waiting, looking very miserable indeed.

"London Rose, I think perhaps I ought to thank you," he said.

"Why?" she asked.

"Because … you made possible my undoing. You made it happen. I can't help thinking you did me a great favor."

Astonished, London waited for him to explain.

"Of course," he said, "I ran across the recipe while reading through archives at the *Bayerische Biermuseum* here in Bamberg. It looked marvelous, and it seemed a shame that it hadn't ever gone into production and was lost for so many years, and …"

Preiss shrugged wearily.

"I saw no harm at all as claiming it as my own. Who would I hurt by it, after all? In a way, I suppose I thought I was doing the Leitner family a posthumous favor by bringing their creation back to life. A lie is a lie, of course … but I managed to persuade myself otherwise."

Preiss paused for a moment.

"Yesterday afternoon, Sigmund was already quite drunk by the time he came to my booth. I gave him a sample of my beer and told him … well, what I started to tell the audience just now. That the name of the beer was *Illicium*, which was the Latin word for 'enticement,' and that the recipe involved an innovative use of star anise blended with Chinese 'five spice,' and …"

Preiss heaved a long, bitter sigh.

"I had no idea that he'd discovered the same recipe quite on his own. And when I told him about it, he flew into a rage. He considered my theft an insult to the revered memory of the Leitner dynasty and an insult to the art of beer making itself."

He choked with emotion.

"I apologized to him. I tried to take it all back. I told him I wouldn't go through with it. I'd give the Leitner family all the credit they deserved. But he was drunk, and he was furious, and to him what I had done was nothing less than some sort of a personal betrayal. We could no longer be friends, he said, and he would tell the whole story in his upcoming column, whether I changed my mind or not. He stormed away and just left me standing there."

Preiss shifted uncomfortably.

"About an hour later I was walking through the *Maximiliensplatz* considering my situation. I knew Sigmund had meant what he'd said. Even after he sobered up, he wouldn't change his mind. That was just the kind of man he was. And I figured there was nothing I could do about it. He would write his column, and I would suffer the full brunt of his wrath. The best I could do would be to spend the rest of my life and career atoning for my dishonesty. I would survive it, I thought."

He squinted thoughtfully.

"But as I walked past the curtain in front of the stage, I heard a voice from behind it. 'I am the true king of the Hoffmann Fest! I am the true king of the Hoffmann Fest! This year's *Katers Murr* is nobody. The true king of the festival is I!'"

200

Preiss looked back and forth at London and Erlich.

"I crept up onto the stage behind the curtain, and I found Sigmund sitting in the chair on the platform above the beer vat. He was beyond drunk, not even wearing his monocle. He seemed to be quite out of his mind."

"He'd been hit on the head," Erlich explained. "He was delirious as well as drunk."

"Was he? Well. I was seized by an impulse of pure spite and vengefulness. If there was nothing I could do to stop him from telling his story, at least I could humiliate him first. As he kept ranting away, 'I am the true king!' I climbed up the stairs and pulled the lever."

Preiss shuddered deeply.

"I hadn't meant to kill him. But he thrashed around for only a few moments before he fell completely still."

London asked, "Why didn't you try to save him?"

"Because … I was angry, I suppose. And at the same time, I was afraid. I'd made my own situation much, much worse than it had already been."

He shook his head again.

"Anger and fear. It was—what is the English phrase?—a 'perfect storm' of desperate, self-destructive emotion. I wasn't like myself. I acted in a way that I myself could never have imagined. I simply walked away."

He shrugged again and said to London, "I guess that's all there is to tell. But I do want to thank you for unraveling the truth. I must have always wanted to get caught deep down. Otherwise I wouldn't have continued my charade even after Sigmund's death.

"I want you to know something else," he added. "I truly meant it when I said I would miss him. My mourning was perfectly sincere. I meant it very much. I still do."

London stood watching as Detektiv Erlich and his men loaded Preiss into the van and drove away with him.

London was startled by how genuinely sorrowful Helmut had sounded just now.

They really were friends, she thought.

She felt sad that their friendship had come to such a terrible end.

When London returned to the bench, she was delighted to see Bryce sitting there with Sir Reggie and Audrey.

"I got a bit lost in back in the streets," he explained. "But Audrey has told me everything she could."

"Is everything all right now?" Audrey asked London.

"I … I guess," London stammered.

"Nobody's going to arrest us or anything?"

"No," London said.

Then London took out her cell phone.

"I'd better call the captain again," she said. "He won't believe what I have to tell him."

CHAPTER THIRTY FIVE

The *Nachtmusik* was about to leave Bamberg. When London walked up the gangway with Bryce, Audrey, and Sir Reggie, she saw that the crew was already preparing the boat for departure.

"I'll certainly have some vivid memories of this place," Audrey mused as they stepped on board.

"It's turning out to be an interesting voyage," Bryce said.

Too interesting, London thought.

Captain Hays met the group in the reception area.

Shaking his head with wonder, he said, "I'm glad to see all of you back in one piece. We're ready to set sail as soon as all passengers and crew are accounted for. Could you check on that for me, London?"

London took out her cell phone and opened an app showing who was checked in.

"Everybody is still with us," she told Captain Hays.

"Excellent." He raised his own phone and notified the crew to remove the gangway. Then he said, "Oh, by the way, London, that was quite some story you told me over the phone. Are you sure that you've finally caught all the culprits?"

London let out a tired laugh and replied, "If not, I'll leave it to Detektiv Erlich and his team to take things from here."

Captain Hays stroked his walrus-style mustache.

"You know, London—Bob Turner and his, eh, chronicler, Stanley Tedrow, came by my stateroom and gave me their own briefing of the case. I must say, there are a few discrepancies between his account and yours."

"I'm sure there are," London said with a grin.

"For example," the captain continued, "Bob said nothing at all about a dishonest brewer, only a short-tempered security guard wielding a deadly cudgel. The way Bob tells it, he single-handedly nabbed the fellow through an astonishing feat of derring-do. I believe he and Mr. Tedrow have forwarded a written account of their investigatory prowess to Mr. Lapham. Would you like me to get in touch with our CEO and try to set him right as to facts?"

London laughed heartily.

"No, please don't," she said. "Just leave well enough alone."

"Very well, then," Captain Hays said. "I expect you'll sleep well tonight."

The captain headed away to the elevator, leaving London with Bryce, Audrey, and Sir Reggie. For an awkward moment, the three humans didn't seem to know what to say to each other.

Bryce and London exchanged yearning glances.

He wishes we could be alone, London realized.

And so do I.

But Audrey didn't seem to notice any such signals.

Bryce shuffled his feet and cleared his throat.

"Well," he said finally, "I guess I'd better go check how things are in the kitchen. You will let me know if you need anything, won't you, London?"

"I promise," London said.

Bryce sauntered away and disappeared down the stairs.

Audrey demanded, "Are you really going to let that Bob Turner fellow take all the credit for solving the case?"

"Oh, absolutely," London said.

"Whatever for?"

London laughed again.

"I'm just as happy that Mr. Lapham doesn't know much about my detective work. I don't want him to develop expectations. I'm quite happy with my job as Social Director, thank you very much."

"Then your detective work is a secret?" Audrey asked thoughtfully.

"It's definitely better that way. If we ever have to go through another one of these ordeals, I'm sure you'll understand how I feel."

Audrey let out a squeal of enthusiasm.

"Oh, I can hardly wait!" she said.

Then she raised her hand to her lips as if shocked by her own words.

"Not that I hope anyone else will get killed, understand," she said to London.

"Of course not."

"It's just that this has been … well, an adventure. It's made me feel so very alive, more so than I can ever remember. Meanwhile, I'm utterly exhausted. I'm going to turn in for the night. Thank you for an exciting day, London Rose. And thank you for … well, everything else."

London smiled as she remembered what Audrey had said about gratitude earlier today.

"You helped me feel something really important."

"Any time," she said.

Audrey leaned over and scratched Sir Reggie under the chin, then headed away.

London sighed wistfully.

"If only Bryce had hung around for a few moments longer," she said to Sir Reggie.

The little dog let out a sympathetic murmur.

"Well, I guess I'd better make my final rounds for the night," she told him. "We've got to make sure that everybody is occupied and happy."

Sir Reggie followed her on into the Amadeus Lounge, which was quite busy now that all the passengers had come back aboard. The first person she encountered there was Letitia Hartzer, who called out to her from a table where she was having drinks with some friends.

"Oh, London! Exactly who I wanted to see! I'm *so* excited about our upcoming visit to Amsterdam, and I wanted to study a map of the city before we get there. The tiny little dinky map I get on my cell phone is simply not up to snuff. So microscopic, it hurts my eyes. I wonder whether ..."

"I could get you a physical map?"

Letitia chuckled. "Yes, the old-fashioned analog kind, all printed out in wonderful colors on a big, folded sheet of pressed-and-dried wood pulp—*paper*, I think it's called."

"Yes, I believe that is the word for it," London said with a smile. "I'll see if I can fetch you a real honest-to-goodness paper map."

London and Sir Reggie walked over to the library, where she once again found the door closed—and locked.

"I can't believe this," she growled under her breath.

She knocked sharply on the door.

"Emil, are you there?"

Once again, she thought she heard a muffled whispering sound inside.

And once again, Sir Reggie let out a suspicious-sounding growl.

London stepped back and crossed her arms.

"Emil, I'm going to use my master keycard to let myself in there."

There was a scuffling sound, then Emil's voice replied.

"London, just—wait a minute."

London stood waiting until the door opened. Standing inside and looking thoroughly embarrassed were Emil and Amy. Their faces were red. Their hair and clothes mussed. Emil was actually tucking in his shirttail.

"Well," Amy said stiffly, straightening out her own blouse, "thanks so much for your help with my … uh, research, Herr Waldmüller."

"Ahem," Emil said, "I'm always glad to be of assistance, Fräulein Blassingame."

Looking more ridiculous by the moment, Emil and Amy actually shook hands.

Then Amy almost tripped and fell as she brushed by London in a futile attempt at a casual exit.

As soon as Amy was out of sight, London burst into laughter.

"What do you find so amusing?" Emil inquired with as much dignity as he could muster.

"What do you think?" London said with a guffaw. "You and Amy—an item! I had no idea."

Emil looked at the floor and shuffled his feet.

"I am glad it gives you—so much glee," he muttered.

"Is this why you've been behaving so oddly toward me lately?" London asked, trying to calm her laughter. "Is this what you were doing when I found you listening to that *oompah* band this morning, and you lied and said you had some sort of business to attend to? Were you having some kind of a—a *tryst* with Amy?"

"If you must know—yes, I was."

"Why did you have to act so *weird* about it? So furtive and sulky? Why didn't you just come out and tell me what was going on?"

Emil looked genuinely surprised by the question.

"I … I did not want to hurt your feelings," he said.

London sputtered in an effort not to burst out laughing again.

"Emil, listen to me. I'll admit, I had sort of a crush on you for a while. But not anymore. As teenagers like to say, I'm *so over* you."

"Oh," Emil said with a look of startled disappointment. "Well. Why did you not … inform me?"

"I guess I did not want to hurt *your* feelings," London said as her laughter started to wane. "Look I'm glad we've got this out in the open. I mean, we're both professionals, and we're both adults, and we've got jobs to do."

"Agreed," Emil said with clumsy formality.

"We work well together," she added. "I hope that will continue."

"Of course."

"Meanwhile, I've got to get back to my rounds. I came here looking for a map of Amsterdam. Could you lend me one?"

"Yes, I'll get one for you right away," Emil said, looking relieved. He turned to a nearby bookshelf, found a map, and handed it to her.

London delivered the folded paper map to Letitia, who was most grateful.

*

After London finished her rounds for the night, she took her exhausted little dog back to their room, where he fell fast asleep on the bed. With so many things still going around in her head, she didn't think she could sleep yet so she headed up to the Rondo deck to enjoy the night air.

The *Nachtmusik* was sailing along the Main River on its way to the much larger Rhine, which the boat would follow on its way to Amsterdam.

After all the turmoil of the last couple of days, it was good to stand at the railing, feeling feel cool breeze blow through her hair and watching lights from small towns pass by on the riverbank. She let her mind go still and quiet and enjoyed the low, comforting rumble of the *Nachtmusik*'s engine.

Suddenly she thought she heard a voice whispering in the darkness.

"Fern Weh."

She almost turned around to look and see who had spoken when she realized the truth.

It was me.

I said it myself.

It hadn't occurred to her that the mysterious name from a posted ad back in Regensburg was still wafting through some distant part of her mind.

"Fern Weh," she said again. *"Fernweh."*

Said as a single word, it meant "wanderlust."

She knew she still had the tiny slip of paper with the phone number written on it. She remembered the phone message she'd heard when she'd tried to call that number.

"Die von Ihnen erreichte Nummer ist nicht in Betrieb."

"The number you have reached is not in service."

She had to wonder yet again—was there even the faintest possibility that Mom had left that ad and that number, and that Fern Weh was the name she had assumed for her travels? Had London found that number too late to reach Mom, after she had moved on to some new location and some new phone number?

How can I possibly know? she wondered.

How will I ever know?

She felt a craving deep inside—and an urge to do something, anything, to find out the truth.

She took out her cell phone and went online and ran a search on the name *Fern Weh*. While she found thousands of entries for *Fernweh* as a single word, she didn't find any instances of someone using it as a name.

Then she found herself thinking ahead to the next leg of their voyage.

We'll be in the Netherlands, she thought.

Her Dutch was rusty, so she looked up "wanderlust" in an online Dutch/English dictionary:

Reislust

Without stopping to think, she ran a search on the word. Of course, once again she came up with thousands of entries. Then it occurred to her—maybe she should try it as two words, just as the word had been divided in German.

She typed in the words:

Reis Lust

She was startled to run across a website with those two words as its name. She opened it and found herself looking at a single page with three lines of text written in large, cursive letters:

Reis Lust
elke Europese taal
65 Poppenhuisstraat, Amsterdam

London felt a jolt of surprise. She didn't know what to make of what she was seeing. The last line was obviously an address.

But the second line?

She was quickly able to translate it in her head.

any European language

She gasped aloud.

Was it possible that this was another ad for a language tutor—a more cryptic one than the last?

And was the tutor calling herself "Wanderlust" in the language of every country she visited?

And might that tutor be Mom?

If so, was she following a similar route as London through Europe?

It seemed impossible to believe.

And yet ...

London would be in Amsterdam soon. There was no reason in the world why she couldn't go directly to that address and find out what the webpage meant.

I've got to know, she thought.

Then she heard a voice say, "London."

For a moment she wondered whether she'd said her own name. But this time she turned around and saw Bryce's handsome face gazing at her with a broad smile

"I hoped I might find you up here," he said.

"I'm glad you did," London said.

They stood staring at each other shyly but happily for a moment, and thoughts of Mom faded from London's mind.

"Quite an adventure today, wasn't it?" Bryce said.

Then she and Bryce both laughed at his charmingly awkward effort at making conversation.

"An adventure, indeed," she said.

"I suppose you must be getting tired of adventures by now."

London looked up into his warm gray eyes.

"Maybe," she said. "Or maybe not."

She leaned toward him, and he lifted her chin.

Finally, their lips met in a long, delightful kiss.

NOW AVAILABLE!

MISFORTUNE (AND GOUDA)
(A European Voyage Cozy Mystery—Book 4)

"When you think that life cannot get better, Blake Pierce comes up with another masterpiece of thriller and mystery! This book is full of twists, and the end brings a surprising revelation. Strongly recommended for the permanent library of any reader who enjoys a very well-written thriller."
--Books and Movie Reviews (re *Almost Gone*)

MISFORTUNE (AND GOUDA) is book #4 in a charming new cozy mystery series by #1 bestselling author Blake Pierce, whose *Once Gone* has over 1,500 five-star reviews. The series begins with MURDER (AND BAKLAVA)—BOOK #1.

When London Rose, 33, is proposed to by her long-time boyfriend, she realizes she is facing a stable, predictable, pre-determined (and passionless) life. She freaks out and runs the other way—accepting instead a job across the Atlantic, as a tour-guide on a high-end European cruise line that travels through a country a day. London is searching for a more romantic, unscripted and exciting life that she feels sure exists out there somewhere.

London is elated: the European river towns are small, historic and charming. She gets to see a new port every night, gets to sample an endless array of new cuisine and meet a stream of interesting people. It is a traveler's dream, and it is anything but predictable.

In Book #4, MISFORTUNE (AND GOUDA), they cruise into Amsterdam, the land of Van Gogh, with its gorgeous canals, flower-filled fields and exquisite cuisine. But when London discovers a dead body floating in a canal, she, the only suspect, must clear her name. A baffling mystery ensues, taking London all the way from the world of Dutch museums to the murky streets of its Red Light district.

Laugh-out-loud funny, romantic, endearing, rife with new sights, culture and food, THE EUROPEAN VOYAGE cozy series offers a fun and suspenseful trip through the heart of Europe, anchored in an intriguing mystery that will keep you on the edge of your seat and guessing until the very last page.

Books #5, CALAMITY (AND A DANISH), and #6, MAYHEM (AND HERRING), are now also available!

Blake Pierce

Blake Pierce is the USA Today bestselling author of the RILEY PAIGE mystery series, which includes seventeen books. Blake Pierce is also the author of the MACKENZIE WHITE mystery series, comprising fourteen books; of the AVERY BLACK mystery series, comprising six books; of the KERI LOCKE mystery series, comprising five books; of the MAKING OF RILEY PAIGE mystery series, comprising six books; of the KATE WISE mystery series, comprising seven books; of the CHLOE FINE psychological suspense mystery, comprising six books; of the JESSE HUNT psychological suspense thriller series, comprising fifteen books (and counting); of the AU PAIR psychological suspense thriller series, comprising three books; of the ZOE PRIME mystery series, comprising six books; of the ADELE SHARP mystery series, comprising ten books (and counting); of the EUROPEAN VOYAGE cozy mystery series, comprising six books (and counting); of the new LAURA FROST FBI suspense thriller, comprising three books (and counting); of the new ELLA DARK FBI suspense thriller, comprising six books (and counting); of the new A YEAR IN EUROPE cozy mystery series, comprising three books (and counting); and of the new AVA GOLD mystery series, comprising three books (and counting).

An avid reader and lifelong fan of the mystery and thriller genres, Blake loves to hear from you, so please feel free to visit www.blakepierceauthor.com to learn more and stay in touch.

BOOKS BY BLAKE PIERCE

AVA GOLD MYSTERY SERIES
CITY OF PREY (Book #1)
CITY OF FEAR (Book #2)
CITY OF BONES (Book #3)

A YEAR IN EUROPE
A MURDER IN PARIS (Book #1)
DEATH IN FLORENCE (Book #2)
VENGEANCE IN VIENNA (Book #3)

ELLA DARK FBI SUSPENSE THRILLER
GIRL, ALONE (Book #1)
GIRL, TAKEN (Book #2)
GIRL, HUNTED (Book #3)
GIRL, SILENCED (Book #4)
GIRL, VANISHED (Book 5)
GIRL ERASED (Book #6)

LAURA FROST FBI SUSPENSE THRILLER
ALREADY GONE (Book #1)
ALREADY SEEN (Book #2)
ALREADY TRAPPED (Book #3)

EUROPEAN VOYAGE COZY MYSTERY SERIES
MURDER (AND BAKLAVA) (Book #1)
DEATH (AND APPLE STRUDEL) (Book #2)
CRIME (AND LAGER) (Book #3)
MISFORTUNE (AND GOUDA) (Book #4)
CALAMITY (AND A DANISH) (Book #5)
MAYHEM (AND HERRING) (Book #6)

ADELE SHARP MYSTERY SERIES
LEFT TO DIE (Book #1)
LEFT TO RUN (Book #2)
LEFT TO HIDE (Book #3)
LEFT TO KILL (Book #4)

LEFT TO MURDER (Book #5)
LEFT TO ENVY (Book #6)
LEFT TO LAPSE (Book #7)
LEFT TO VANISH (Book #8)
LEFT TO HUNT (Book #9)
LEFT TO FEAR (Book #10)

THE AU PAIR SERIES
ALMOST GONE (Book#1)
ALMOST LOST (Book #2)
ALMOST DEAD (Book #3)

ZOE PRIME MYSTERY SERIES
FACE OF DEATH (Book#1)
FACE OF MURDER (Book #2)
FACE OF FEAR (Book #3)
FACE OF MADNESS (Book #4)
FACE OF FURY (Book #5)
FACE OF DARKNESS (Book #6)

A JESSIE HUNT PSYCHOLOGICAL SUSPENSE SERIES
THE PERFECT WIFE (Book #1)
THE PERFECT BLOCK (Book #2)
THE PERFECT HOUSE (Book #3)
THE PERFECT SMILE (Book #4)
THE PERFECT LIE (Book #5)
THE PERFECT LOOK (Book #6)
THE PERFECT AFFAIR (Book #7)
THE PERFECT ALIBI (Book #8)
THE PERFECT NEIGHBOR (Book #9)
THE PERFECT DISGUISE (Book #10)
THE PERFECT SECRET (Book #11)
THE PERFECT FAÇADE (Book #12)
THE PERFECT IMPRESSION (Book #13)
THE PERFECT DECEIT (Book #14)
THE PERFECT MISTRESS (Book #15)

CHLOE FINE PSYCHOLOGICAL SUSPENSE SERIES
NEXT DOOR (Book #1)

A NEIGHBOR'S LIE (Book #2)
CUL DE SAC (Book #3)
SILENT NEIGHBOR (Book #4)
HOMECOMING (Book #5)
TINTED WINDOWS (Book #6)

KATE WISE MYSTERY SERIES
IF SHE KNEW (Book #1)
IF SHE SAW (Book #2)
IF SHE RAN (Book #3)
IF SHE HID (Book #4)
IF SHE FLED (Book #5)
IF SHE FEARED (Book #6)
IF SHE HEARD (Book #7)

THE MAKING OF RILEY PAIGE SERIES
WATCHING (Book #1)
WAITING (Book #2)
LURING (Book #3)
TAKING (Book #4)
STALKING (Book #5)
KILLING (Book #6)

RILEY PAIGE MYSTERY SERIES
ONCE GONE (Book #1)
ONCE TAKEN (Book #2)
ONCE CRAVED (Book #3)
ONCE LURED (Book #4)
ONCE HUNTED (Book #5)
ONCE PINED (Book #6)
ONCE FORSAKEN (Book #7)
ONCE COLD (Book #8)
ONCE STALKED (Book #9)
ONCE LOST (Book #10)
ONCE BURIED (Book #11)
ONCE BOUND (Book #12)
ONCE TRAPPED (Book #13)
ONCE DORMANT (Book #14)
ONCE SHUNNED (Book #15)

Made in United States
Orlando, FL
06 July 2022

19451542R00136